THE PRICE OF POSSESSION
A Reverse Harem Tale

I0664062

Pizza Shop Exorcist
Book One

by

Dakota Brown

THE PRICE OF POSSESSION
A Reverse Harem Tale

Pizza Shop Exorcist, book 1

Dedication

This one is for David B. Riley.
Thank you for publishing my first stories way back. Thank you for your friendship through the years, and everything else. You will be missed.

Acknowledgments

Sending a shout out to my team: My PA Becky Hodges, Lizzy, Shoshanah, Justinn, Sean, Jen, and Therese. You all keep me sane–relatively, because, let's be honest, what is even sanity for an author–and on track. Thank you so much for all the things you do for me. I also want to thank my cover artist. I absolutely love what she created for this series.

Every book is a journey, and let's be honest, last year was an adventure. This year is looking to be one, too. I just hope that those hobbits have about gotten that ring thrown into the volcano so we can get on to the good parts of the quest in our everyday lives and move past all the bad stuff. Writing these adventures has kept me going through the last twelve months, giving me a lot of positives to focus on and escape into. Hopefully, they've provided some escape for you as well.

I had a ton of fun writing Chris Price and her guys. I hope you enjoy reading about her, because I have lots more planned. I needed some snark in my life, and this character provided ample outlet.

Take care of yourselves, dear readers, and I'll see you around the internet.

Chapter 1

Price

The aroma of garlic and tomatoes strengthened as the door to my office opened. I glanced up from the computer monitor I squinted at. "What's up, Billy?"

"Chris, one of the customers is hassling Stacy." My restaurant manager had deep furrows in his brow and his dark eyes sparked with anger. The only person who hated customers disrespecting the servers more than him was me.

Slamming my boots down onto the floor from where I'd had them propped up on the back of the desk, I shoved my chair backward and stood, a feral grin on my face. "I love it when they're dicks while I'm doing paperwork."

A smirk broke through Billy's frown. "Get'em Boss Lady," he said as he followed me out of the office.

I stormed through the kitchen, though I didn't take time to talk to my employees like I normally would have. Right now, I was out for blood. I headed into the dining area.

Stacy stood by a corner table shooting a desperate look toward the kitchen. Her expression lightened when she saw me. The man yelling at her increased his volume and I could hear him shout over the 80's rock blasting through the speakers. White man, early forties, clean cut hair, wearing jeans and a polo. Great, not even an interesting challenge, just an average asshole sitting at one of my tables.

There weren't a lot of people in the pizza parlor yet, as it was relatively early, but he had already caught an audience. I was sure he was loving that. I just felt bad for his kids for having such a horrible role model. His wife didn't look any more pleasant than he did, so maybe the two boys

1

sitting there looking uncomfortable were completely screwed.

"You're completely incompetent..." the man declared as I approached.

"Hey, asshat, what's your problem," I snarled as I kicked out the chair next to him, stomped my combat boot down on the seat and leaned well into the man's personal space.

He turned and I swear he was frothing at the lips.

"Who the hell are you?"

"I'm the bloody owner, asshole. Who the hell are you?"

That stopped his tirade for a moment while he tried to process the image I presented to him. His gaze traveled up my five foot two frame. It wouldn't have been intimidating, but his eyes widened at the bleached blond hair, shaved sides, spikey top and a few extra piercings. The angry glare combined with the black leather jacket–anarchy symbol on the front–and acid washed jeans and combat boots certainly gave him pause–I owned the throwback to the eighties persona.

"Your server..."

I cut him off as he jabbed his finger toward her. "I'm gonna stop you right there. You're being a dick. Don't care what the problem is, there are other ways to resolve your issues than beating up on the wait staff."

He opened his mouth.

"Is it going to be polite?"

"What?" he stammered.

"The words about to come out of your mouth. Are they going to be polite?"

He shot to his feet so he could tower over me. I grinned and hopped up on the chair.

"You listen here, I'm the customer and I demand respect." He shook his finger at me.

"You can demand it all you want, but you've done nothing to earn it. You can't come in here and throw at temper tantrum like a child and expect to get respect."

His eyes widened and he whirled away. "We're leaving!"

"Mate, you gotta pay for your pizza first."

"It's not even what I ordered."

"Yeah, and if you hadn't been a dick about it, we mighta worked something out. Now you're going to pay for your pizza and tip the waitress really nicely or I'm going to call the cops. Retail theft is illegal in Santa Fe, and, well, everywhere."

The man's jaw dropped, and I grinned. "Pay for your food, tip the lady, then get out and never come back."

The kids got out of their chairs and one of them tugged at his arm. "Just pay, let's go."

Their mom was staring at me like she couldn't decide if she should scream and run in fear or go all self-entitled on me.

The man must have decided I was serious. He pulled out his wallet, grabbed out a bill, threw it down on the table, and stormed toward the exit. I glanced down, making sure it was enough to cover everything, before watching as they left.

"I'm leaving a bad review!" he shouted.

"I'll look forward to ripping you a new one online, too," I shouted back. "Fucking tourists," I muttered before grabbing the hundred-dollar bill and handing it to Stacy. "At least he tipped you well."

Her eyebrows rose. "I'll make change for the pizza."

"Naw, mate, don't worry about the pizza. Tip's all yours. Just clean off the table. Jerks." I hopped off the chair and stomped back toward the kitchen to a round of applause from our regulars and some mystified looks from a few out of towners.

3

The tourists were typically pretty easy to tell in Santa Fe, and we catered to the local crowd. They were a loyal group. They also knew I took good care of my staff. The secret to Price's Pizza Parlor, happy staff, and secret family recipes for the crusts. The nostalgic nod in the décor, music—and the owner—toward the eighties punk scene didn't hurt, either. Especially in Santa Fe.

"Thanks, Chris."

"Sure thing, Billy. Thanks for grabbing me. Always a good time." I shot him a grin, and answered a few smiles from my cooks, before shutting myself back into my office. This paperwork was the worst part of having a business. Yet again, I debated training Billy for this job. I liked staying active with the shop, but to be honest, I'd rather be in the kitchen than in the office.

I had settled back into the payroll when Billy cracked my door open again. My stomach grumbled when the heavy scent of garlic hit me. Maybe it was time for lunch. Dinner? I glanced at the clock. Dinner.

"Yeah?"

"There's a priest here to see you," he said uncertainly.

Fuck.

"Black guy? Ordered a basil and mozzarella with a beer?"

"Yeah." Billy nodded. "Then he asked for you."

"'Kay, make his small a medium. On the house. Throw a ginger beer on the order and I'll meet him in a minute." Good time for dinner, I supposed, though I clenched my jaw and wondered what Darius wanted with me. He and I went way back, thick and thin and all that, but when he showed up, he usually wanted something, and if it was something he couldn't handle, it was going to either be very interesting, or very dangerous. Possibly both. I hadn't seen him since I'd officially given up my old life five years back. Despite the lack of contact, he was arguably my best friend. Perhaps by default since I didn't have a lot of friends left these days. We had drifted apart after our misspent youths, but he had still turned up now and again. At least until after my family had gotten killed five years back. Then it had seemed like he had ducked away for good.

"Sure, boss."

I shot Billy a thumbs up and made the final entries on the payroll. I was definitely teaching Billy how to do this.

Once I finished, I headed out into the kitchen. A few of my cooks gave me curious looks. I shrugged. "Gotta atone for my sins, I guess." A cocky grin had them laughing as I left the kitchen.

Mandy was just giving Darius our pizza when I hit the dining area. Our drinks already sat on the table of the small corner booth.

He looked up when I approached, a broad smile easing his pensive expression. I hadn't seen Darius in five years, but not much had changed. Perhaps a hint more gray in his short cropped brown hair and in the carefully trimmed beard and mustache he wore. I hadn't seen him in anything but his black clothing with the white collar since he'd taken his vows, though a priest walking into an eighties throwback pizza joint amused the hell out of me.

I smiled tightly back. "Mandy, I'll shout if we need anything, otherwise leave us alone, okay?"

"Sure, Chris." She glanced at Darius and he nodded that he was okay, and the waitress split.

"Price, good to see you." He pushed a plate toward me, and I helped myself to the pizza before answering.

"Yeah, always good to see you, too, mate. What's up?"

"I'd stick to the platitudes, but I don't want to get eviscerated." He chuckled.

I winked and took a bite of my pizza, groaning softly in pleasure. I really did like pizza. Never got tired of it.

"We've got an interesting one down at the jail."

5

I arched an eyebrow and took a drink, waiting. He was going to ask for help and I was going to tell him no, because I was out. Done. Not getting dragged back in. Gone respectable and all that.

"The demon wants out. Is practically begging us to send it home. I can't get it out of the guy's body."

My other eyebrow shot up to join the first. "Say what?"

"The demon wants to be exorcised. I can't get it out. The guy is hanging onto the creature somehow."

"That's...not how it works."

Pizza forgotten, my mind whirled around the possibilities and came up blank.

"Yes, I realize that."

"Did you try, uh, asking the demon why it was stuck?"

"It can't tell us. Mostly it's not even able to talk or control its host, which is also weird. The signs all say the demon has been there a while, but it has been reduced to begging for release."

"That's bizarre."

"Yes."

He didn't say it, but obviously that is why he had walked through my doors. He wanted me to have a go at releasing the demon. Trouble was, that wasn't my gig anymore.

"Darius..."

"Chris, please. I wouldn't ask if it wasn't important."

"More to it than just one stuck demon?"

He nodded.

"Care to fill me in?"

"I can't. It's an ongoing police investigation. If they want to tell you more, that's up to them."

I sighed, remembered my food, and put some attention to filling the void in my gut while I considered Darius' predicament. I should be sending him packing. *Best* friend or not, Darius usually brought trouble with him.

"You know I quit, right?"

His shoulders slumped. "Chris..."

I waved my hand, "yeah, yeah, I know. Tried everything, can't think of anything else, I'm your only hope, etcetera."

Darius sighed. "I've said it before, and I'll say it until the day I die. I'm sorry I dragged you into all of this."

"I'm not sorry you dragged me in, just never expected you to abandon me, or I might not have followed in the first place." He knew I didn't mean him joining the priesthood. That had happened long after.

There was nothing he could say, so he simply nodded sadly.

"S'okay, mate. I forgave you a long time ago. Guess I'll let you drag me back in." Cursing myself as I finished off my pizza and sucked down the ginger beer, I tried to prepare myself for an exorcism.

I was good. Maybe one of the best, and for five years I'd managed to leave all that life behind and focus on my family's pizza parlor. They'd died in a fight with a demon prince they'd had no business even being involved with. That part had been accidental. My folks, bless 'em, were as normal as you could possibly get. How they'd come up with me? Well, if I didn't look just like them, I'd suspect I was a changeling of some sort.

Note, I'm not. I checked. Handy spell, that.

Darius still blamed himself for the incident with the demon prince, though it had happened several years after he became a priest. I blamed me. Either way, it was five years past and I'd managed to focus on the family business and not get involved with anything more esoteric than a couple of really awful boyfriends. The last of which had a restraining order on him, and I'd been done with that for over a year. Determined that it would be just me, myself, my vibrator and I, for the near future, I was happy to focus on pizza.

"So, how'd the cops take an actual demon landing on top of them? And how'd they know to call you?" That was a curiosity. Outside of the religious types and a handful of folks actually in the know, as it were, most people thought demons weren't actually real. I was one of those in the know and I didn't even fully understand what all was out there.

Darius concentrated on a slice of pizza for a minute before he shrugged. "This is technically not information I'm supposed to share, but one of the cops on the detail that brought the man in happens to go to my church. He's quite religious and the incident freaked him out enough that he came to me. Obviously, I recognized the signs of possession and got him to take me in to see the man. The deputy in charge of the investigation is not what you would call a believer, but she's also willing to accept something that's so obviously in front of her eyes."

"Huh. Wonder how they'll explain this in their official paperwork."

"Not my problem." Darius chuckled.

"No. Guess not."

Finishing the last of his side of the pizza, Darius stood and pulled out his wallet.

I shook my head. "Pizza's on the house. Tip the waitress."

He smiled, threw a twenty on the table, and gestured for me to lead the way.

I waved at Mandy before heading for the door. "I'll be back!"

A few of the nerdier students of the eighties laughed at my inadvertent movie quote. We had 'quote wars' night a couple of times a month, and the tables that managed the most entertaining quotes would get discounts on their pies. We were generous, but the locals really got into it and it wasn't hard to award the discounts liberally on merit.

The evening heat smacked into me when I left the airconditioned building. Only an extreme dedication to 'the look' kept me in my leather jacket with the pizza on the back and the anarchy symbol on the front.

Fortunately, while my car looked like it was a piece of shit, the air conditioner worked really damn well, and the engine was big enough to power it. Got next to nothing for fuel economy, but I didn't typically have to drive far, anyway.

I got into the gray sedan. Darius had parked his small Honda next to it. Though I knew the way to the jail, I followed just in case they had taken the prisoner someplace else. I wasn't sure how I felt about being on the police radar, though. I'd moved back to Santa Fe to get away from my demons, not find new ones.

Sure enough, Darius headed west out of Santa Fe proper. The houses thinned out as we drove out into the flat openness of the desert. A few miles down the road, a quick swing south, and we were at the sheriff's office. They would have a holding cell there, so I guessed we weren't actually going to the jail itself. Suited me fine. An exorcism in a jail just seemed like an even worse plan than doing an exorcism at all.

I parked next to Darius, quickly shed the handful of knives I had in various pockets, and slid out of my car.

A deputy sheriff, her nametag said McClellan, met us at the door. She shook Darius' hand before eyeing me. I looked up at her. She was taller than Darius, probably at least six foot. Her dark hair was pulled back in a bun, and she had a deep tan to her skin and high cheekbones that made me think she was part Native.

"This her?"

Darius nodded. "If anyone can figure it out, Chris Price can."

Deputy McClellan looked skeptical, but she shook my hand anyway before leading us through a door that required a keycard, and back into the main part of the building. The carpet was old, but serviceable, the paint job relatively new, and the occasional artwork southwestern.

We went down the hallway and back into another room guarded by a keycard reader. I'd been on the wrong side of the law in enough minor scrapes to be a touch nervous, but this time I wasn't in cuffs, so hopefully getting out of here wouldn't be a big deal.

Darius, as if sensing my unease, glanced at me and winked.

I shook my head and flipped him off.

He chuckled. Deputy McClellan ignored us.

This room looked like a typical interrogation room, concrete floor, paint chipping on the cinderblock walls. Normally there would be a table and a couple of chairs, but this room was empty other than the man tied to a chair in the middle of a chalk drawn circle. Out of habit, I inspected Darius' containment spells and found them adequate. Though if what he said was true, the demon would probably have respected a lesser containment. Still, better safe than sorry with these things.

The man's eyes tracked me, but they were human eyes, human anger, a hint of human fear.

I studied the bound man. He was white, younger than me by a few years, and had a scar on his cheek. His dark hair was matted to his head with sweat, and his gray T-shirt was stained at the armpits and a damp spot went down his chest. I approved of the torn jeans, but they were dirty. He wasn't wearing boots or socks. Handcuffs secured his hands to the chair, and leg cuffs did the same to his legs. I could see where his skin had chafed a little.

I held out my hand and Darius slapped a bottle into it. He knew what I wanted. It was even, conveniently, in a squeeze bottle. A bit more respectful than the honey bear bottles I'd used to use for holding holy water, but still...

Flipping up the cap, I saw the guy's eyes widen. Obviously, this wasn't new to him. I squirted him with the blessed water and he screamed, back arching as he tried to come away from the chair.

I intoned the first few phrases of the exorcism.

"You'll not have the demon, he's mine!"

"Mate, you're one fucked up S.O.B."

He laughed at me.

"Yeah, never thought I'd say this, but I actually want to talk to the demon." I stepped over the containment circle and punched the asshole in the face.

The punch wouldn't necessarily have done it, but his head jerked back into the solid chair, and I suspected the demon helped because the man's eyes rolled back in his head.

I shook out my fist and hoped I wasn't going to get in trouble for torturing a prisoner.

"So, now I'd like to talk to the demon inside this asshat's body," I said, hoping the demon would reply.

"Please, please, please get me out," the demon hissed through the unconscious man's teeth.

"You're stuck? The exorcism didn't work?"

"Yes, stuck."

"How?"

The demon rolled the guy's eyes and he tried to speak but couldn't.

"Interesting."

I stepped back out of the circle and glanced at Darius. "Got some incense?"

"I have a smudge stick," he offered and pulled a bundle of sage out of his pocket.

"Have to do." I took it and pulled out a lighter.

Everyone watched as I lit the bundle and let it start smoking. Once it was smoldering appropriately, I stepped over the binding circle again, watching as the smoke hit the edge of the spell and spread out, skirting the edges. The fresh smoke that burned inside the circle acted normally.

I waved it around the guy and spoke the words of a reveal spell.

The smoke circled around the man as I smudged him before settling against his chest. There, I saw something I hadn't noticed before. A charm on a necklace.

"Well, that's new." I reached out and grabbed the charm, jerking it from around the man's neck, just as he woke back up.

He howled in rage as the chain snapped.

I stepped back and ran smack into the containment spell. My heart sank and my blood ran cold. Shit...that's not how it was supposed to work. Among other things, the creature should not have been able to get through my personal wards without my permission.

Oh, thank the void, a voice sounded in my head. *That man is vile.*

"What the fuck." I squirmed as the demon slid into me, slipping around under my skin, settling in, but not taking control.

"Chris!" Darius exclaimed.

"Give it back," the prisoner snarled at me. "It's mine. I earned it."

"No, mate, my demon now. Why don't you go fuck yourself?"

The prisoner went crazy, screaming curses and fighting against his restraints until his wrists went bloody, then he kept fighting.

"Darius, think you're going to have to let me out, and get him taken care of. I've, uh, got the demon now."

"I can see that," he replied, not breaking the circle.

"No, really, like, the demon isn't in control." I held up the charm I had clenched in my fist. "I think we need to exorcise this."

"We need to sedate the prisoner," the deputy said. I hadn't noticed the other person who had joined us. In fact, I was having a hard time focusing on anything except the hunger coursing through me. I'd just eaten, so I knew it must have been the demon's. I almost felt sorry for it.

I tried not to double over and clutch my stomach. That would not be a good way to convince Darius I was okay.

The circle broke and I stumbled backward.

Darius caught me as I crashed to the ground. He ran his thumb across my brow in the sign of the cross. I could feel the holy water burn my skin, but it was mild, more irritating than painful.

I hissed anyway. "Darius, just, give me a minute, hmm?"

"Chris, the longer it's in you..."

"Mate, it's in the charm. It's projecting through me because I'm in possession of the charm."

"Are you sure?" His concerned face blocked out the harsh florescent light from the bulbs in the ceiling.

"Pretty sure."

He leaned back and helped me sit up.

"Look, let me take it back to my place. I've got a permanent circle in the basement. I'll see if I can cast it out of the charm and send it on its merry way back to hell."

"I'm going with you."

"Yeah, sure, whatever." I tried, again, not to hunch as pain rippled through me in an expression of the demon's hunger.

Deputy McClellan stared at me, eyes wide when I finally stood up with Darius' help.

"We'll take this part of it from here, Deputy," Darius said.

"Thank you, Father. Ms. Price. I'll show you out."

I nodded, distracted, trying to walk normally as I followed the Deputy and Darius out of the Sheriff's office. I barely even noticed the heat when I got into the car. The steering wheel probably burned my hands, but it was all I could do to focus on the road and follow my friend back to my house. I probably wouldn't have made it in the state I was in if I hadn't been following Darius.

Still, we finally pulled onto my family's land. It wasn't much, just a few acres and a fairly nice adobe house. I'd grown up here, and now it was home again since I was the only Price left to claim it.

I parked, managed to remember to turn the car off, and fumbled with my keys.

Darius picked me and the keys up from the ground and carried me to my house.

"Chris, are you sure you're okay?"

"No, mate. I'm fucking famished." I blinked a few times. "No, the demon is famished. I'll be fine once I can set this thing down."

"Why wasn't the prisoner affected like this?"

Drugs, the demon supplied.

"Probably high," I muttered. "What do you eat, anyway?" I asked aloud.

Energy. I'm doing my best not to harm you.

"Great."

"What did it say?"

"It feeds off energy. It's doing its best not to hurt me, but I don't think it can help whatever it's doing to me."

No.

Somehow, we were already in my basement. Darius carried me to the center, and I dropped the charm on the workbench. Though he'd never been down here before, Darius knew what to look for and backed me out of the circle that was permanently inlaid into the concrete floor with a

14

band of silver. That had cost me a small fortune, but after the mistakes of my past, I had dished out the money to craft a solid containment for my workspace.

The crippling pain cramping my stomach eased and I heaved a relieved sigh.

"Thanks."

"Of course, Chris. Can you still hear the demon?"

I waited for a few moments for it to talk to me, before shaking my head. "No."

"Good. So, how do we cast a demon out of a charm?"

"Fuck if I know."

"Got any resources that might tell us?"

I shook my head. "I got out, Darius. I have a few things to put up wards, because I'm not a total idiot, but I got rid of the rest."

He stared at me. "Seriously?"

"Well, I mean, I know where it's at. But it's not accessible for a reason."

Darius ran his hand over his short hair and sighed. "That was smart, but also inconvenient."

"Why don't you try a normal exorcism. If it doesn't work, I'll put some thought into it. The charm is safe here, anyway."

Clearly unhappy with my suggestion, he still agreed. Yet again anointing me with holy water and the cross on my forehead. This time there was no unpleasant tingle.

He studied me and I nodded. No demon.

"Okay."

Darius performed the rite, but with no body, and no real resistance, we couldn't tell if it had been successful.

Sighing, I stepped into the circle and clutched the charm.

Hunger washed over me again, and I doubled over.

Must destroy the charm. Bound.

The demon's voice had faded, but it was still there.

"Nope, he's bound. We gotta release the binding somehow," I stated through gritted teeth. I dropped the charm back on the table, almost able to feel the energy drain this time since I was looking for it.

Since I didn't have the charm in my hand, I managed to get out of the circle without Darius breaking it. That was a good sign.

"It's getting late," I declared. "I'm going to eat again, and then pass out on my face. Unless you're staying, you might want to head back to your church and, I don't know, meditate on the problem or something. I'll see if I can find something to help tomorrow."

I knew just the spell, but Darius didn't need to know what I was up to. This particular spell typically found me all sorts of trouble along with the answers I sought. He might have had an idea of what I was up to by the long look he gave me, but ultimately, he gave in to my plan. I walked him to the door.

"I'll check in with you tomorrow."

"Sure, Darius. See you then."

"Be careful, Chris."

I didn't bother to reply. We both knew I didn't know how to be careful. Not really, or I wouldn't have gone with him today.

Darius walked to his car, a distinct, probably guilty, hunch to his shoulders. We locked gazes for a moment when he turned to look at the house again, before he got in his car and drove away, leaving me alone with a bound demon in my basement. Kind of like last time.

Fortunately, this time, I really did think the demon wasn't out to hurt us. That would certainly be a first for me.

My stomach growled and I headed for the kitchen.

Chapter 2

Price

My senses full of the scent of old books and heavy incense, I followed the magical tug on my chest as the spell I'd cast at home led me to what I needed most at the moment. Hopefully, whatever it was, was actually the way to release the demon from the charm and not some other thing. I'd focused my intent as clearly as I could manage, and though I often had mixed results with this spell, I felt pretty good about this casting.

The pull had taken me from my house to the downtown tourist district. I wandered past the artsy stores until the tug led me to, I shit you not, the metaphysical store. The froufrou one I'd never been in. What the hell?

I almost didn't go in, but the pull from the spell was pretty clear so I pushed open the door and tried not to wince as the nearly physical wall of incense aroma hit me.

Still, even though my senses should have been overwhelmed, I could smell the original scent that had clouded my nose the whole way here. Musty books and heavy, spicy incense.

I barely looked around at the crystals, rocks, candles, dream catchers, and other things that littered the shelves. The pull still tugged at me until I ended up at the counter, staring at the man who until I'd walked up to him had been reading a book. He had bronzed skin, liquid brown eyes I could get lost in, and medium length wavy black hair that just begged me to run my fingers through it.

"Hello," he said and something like a middle eastern accent washed over me.

I managed to snap out of my flat-out stare as the spell released me.

"Hi," I managed, feeling more than a bit flustered. I hid my embarrassment behind sass. "Got any *good* books?"

He arched his eyebrows before he curled his lips. "A few. What do you need?"

"Um." I glanced over at the store's copious book collection and sighed. It was all new age stuff. That was all well and good, but they likely didn't have what I needed there. Why had the spell brought me here? "Something to release bindings?"

"Perhaps you should find an exorcist. I hear the local catholic church has one." He sounded bored.

"I am an exorcist," I snapped before I could stop myself. "I can get a demon out of a person, but I don't know how to get one out of a charm that it's bound to." That was more than I had wanted to say. Damn it.

The renewed interest in the man's eyes made me squirm a little on the inside. He had a way of looking straight through you that I didn't see much anymore.

Without a word, the guy turned and went into the back of his store.

Wondering if I'd pissed him off, or if I should run, I edged back from the counter until I was at the book rack. Maybe there was something here.

"Does the demon wish to be released from the charm?"

"Fuck, mate," I exclaimed as I jumped out of my skin. I hadn't heard him return or come up behind me.

Amusement glinted in his eyes when I turned to glare.

"Yes, it would very much like to go home. Complicated, long story." I hoped he wouldn't ask. I was honestly shocked he seemed to believe me about the demon. Most people didn't.

"Do you have holy water?"

"Yeah." Darius had left that and the sage with me.

"Sage?"

I nodded.

"A focus crystal?"

"No."

He held out his hands, as if he had anticipated that. In each palm was a crystal, the left a smokey quartz, the right citrine.

I chose the citrine. No idea why.

He set the quartz back on the display and gestured for me to follow him back to the counter. I did, trying not to notice how fluidly he moved, like a dancer maybe. Not to mention the way his wavy hair brushed the collar of his T-shirt or the way his jeans fit his ass. No, I was definitely not staring at his ass. What the hell was wrong with me? I was not looking for any sort of relationship, not even a one-night hook up. Well, he was easy on the eyes. I shrugged and wondered how much the damn crystal was going to cost me, or why I needed it.

The guy pushed a leather-bound book across the counter. It was open, the pages handwritten and yellowed with age, but reasonably well preserved.

I studied the words on the page, grateful they were in Latin, and grateful I could read it.

My new shopkeeper friend watched, not saying anything, as I read through the instructions.

"Huh, okay. So, how much is this going to cost me?" And I wasn't completely worried about the monetary cost. Someone who actually had real magical texts might not even deal in currency.

"The book is a loan. The crystal is ten dollars."

"You're really going to trust me with this?" I raised my eyebrows.

He lifted one shoulder in a lazy shrug. "I can find the book if I need to track it down."

"Oh." Maybe it was blood marked? What was a guy who had a blood marked book doing working in a new age store? I wasn't sure if I wanted to know or not.

"Tell me, do you roleplay?"

I stared at the shopkeeper, my brain trying to make the switch from Latin incantations to questions about roleplaying.

"Like, whips and chains? Kinda personal for someone you just met, don't you think?"

He chuckled. "Tabletop."

I tilted my head.

"With dice?" His amused smile pissed me off.

"Oh, that kind of roleplaying. No, gave that up ages ago." *Duh*, I thought to myself. He meant gaming. I had skipped straight from the role players are nerds phase straight into the full on occultist phase, and missed the pretending phase.

"Pity." He shrugged.

"Right. Um, why? Kinda out of the blue, you know."

"I'm looking for a new group, and it struck me that a *real* exorcist might be fun to play with."

His tone was a bit more suggestive than I had anticipated and instead of irritating me, it sent tremors of need down my spine. Fuck that. "I am a real exorcist," I bit back. I tried to stay chill. I wasn't sure it worked.

"Of course."

I glared at him. "There might be a local group around here somewhere."

He didn't reply.

Vaguely irritated, and not sure why, I paid for the crystal. I thanked him for the book and headed back to my car. The entire drive back to the house, I had the nagging suspicion I'd missed something I needed in the store. Still, the spell was reasonable, and it actually shouldn't be too hard to accomplish my goals.

Those thoughts occupied me on my on my drive back to my house. I made a cup of coffee once I was inside and studied the ritual. It was straightforward and I likely had a copy of a similar ritual in one of my books. Still, I didn't have my books and I did have...I hadn't gotten his name. Huh.

Well, time to go release a demon. I took a beeswax taper from my drawer, grabbed the book and the crystal, and went down into my basement.

Though I wasn't real keen on the idea, I had to cross the barrier to set up the spell. I left the book on the table by the door, took a deep breath and crossed into the protective circle.

It was a risk every time I crossed the barrier, but the demon was currently bound, and I'd be out before I invoked the spell.

The top of my work bench was slate, and I quickly but carefully drew the proscribed sigils around the charm to direct and contain the energy. I set the crystal, lit the candle and the sage bundle and, after one more look to make sure I'd gotten it right, stepped back out of the circle.

"All right, demon, let's get you out of there so I can be done with this whole nonsense." Taking a deep breath and centering my personal energy, I began the incantation.

I could feel the bindings on the spell resist my efforts to unravel them, and I began the incantation again with more feeling now that I had the shape of the spell in my mind.

On the third repetition, I felt the bindings give. Energy flashed visibly, contained by the protective circle but still causing me to flinch away. A sharp crack split the air.

When my vision cleared, my gaze darted to the table. The candle had melted away, and the citrine crystal had shattered almost into powder. The charm itself was a puddle of silver.

A soft groan pulled my attention to the floor. A body lay there, curled on its side, back to me.

"Hello?"

"Thanks for that." The voice was still masculine, so was the form of the body. "It was getting cramped in there."

Instead of the triumphant, "I tricked the humans" voice I had expected, the demon just sounded exhausted and grateful to be out.

"Are you okay?" I snapped the book shut and put it on the bench by the door before walking over to the edge of the circle.

"Not really," the demon replied.

"You ready for me to send you back?" That might be the easiest way to fix any other problems the demon might have.

"No. Need to answer your priest's questions. Let me rest first." The demon's voice was smooth, like liquid silk, and the way it caressed my skin sent shivers down my spine. As good as it sounded right now, I couldn't imagine what he might sound like when he wasn't starving and freshly released from being bound.

"How do you have a body?"

"Not all demons have to possess someone to be present on the material plane. Just the ones you commonly deal with." He didn't roll over, so I couldn't get a look at his face, but his back was nicely muscled, deeply tanned, and his ass was very firm. I tucked my hands under my arms before I did something I'd regret in my quest to touch the alluring demon. That desire really should have been my first clue as to what kind of demon lay on the ground in front of me.

"Okay, I'll let Darius know you want to talk to him then, and, uh, let you rest."

"Thank you." The effort the demon had to put into saying those words made me worry that he might not actually last long enough for Darius to get here. I suspected the priest would be busy until the evening. Why was I even worried about a demon? That probably should have been my next clue.

Shaking my head, I grabbed the book and forced myself out of the basement and into my kitchen. Some of the demon's hunger must have worn off on me because I was also starving. I settled for a protein drink and sent a quick text off to Darius.

He didn't reply, and I settled in with my new reading material and some coffee to wait.

Dakota Brown

Chapter 3

Malak

I couldn't get my mind off the intriguing creature that had walked into the shop not long ago. I could tell she often wore her bleached hair up in some sort of mohawk, though it was currently unstyled. The sides of her head were shaved close and I had the strongest desire to track her down just so I could run my fingers over the short hair.

The scent of rain, an intense warning of an impending storm, lingered on the air even after she left. It was as if the memory of her was so strong, that it was all I could smell, even over the incense that permeated the air.

She wasn't tall, but I wouldn't have called her petite. She looked like she could probably handle herself in a fight and there was something extra about her that I couldn't put my finger on. There was no doubt in my mind she was an exorcist as she claimed and that she probably wouldn't have any issues dealing with this demon problem she had. Still, something drove me to want to help her. Though, I doubted she'd welcome an intrusion.

It was fortunate we only had one other customer in the remaining hour I had agreed to take care of the counter before Olivia returned, and they hadn't needed much attention. I simply could not tear my thoughts away from the woman. I hadn't even gotten her name. Of course, she had my book, which I'd hastily thrown a blood mark on when I'd decided to lend it to her.

We had quite a few occult volumes in the back that were for sale, but I also had a handful of my personal collection here, as well. Many that we sold were from my collection over the years. Either they were uninteresting to me, or I knew them so well I no longer needed them. Occasionally someone turned up who wanted something more than the new age stuff we typically sold. Even more occasionally, I sold them one of the books from the back. Most of the lucky few who turned up in search of something different were from the small local supernatural community and had been sent to me by someone else.

The bell chimed and Olivia, the co-owner, walked in. She was far more into the new age aspects of the occult and managed most of the content of the store. We had met years ago, when I'd saved her from dying after being attacked by a werecat. She hadn't avoided the transformation, but at least she hadn't died in the process.

I couldn't help but contrast her to the exorcist I'd just met. Tall where the other was short, dark where the other was pale, curvy where the exorcist was slender.

"Malak, what's up?"

"What makes you think anything is up?" I leaned back in the chair I was perched on and crossed my arms.

"You've got some sort of weird ass dreamy look in your eyes. Whoever it is, you should call them. Haven't seen you that interested in anyone else, well, since we met."

I frowned, trying to think of a way to deny her accusation and completely failing.

She laughed, the hearty sound bringing a sheepish smile to my lips. "Guess I'm learning how to read you after all these years."

I sighed and shook my head. "A woman came in looking for one of the special books today. She does seem to have caught my interest."

Olivia came around the counter, beginning the process of taking over for me. "Do tell."

"I'm not sure there is much to tell. She wasn't here long. I even forgot to get her name. Apparently, she's an exorcist."

"Oh, another occultist. I can see why she got your attention, Mal."

I shrugged.

"You know anything about her?"

I ran my hand through my hair and scuffed my foot on the floor, a little embarrassed. "I blood marked the book I lent her. I can find her if I need to."

My friend chuckled. "Don't wait too long, Mal. I've got a feeling. Why don't you just track her down, see if she needs your help."

I had been thinking that same thing, so the idea stuck with me.

Sighing, I shook my head. "Maybe I will."

"Get out of here." She shooed me toward the door. "Go find this new friend of yours. I want to meet her sometime soon."

"Okay. I'll see what I can do." Leaving at Olivia's insistence, I headed home. I lived close enough to the square that I didn't need to drive, and with limited parking it was easier not to. I walked toward my small house, lost in thought.

Fortunately, I managed to avoid knocking anyone over, though the old Native man who played some sort of pipe did have to scramble out of my way. It took me a few strides before I realized what I'd done. I turned around and apologized to him. We'd spoken on more than one occasion and I suspected he would forgive me.

Otherwise, I made it back to my house in a fog that drove home how necessary it was to speak with the exorcist at least once more. There was just something about her that called to me.

Now I just had to track her down. Not difficult.

I pulled out a pendulum and an old-fashioned paper map, speaking a few quiet words of connection between the pendulum and the book I'd marked.

There was no hesitation once I spoke the final word of connection. The pendulum, well attuned to my own energies, homed in on the book and pointed to its current location. A spot not too far outside of town.

I noted down the address and headed for my car, hoping my exorcist wouldn't mind the intrusion.

Chapter 4

Price

I'd just started studying a really interesting discovery ritual when my doorbell chimed.

Darius always knocked, so it couldn't have been him. I put the book on the coffee table and went to the door. The view through the peep hole showed the owner of the spell book. He really could track it down. Interesting.

I opened the door. "Howdy, mate."

He smiled, and I tried not to get lost in his liquid brown eyes.

"I wanted to check and see how you were doing with your demon." He looked away before I could, releasing me from his stare, and studying the door frame.

"Fine, I guess. He wanted to talk to a priest and then I can send him back." At first, I thought the door frame was an odd thing for him to be looking at, but I watched his gaze and it flicked from one supposedly invisible sigil to another as he traced the warding I'd placed on the entryway. Very interesting.

"A priest?"

"Guess even demons want confession sometimes."

"I see," he replied dubiously.

"Great book. Thanks for lending it to me."

"You're welcome."

I left the door open and stepped back, making it clear he could come in, without actually inviting him. His lips moved but he didn't say anything out loud. I frowned, but then he stepped across the threshold, glancing around curiously.

"I must say, your taste in décor does not match your taste in attire."

Laughing, I shook my head. "Naw, you should see my room. It matches. The house, still mostly my parents' decorations. I never bothered to change it up."

I currently wore my normal ripped jeans, combat boots, and throwback band T-shirt. My jacket was on its hook by the door. The T-shirt showed off the knotwork tattoos that spiraled up my arms. Protective runes hid in the artwork. The tattoos hidden under my shirt were much earlier works and far more in line with my punk beginnings. The knotwork had been a later addition. The artist had suggested it would meld well with the runes I'd wanted inscribed on my body. She'd been right.

"That makes a great deal more sense," he allowed.

He followed me into the living room where I'd been reading, and I handed him his book back.

"I would have brought it back later tonight, or tomorrow. You didn't have to come out this way." I lived out of town a bit. Not far, just enough to have some space around me.

"It was no trouble. I was curious, and I thought it might not hurt to check on you in case the unbinding went poorly."

"Seemed to work fine."

He touched my shoulder and I stiffened and turned to glare at him. He captured my gaze with his, fingers touching my chin lightly, though I suspected he would have grabbed my face if I'd tried to turn away.

"What?" I demanded after a moment, voice hoarse. My insides were doing all sorts of interesting summersaults I hadn't expected. His scent washed over me, the same scent

I'd gotten caught up in when I'd cast the spell yesterday, heavy spice incense, and old books. Surely, not...

"Just checking."

I cleared my throat and pulled away from him. "Demon's in the basement if you don't believe me."

He followed when I headed that way to show him. That definitely should have been my last clue. Randomly inviting a stranger into my basement to see a demon was not a normal behavior. I certainly didn't think of that until much later.

I'd left the light on so the demon wouldn't be in the dark. Not that I knew if he would have cared or not. He lay basically where I'd left him, though he had shifted to his other side and now faced the door. Not that I had necessarily expected otherwise, but he was still quite naked, and I tried not to peek. Naughty Chris, don't ogle the demon's bits.

His eyes snapped open and he studied both of us.

"Finally," the demon purred.

We both had a moment to say 'what?' before a wave of pure lust washed over me.

I whimpered, stomach tightening with need, vision going hazy for a moment before I found myself shoved up against the wall, legs wrapped around...shit...I didn't even know his name...his lips pressed to mine. We devoured each other, my hands buried in his hair, one of his cupping my head, the other squeezing my ass.

I chased his tongue with my own, tasting him, deepening our connection until I noticed some of his teeth were awfully sharp. Coming up for air, I broke off our kiss, chest heaving, heart racing. He kissed along my jawline before nibbling his way down my neck. I was not quite convinced I'd felt anything strange until he pressed his teeth into my neck, not quite breaking my skin.

"Fuck," I groaned. I supposed if I was going to die, I'd enjoy it. There was literally nothing I could do to defend myself, and I wasn't sure my personal wards would kick in.

He froze, simply going still, not even breathing for a moment.

"I'm sorry," he finally breathed out, lips moving against my neck. "I have no idea what came over me."

"Not sure it was your fault." I tried to get my body to cooperate, but though I thought I should be pulling away my legs remained firmly wrapped around the guy.

"I'm literally starving over here, could you carry on?" The demon's voice caressed my ears. If I hadn't been turned on, and soaked between the legs before, I certainly was now.

My new friend pressed me back into the wall and if what I felt pressed between my legs was any indication, he probably had exactly what I needed to make me very happy. Unfortunately, his teeth were still pressed against my neck.

"I'd rather you kissed me, than bite me, if we're going to do this," I managed through the lust induced fog in my brain. I should be freaking out. Make out sessions with random dudes wasn't necessarily out of the ordinary for me, at least not in the old days. The last five years had been pretty tame in comparison to my youth. I often hadn't even bothered with names, and I wasn't going to take the time to get one now. Vampires on the other hand...this was a first.

He managed to pull himself away from my neck and we went back to devouring each other's lips while the demon purred in the background.

Something broke through our lusty haze and we both froze again.

Loud pounding on the door.

"Darius." I groaned.

"Boyfriend?

"The priest I mentioned."

"Ahh." He ran his thumb lightly over my lips, before tracing my cheek with his fingers, then running them down my neck.

I shivered, tightening my legs around his waist. My heart raced, and more than a little fear settled into my gut which did nothing to cool my ardor.

"I should probably go, anyway," he said, meeting my gaze with his own, and I thought I heard regret in his voice. "I did come simply to check on you and see if you were done with my book. If I had known you had an incubus in your basement, I might have come prepared."

"With condoms?" I quipped.

His eyebrows almost disappeared under his hairline before he laughed. "No, some sort of resistance to your demon's," he hesitated. "Charms."

"To be fair, I didn't know, either." Now that my mystery shopkeeper had me pressed up against the wall, I really didn't want him to leave and I was pretty sure that had more to do with my months of celibacy than the demon's desire to be fed.

My front door clicked.

"He's never actually needed a key to get into most buildings," I explained at the vampire's surprised look.

"Some priest." He settled his hand more firmly on my neck, not letting me down. And I understood I only had moments before things could get dangerous for me and for Darius.

"Look, I'm not going to say anything. Vampire hunting isn't really my gig, so, you know, unless you want to answer some really awkward questions maybe let me down."

He studied me for a moment longer before holding me while I unwrapped my legs from around his waist. He supported me while I tried to get my legs to hold me up again. After one more long, searching look that hopefully convinced him I wasn't going to share his secret with the world, he stepped away.

I'd mostly succeeded in getting my body under control by the time Darius came down into the basement, though we probably both looked a little disheveled.

"Price?" He took in my new vampire friend before glancing over at the incubus now sitting cross legged in the circle.

I followed his gaze and almost had to cover my eyes or risk drooling on myself. The demon was very well endowed and very happy with the situation he'd put me in. Not that I wouldn't have been happy to make out with the vampire, well before I knew he was a vampire, anyway, without the demon's help.

"So, he's still here then." Darius seemed to have forgotten about my other guest for the moment.

"Yeah." I cleared my throat. "He wanted to talk to you."

"So, Demon, what did you want?"

"This demon has a name." The incubus climbed to his feet.

"And what do you wish to be called?" Darius crossed his arms over his chest.

"My name is Sabianamon. You can call me Sabian."

The power of his name washed over me. Had he really just given us his real name? Seriously?

I met Sabian's light amber gaze. He smiled and my panties would have melted off if such a thing were actually possible. Fuck. My knees wobbled, and I had to catch myself on the wall.

"Sabian," Darius said slowly.

"Yes." Fortunately, Sabian's impressive erection was fading back to merely an impressive dick, which was a little less distracting. Not a lot less, considering I'd just been about to tear a vampire's clothing off and I was still completely aroused. If I could have given the incubus a towel, or something, I would have, but I didn't want to break the circle. He was having a big enough effect on us as it was.

"You wanted to see me?"

"They're running drugs. I think you knew that. My memories are a little hazy and incomplete."

"Yes. Your host was the first we actually managed to catch."

Sabian shuddered, a full body motion that managed to convey the depth of his revulsion, and also remind me of a dog shaking.

"They are summoning demons, binding them into charms, and handing them out to their people."

I shared a concerned look with Darius before he turned back to the demon. "Why?"

The demon shrugged. "If you could be faster, stronger, and more bullet proof than your competition, wouldn't you be at least interested in the idea? Especially if the cost was much lower than normal possession?"

"He's got a point," I agreed.

"Anything else you can tell us to help stop this?"

Sabian shook his head. "Unfortunately, no. Not that I don't want to, I just don't remember anything else. The bindings are cleverly done."

"That someone with the kind of skill necessary to bind demons in such a way is working with a drug cartel is concerning," the vampire offered.

That brought Darius' attention back to him.

"Who are you, anyway?"

"Malak Naji," the vampire offered. "I lent Ms. Price the spell to unbind the demon."

Oh, that was his name. Malak, huh. I realized he also hadn't known my name until Darius had said it. It took a great deal of effort to keep from laughing.

Something must have shown on my face because Darius shook his head. "Chris, you're something else."

"What?" I asked innocently.

His gaze flicked between me and Malak for a moment before he shook his head again. "I'm well familiar with that flushed, disheveled look of yours."

"Um, well, to be fair, Sabian's an incubus, and he's starving, so it wasn't my fault. Or his." I pointed at Malak.

"Right." Darius gave Malak a long hard look before glancing back at Sabian. "Ready to go back?"

Sabian shrugged and glanced between me and Malak before returning his attention to Darius. "I'd actually kind of like to stay."

"Of course, you would," Darius grumbled.

"I'm not a crossroads demon where souls are involved, or even out to make a deal. I just haven't been up here in at least an age. Might be fun to look around. I'm not even particularly evil." He gave Darius a winning smile. "Besides, I might be able to help with your drug cartel."

"How?"

The demon shrugged. "I don't know. I simply might be able to help. I'm harmless."

"You had my best friend making out with a total stranger," Darius pointed out.

"Uh, mate, that's not really so out of character, right? At least he's a hot stranger." I grinned when Darius shot me an annoyed look. Why was I defending the demon, again? "Besides, I was enjoying myself. Pretty sure Malak was, too."

Malak chuckled.

"See, harmless." Sabian did his best impression of a puppy dog, turning his amber eyes fully on Darius.

"You're begging me to release you and let you hang out with my best friend? Seriously?"

"I already gave you my name. What else do you need? She's basically my master now."

"Naw, you can leave the dungeon mastering to Malak." I snickered at Malak's startled expression.

Darius frowned at the vampire. "What?"

"Role playing." Malak sighed.

The demon purred. "I like whips and chains."

"Why is everyone suddenly going right to whips and chains?" Malak exclaimed. "Dice, lots of shiny little dice, and books, and beer and pizza. No whips and chains."

I doubted Malak was actually consuming pizza, but then, I had also thought vampires were allergic to sunlight and that was obviously incorrect. The thoughts didn't stop my laughter.

"You'd like it," Sabian retorted.

"What?" Malak and I blurted at the same time.

"I can always tell what people will like." He gave us both a lazy wink. "Otherwise, I wouldn't have encouraged you to kiss."

"Learn something new every day. Eh, mate?" I nudged Malak.

He sighed again.

Darius chuckled. "I'm tempted to let your demon out and leave you three alone. Might be good for you to date a nerd instead of your normal type."

If he knew Malak wasn't just a nerd... I wasn't about to break my promise to Malak though, even to my best friend. Not without a really good reason. Then I got a look at Darius' expression. Was he serious?

"Oh please," Sabian begged. He went so far as to drop to his knees and clasp his hands up in an imploring gesture. "I promise to behave."

"Define behave," Darius ordered.

Whoa, he was actually considering it. He must know something I didn't, because I wasn't nearly as convinced as the priest seemed to be. Maybe the investigation really was that desperate.

"Well, I won't harm Chris, or Malak, or you." He hesitated, thinking. "No inciting orgies unless it's in defense of you three." He sank back on his heels, head tilted. "What do you want me to promise?" he finally asked.

"Incubi are not harmless," Malak offered. "But he's nearly got me convinced he is, at least to us. Demons are notoriously devious, but he did give us his name. That negates a great deal of his power should we chose to use it."

Mmmm, Malak was considering an 'us' in this equation. I might get my hands on him, after all. What the fuck was I thinking? He's a vampire. My brain did mental yo-yos while I tried to come to terms with my conflicting desires. None of them necessarily involved letting an incubus loose in my life, however.

Darius shook his head. "Here's why I'm considering this, demon."

"Sabian," the demon corrected.

Darius hesitated for a moment before shaking his head. "Fine, Sabian."

The demon purred when Darius said his name.

What the fuck? Did he actually get off on being controlled? Shit, was he a sub? What on earth were we getting into? I could already tell Darius was going to let him stay.

"Here's why I'm considering your request. We might actually need your help with the drug cartel. If you'll help us, and the other things you promised, then I'll let you out."

I wanted to object, because obviously Darius wasn't going to take an incubus to church, so he would be staying with me, but though I thought the words, they didn't cross my lips. What the hell. Might be fun to have a well-endowed incubus around. My vibrator was only so satisfying. As if sensing my thoughts, Sabian's gaze wandered over to me and he grinned.

"I agree, I'll help as much as I can." He bounced to his feet.

I managed to keep my eyes on his chest, but it was tough.

Darius glanced at me.

"You know he'll have to feed off of sex, right?" I pointed out.

"Isn't that what your dungeon master is for?"

That was a little callous, but that was Darius. When he got focused on a mission he tended to forget that people were, well, people and not tools.

"I mean..." I shrugged. "That's probably up to him."

I glanced at Mal who looked a little shell shocked at the turn of events, but not exactly unwilling. The demon's influence? Or something else?

My brain was so tweaked out by the bizarre turn of events that I was having a hard time finding words.

"You've never had a problem with sex with random guys in the past. That change?"

I narrowed my eyes at Darius.

"Why exactly do you want to keep the incubus?" I ignored his other question.

"Sabian here is the first demon the cops have come across that they were able to catch, but the increase in activities with the drug cartel have been immense recently. They're loosely associated with human traffickers. If we can't get it stopped before this spills over, it could get pretty bad for a lot of innocent people."

Huh, maybe he did actually have a real reason for keeping the demon around.

"If Sabian can give us an edge, we might need it. Obviously, I have to leave him with you. I'm not judging, Chris. I have no ground to stand on in that regard. I just know you used to like sex, and I feel like they'll probably be a step up from your usual hookups."

"I..." Was I really agreeing to this? Yeah, I was. Human trafficking, that was bad shit and demons getting in on it was even worse than the drugs. Darius was right. We had to get this stopped. "Okay, mate. Just remember, I'm stuck with the demon because of you. You can not come back later and try to get all righteous on me or some shit."

"Promise," Darius replied.

I glanced at Mal, who had settled back into an interested but somewhat impassive expression, as if we weren't talking about using him to help me feed an incubus. Mal glanced at me, winked, and went back to studying Sabian. Maybe he wasn't that upset about it. Come to think of it, willing hookups might be hard for a vampire to find. At least with someone who knew what he was.

Darius took a deep breath, then slid his foot across the circle, breaking the containment spell.

Sabian squealed in glee, threw his hands up, and scampered over to my side. I'd never seen a six foot something tall man scamper before, but he nailed it. Then he sank down next to me and wrapped his arms around my leg, resting his head on my thigh and staring up at me adoringly.

I gaped at him, not even sure what to say.

Malak chuckled.

Darius sighed. "I'm not sure if I should be apologizing or not, Chris."

"Don't know. Looks like I'm in for a good time."

Darius actually blushed.

"Is that something a man of the cloth is supposed to promote?" I couldn't help but needle him a little. "Demons, lewd acts, leaving me with a dungeon master."

Malak sighed.

Darius gave Malak another searching look before he shook his head. "You haven't had a lot of luck with humans, maybe the demon can change things around for you."

I almost choked. "Yeah, definitely think that's not something a priest is supposed to say."

Darius grinned. "Hell, Price, he might be safer to let loose in Santa Fe than you are."

I could not come up with a proper retort because, maybe, just maybe, he was right. "Yeah, thanks for that, mate. So, change of subject. Sabian..."

The demon purred, the sound going straight to my groin. My legs nearly buckled, and I was almost grateful when Malak aborted his move to grab me, or Darius might have gotten an eyeful.

"Could you keep that under wraps for a bit, mate?"

"Sorry," Sabian replied contritely.

"I'd make a quip about innocent eyes, but Darius isn't nearly as pure as his profession makes him out to be." I glared at my friend.

He shrugged, not denying it.

"Anyway, Darius, could you get some clothes for our new friend here? I'm quite certain I have nothing in his size. Well, maybe a robe, but that's probably about it."

"Sure, Price. I'll pick a few things up. Bring them by tomorrow afternoon?" He waggled his eyebrows.

I managed to refrain from blushing. "Hey, you're the one leaving me with a starving incubus."

"You want me to send him back to hell instead?" Darius asked. "If you don't want him around, I'll make him leave."

Sabian tightened his arms around my leg, but as far as I could tell, he wasn't otherwise using any of his powers on me. My personal wards would protect me from most anything that would harm me, which is how his power before had gotten through–he'd meant no harm. I'd never put the wards to the test against a vampire before, so I wasn't sure how effective they would have been if Malak had gotten his teeth in my vein. Maybe if he'd actually been trying to hurt me, but he hadn't been. Just caught up in the lust like me.

"Naw, guess he can stay."

Sabian let out a relieved breath.

"Malak, nice to meet you," Darius said. "She's a handful, hope you're up for it." He headed for the stairway. "You might want to go upstairs first, more comfortable."

"Darius!"

He chuckled and hurried up the stairs.

"Fucker," I muttered.

We stood around in uncomfortable silence until I heard the front door close then I glanced at Malak, not entirely sure how to proceed.

He clasped his hands together, partially avoiding my gaze, obviously not quite sure what to do next, either.

"Ms. Price…"

"Naw, mate. You had your tongue in my mouth. Think that means you can call me Chris."

"Okay," he replied, laughing. "I typically go by Mal."

"Great."

"I should probably leave."

Damn it, I'd actually wanted him to stick around. Wasn't going to force the issue, though. That certainly wasn't fair.

"Sure, if you want."

He tilted his head. "Do you want me to stay?"

I shrugged. "Hungry incubus and all, might be useful to have you around." Sabian tightened his grip on my leg again.

Mal's eyes widened. "I'm not sure you need me if you have a hungry incubus."

"I'm still too close to starving," Sabian interjected. "I could hurt Chris, or even you, if I fed directly from you."

"Well, in that case, you gotta stay." I smiled at him.

Mal shifted on his feet and shoved his hands in his pockets. "I could," he said slowly.

"Only if you want to," I felt I had to add.

He gave me a lopsided smile. "I have no objections per se, I'm more surprised you want me to stick around. I bite, after all."

"Ah, well, only live once, I guess. Never had a vampire before."

He took a step closer, and I held my breath. He reached out, tracing his fingers along my temple, through the shaved hair on the side of my head and down my neck, making me shiver, speeding my heart.

"I've never had an exorcist before," he replied softly.

"We're something else." I grinned.

"I can tell."

"I'll stay until the morning," he offered. "Then I'll leave you with my phone number. It'll be your choice if you want to see me again."

"What if you don't want to see me again?"

"You're the most interesting person I've met in quite some years. I'm already convinced I'd like to get to know you better."

"Even if I don't role play?" I teased.

"I'm positive I could change your mind. And who knows, maybe Sabian would enjoy it."

I'd somehow nearly forgotten about the demon clinging to my leg. Mal had captured all of my attention.

"I'm up for anything, except being starved," Sabian replied.

"Hint taken," Mal answered and held out his hand. "Care to show me your bedroom? I'm curious what a space you've decorated looks like."

"Just, uh, don't judge the mess. Haven't had anyone to impress in a while."

"Promise."

Dakota Brown

Chapter 5

Price

Mal held my hand as I led him and Sabian down the hallway to the back corner of the house where my room was. Sometimes I thought about moving into the master. Then I thought about dealing with my parents' things. Note, I still slept in my old room.

Not much had changed since my mother had turned me loose with black and white paint. The walls were black, the trim and the ceiling white. I'd since painted wards all the way around the room, making it extra warded in addition to the house wards. I'd done the same with the basement, but for different reasons.

Both Mal and Sabian passed through with no difficulties. That made me a little uneasy.

"Hey, Mal, how'd you get in the house, anyway. Wards should have kept you out."

The vampire turned from his contemplation of a poster of one of my favorite eighties vampire flicks, and glanced at me, eyebrow raised.

I blushed a little and shrugged. "You ever actually seen that movie?"

He rolled his eyes. "Yes."

"One of my favorites. Sue me."

"I promised, no judging."

"Right. I never redecorated after I moved back in."

He smirked at me.

"So, wards?" I changed the subject away from my childhood décor.

"I may have altered my personal protections so that the wards would not recognize me as any sort of threat."

My jaw dropped. "Wait, you can do that?"

"Well, I can," Mal answered. "I very much doubt too many others have the ability."

"Whoa, wait a minute. How do you know that?"

"I'm an occultist. I should have thought that would be clear from the reading materials I lent you."

"So am I. Never knew you could do that with wards."

"Chris, I'm considerably older than you are. I have probably forgotten more about the occult than most people know."

"Oh, right. How old?"

He gave me a cagey smile before turning his attention back to the décor.

Sabian also glanced around, before he found a corner to curl up in and just sort of faded from my awareness.

My phone chimed, distracting me from the pile of clothing in the corner I'd intended to shove in a closet. I fished it out of my pocket and read the text.

"Hey, before you leave, can we send a picture of that ritual to unbind the demons to Darius?"

"Yes."

"Great, thanks."

Mal stepped over to me, took my phone and turned it off before tossing it onto my window seat.

My heart raced as he stepped back into my space and brushed his fingers over my hair. I was definitely a little afraid of him and I was fairly sure he knew it. If he had tricked my house wards, I suspected my personal protections wouldn't respond to a threat from him, either.

Still, I kissed him back when he pressed his lips to mine, and soon I'd forgotten my fear as my tongue chased his, his lips melding to mine.

I wrapped my arms around him, running my hands up under his shirt and across his muscled back.

Mal held me tightly, one hand pressed between my shoulder blades, one cradling my head, somehow making me feel as if I were the most important thing in the world to him at that moment. Only one other lover had made me feel that important, and the emotion nearly brough tears to my eyes.

"You all right?" Mal broke off our kiss to whisper. He ran his thumb across my cheek. Apparently, I had teared up.

"Yeah, mate. I'm fine." Shit, that would take some getting used to if we got up to this again. I wasn't used to someone so perceptive. I guessed a vampire would have to be to survive.

Mal ran his hands down my shoulders, caressing my upper arms, then down my sides.

I moaned softly and pressed against him. He slid his fingers under the hem of my shirt and tugged gently. I raised my arms, wishing I'd had some sort of idea this morning that someone else would be undressing me. I would have worn the lacy underwear.

Mal tossed my shirt aside before letting his eyes roam over my inked skin. He traced his fingers up the knotwork on my arms, pausing over the hidden runes, before lightly brushing his hands down my front, exploring the ink.

Before I could say anything, he turned me so he could see my back.

I wondered if my art had completely distracted him from our intentions, but then he unclasped my bra. I let that slide off my arms and fall to the ground.

He finished investigating the exposed tats and returned to caressing my skin with his hands. Mal pulled me backward so my back was pressed against his chest, one hand went to my chest, gently massaging my breast, while the other cupped my chin and tilted my head back, baring my throat.

My heart skipped a beat when he lowered his lips to my neck, but he only kissed me, lips gentle as he kissed to the curve of my shoulder. I relaxed into his embrace, letting him have my body for the moment. He knew what he wanted, and for once I was happy to surrender control for a time.

"You are beautiful," he murmured, lips against my skin.

"Bet you say that to everyone." I jumped when he tweaked my nipple, annoyed at my quip.

"Only when it's true," he growled back at me, biting at my shoulder.

"Thank you," I replied, chastised.

He really was skilled. I hadn't even lost most of my clothing and he already had me far more hot and bothered than just about anyone else I'd ever been with. I was starting to think I'd seriously been missing out.

Mal's hands wandered lower, tracing across my stomach, before unsnapping my jeans.

I was about to pull away so I could slide out of my pants when he ran both hands to my hips, hooked my jeans, and slid them off me, sinking down to the ground behind me on his knees.

Shit, he was smooth. He even carefully lifted my leg with one hand, while supporting my waist with another so I wouldn't stumble. Yay for a man with experience.

Mal caressed my legs, turning me back toward him and now he was staring straight at my pussy, a pleased smile curling his lips.

He smoothly rose to his feet and pushed me backward until my legs pressed against my bed. I sat and he gently pushed my shoulders back until I was laying down, legs hanging over the edge, with him standing between my knees. He leaned over me, one hand cupping my breast.

Then he stopped, tilted his head, and stared at my bedspread. My rainbow colored unicorn bedspread. It was old, but still serviceable.

"Uh, went through a phase."

He grinned and turned his attention back to me. "No judgement, remember?"

Turning my attention away from the remnant of my childhood, I tugged at his shirt and he let me pull it off.

"For a nerd, you sure do have a lot of muscle." I let my admiration show in my tone.

His laugh went straight to my core, tightening things that were already aching for attention.

I traced my fingers down his chest, following the line of a faded scar. If what I'd felt from his back was any indication, he had a few more back there.

Possibly intentionally, Mal distracted me from questions by dragging his hands down my sides until his hands were on my hips. He knelt between my legs, kissing my thigh as he worked his way closer to my poor, neglected clit. I opened for him, groaning in pleasure as his tongue flicked along my lips.

I cried out when he focused on my clit, squirming at the intensity, clutching the bedspread. He held me still, hands on my hips, while his extremely skilled tongue worked me to the edge of what promised to be an intense release. My legs trembled, heat pooled in my core, my extremities tingled, I cried out as Malak took me over the edge, seeing stars as my body shattered.

By the time my vision cleared, and I'd caught my breath a little, Mal had shed his pants. He crawled up the bed over me. I admired his lean muscles, and yeah, he was just as well-endowed as I'd anticipated.

I licked my lips before meeting his eyes.

He gave me a questioning look, and I held out my hand inviting him closer. "I've got an implant, but..."

"Vampire," he said. "No babies, no diseases."

"Convenient."

"Mostly," he agreed.

I pulled him to me, pressing my mouth to his, tasting me on his lips. I'd always enjoyed that. We devoured each other's lips for a time before he pressed himself against my opening.

"Still okay?" he asked.

"Yeah, Mal."

He smiled and slowly pushed into me.

Moaning, I tilted my hips, enjoying being stretched, taking him as deeply as I could. He slowly slid out of me, then picked up the pace. It didn't take long before I was building toward another orgasm. Mal panted as he thrust into me. I hooked my leg over his back, digging my nails into his shoulder. He rumbled in pleasure.

It surprised me at how long he lasted after everything we'd already been through that evening, but when he finally did stiffen, he brought me over the edge with him. We crashed through our releases together, and when I came down from that high, I found myself cradled in Mal's arms. It had been so long since anyone had held me after sex, he almost got tears again, but this time I really did fight them off.

"That was probably some of the best sex I've ever had."

"Thank you," he murmured, sounding sleepy.

"Hey, Mal? Do vampires need to breathe?"

"No, but if I don't breathe during sex, it usually freaks people out, so I taught myself to remember to." Clearly, he had known where I was going with my question. He kissed my neck and I snuggled more firmly against his chest.

"Any other pressing post sex questions?" He nibbled at my ear.

"I'm sure I'll think of something eventually."

"Sabian, how are you feeling?" Mal raised his voice slightly.

Shit, I'd forgotten about the incubus. Wasn't the first time I'd gotten laid with an audience. I just usually didn't forget they were there.

"Much better," he purred from where he lay somewhere on the floor out of sight. "Feel free to keep it up, though."

Mal ran his hand over my hip. "Not a terrible idea."

Startled, I shifted so I could meet his eyes. "Seriously?"

"If you want."

"Hell yes."

He laughed. "We'll make sure our incubus is quite full before we get our own rest."

"I think that sounds fantastic."

His lips met mine again, and I wondered how long he could keep going. Maybe there were a few advantages to fucking a vampire.

∞ ∞ ∞

When I woke the next morning, sunlight filtering in through curtains I hadn't remembered to shut, I expected to be alone, not curled up spooned in someone's arms.

"You know," I said softly, once I was aware enough of my surroundings to be semi-coherent, "if you spoil me too much, you might not be able to get rid of me."

Mal tightened his arms and kissed my bare shoulder. "I'll take that chance."

"Okay, pressing vampire question number two. Sunlight?"

He chuckled. "Only a problem for vampires in movies."

"Huh."

"Do you want me to make you breakfast?"

I froze for a moment before I rolled over so I could face him. "Seriously?"

"I like to cook."

"Can you eat food?"

"Not really. Doesn't mean I don't like preparing it."

"You really are trying to spoil me."

Mal grinned. "Yes. It's my diabolical plot to get you back in my bed again."

"Technically it's my bed."

"Unicorns and all," he teased.

"Hey, no judging."

"I'm not. I like unicorns."

"Really?"

"They're quite fierce."

"Wait, are unicorns real?"

He gave me that enigmatic grin before he kissed my forehead and climbed out of bed.

I watched while he dressed, enjoying the fluid grace of his movements.

"Do you want breakfast?" He directed that to the floor.

I'd forgotten about Sabian again. I wondered if he was doing that on purpose or if my defenses were just that low right now. If so, I was far too comfortable with a demon and a vampire sleeping in the same room as me. Though, to be fair, neither of them had hurt me. I rubbed my neck. Mal must have been holding back last night. I hadn't noticed him display any hint of fang the entire time. It almost made me feel bad, but I wasn't sure I was quite ready for that level of connection with him.

The two of them left my room together, Sabian still naked. He probably didn't care, but I needed to find him a robe, which meant I needed to venture into the time capsule of my parents' bedroom. I was certain dad would have had a robe that would be close enough in size for Sabian to wear, at least until Darius arrived with clothing for the demon.

I stretched deliciously sore muscles and debated staying in bed until breakfast was ready. No, at some point I was sure Sabian would go outside. I did not need him to be parading around my property starkers.

Groaning, I rolled out of bed and hit the bathroom to freshen up. I pulled on my normal clothes and stumbled back to the master bedroom. Hand on the doorknob, I hesitated. Did I want to be caffeinated first? It wasn't so much the room itself, and the belongings, that kept me out of my parents' bedroom. It was the memories, the nightmares that followed. Their scent lingered on the air all these years later. The light perfume my mother had worn on special occasions. The spicy aftershave Dad enjoyed. The scents sparked the memories, and the nightmares always chased them. I was in for a rough few nights, but it wasn't anything I hadn't dealt with before.

Deciding just to rip the band-aid off, I opened the door and stepped inside.

I tried not to look around at the heavy wood furniture, the southwestern patterned comforter on their bed, now coated in a layer of dust, the comfortable armchair I still debated about dragging out into the living area. It smelled like my dad's aftershave though and I didn't think I could handle that.

I hurried over to the closet, flipped on the light, and grabbed my father's summer robe out. It was black, fuzzy, and light enough to be comfortable in the warmer parts of the year. Sabian was bigger than my dad had been, but not by a whole lot. It should fit well enough.

Trying not to bring the robe to my nose so I could smell it more deeply, I flipped off the light, shut the closet door, and hurried out of the room, running from the memories. Friday night movies with my family, walks in the desert, ice cream in the square.

Shuddering, I made my way back to the kitchen and thrust the robe at Sabian.

"You don't like the view?" He pouted as he took the clothing from me.

"Naw, view's great. Just, probably don't need the neighbors ogling you should someone happen to be close enough to see."

He smirked and slid his arm into the sleeve.

Something of my mood must have come through, because Mal came over and put his arms around me. I snuggled into him, shock at his consideration warring with my desire not to burden him with my problems.

Mal seemed to know I didn't want to talk about it, and didn't ask, just held me tightly for a minute before going back to cooking.

Who did that for a virtual stranger, anyway? Apparently nerdy occultist vampires did. Never would have guessed.

I hopped onto the barstool at the island, determined to ignore the wash of sadness until it went away. That usually worked. Eventually.

"What's for breakfast?"

"Pancakes and bacon. That's about the best I could do with the ingredients you had available." Mal handed me a plate.

"Pretty damn good since I didn't have mix."

He gave me a horrified look.

I grinned.

Sabian, now clothed, sat next to me and Mal gave him a plate, too.

"Gods, these are perfect." I moaned, eyes closed in bliss. "You know, I have space, might as well move in, I need this every morning."

I opened my eyes to see both guys staring at me. Sabian looked enraptured, eyes a little wide, lips parted in ecstasy.

Mal's expression was a bit more predatory, but definitely interested.

Could Sabian feed off of my pleasure just from eating good food? If the expression on his face was any indication, the answer was yes. Guess it was polite to feed my guests.

At that thought my attention returned to Mal.

He sipped some coffee, looking pleased.

Breakfast went quickly, and Sabian offered to clean up. Hoping he somehow knew how a dishwasher worked, I left him alone in the kitchen while Mal and I went to get that picture of the ritual so I could send it to Darius.

I turned on my phone and followed Mal into the basement where he'd left his book last night.

"I feel like I should apologize, mate." I twisted my hands nervously.

"For what?" Mal tucked his book under his arm and glanced at me.

"Dragging you into all of this."

His eyes glinted in amusement. "Did you miss the part where I enjoyed myself last night?" He brushed his fingers across my cheek.

"Uh, no." My face heated slightly. "Just, uh." I shrugged, not able to articulate what I was feeling.

"I'm glad I came over to check on you." He leaned in and I angled my neck so I could meet his lips. He wrapped his free arm around me, pulling me against him as we kissed. I leaned into him, clutching at his shirt maybe a little desperately.

He released me after a few minutes, a smile crinkling the corners of his eyes.

"Let's get this spell sent to your priest."

"Yeah." I gestured toward the stairs. Light would be better in the living room.

Once we were upstairs, Mal opened the book to the right page and I snapped a few pics and texted them to Darius.

He replied with a thumbs up a moment later and a quick question.

Darius: *You okay?*

Me: *Fine. Thanks.*

Darius: *See you in a few hours with some clothes for your guest.*

I replied with a thumbs up and handed my phone to Mal. "Number?"

He quickly entered himself into my contacts and handed my phone back. "I should be going. Olivia might get concerned if I don't at least show up for a few minutes today."

"Olivia?" *No, we will not be jealous of women in Malak's life*, I told myself. *You literally have no claim on him.*

His lips twitched and I thought he might be fighting a grin. "She co-owns the shop. She does most of the work, but I stop in most days and I work the counter on days she wants off."

"Ahh." *See, nothing to be jealous of,* I told my stupid brain. "Yeah, I probably should put in an appearance at work at some point, too."

"Sabian, it was nice to meet you."

The demon looked up from the sink. Clearly, he hadn't known how to use the dishwasher, but he did know how to do dishes by hand. "Yes. I'll see you soon, Mal." He grinned at the vampire. "Thank you for breakfast."

I walked Mal to the door.

He wrapped me in another soul-feeding hug and gave me a relatively chaste kiss. "Call me if you want. I hope to see you again, Chris Price."

I didn't reply, just watched him leave. He drove a hybrid. Go figure.

Once Mal had left, I wrapped my arms around myself and shivered, feeling a little empty. That was a weird feeling for me. Usually, I was glad to get a lover gone and get back to my life. Now I felt a little lost. I wandered back to the kitchen.

"What are we doing today?" Sabian came around the counter and stood next to me.

"Um, not much until Darius gets here with some clothes for you."

"I've heard so much from some of the other demons who've come back from being topside. I want to see it all." He bounced on his toes.

"Okay, great. Rule number one, though. Don't tell anyone you're a demon."

"Duh."

My jaw dropped and then I shook my head. Right.

"I guess I don't have any other rules. I'm not good at following them, anyway. Here, um, let me show you the TV. I need to do a few things around the house. We can head out once you have some clothes."

His face lit up and I found myself smiling in return. Maybe not quite as empty as I had thought.

Chapter 6

Price

Darius arrived a few hours later. I was outside, trying not to get sunburnt while at the same time enjoying being in the fresh air.

"So, how's the demon?" he asked by way of greeting.

"Does dishes, so I guess he can stay. Currently learning about the world through the TV."

"Lord help us all," Darius intoned.

I laughed.

"And your dungeon master?"

"Dear God, Darius, seriously?" I sputtered.

He smiled and crossed his arms.

"Well, he cooks."

"By the pleased expression on your face, he does more than cook."

"You really want the details?" He was going to get an earful if he kept pushing. When he didn't reply right away, I shrugged. "He knows how to take care of a woman."

"Good."

"Tell me you brought some clothes for Sabian?"

"I did my best without him actually there. By the way, are you aware that incubi are shape shifters?"

I raised my eyebrows. "Oh really?"

"Yes. In fact, an incubus is merely a lust demon who has taken male form instead of female form."

"You mean he's a succubus, too?"

"If he wants to be."

"Okay, then." I pinched the bridge of my nose. "Can't say I knew that. Not my area of expertise. Skipped right over the sex demons and focused on the ones I thought I was more likely to meet."

Darius chuckled. He grabbed a few bags from his car and followed me into the house.

"Sabian! Company."

We met the demon in the living area and Darius held out the bags to him. "I just got some basics. I hope they fit."

The demon looked in the bags and his eyes lit up. "Thank you, priest."

Now I was curious what Darius had gotten that made the demon so happy.

It turned out that Sabian was simply easily pleased. A couple of pair of jeans and some plain T-shirts, underwear, socks, and hiking boots. Darius had done very well guessing the demon's size, or the demon had simply adjusted himself to fit. I didn't want to know at this point.

He also had zero sense of modesty. After Sabian inspected all of the clothing he shed the robe and dressed in the living room. It wasn't exactly as if we hadn't seen him naked already, it just surprised me. Darius simply shook his head and turned his attention outside while Sabian slid on his new clothing.

The T-shirts were just tight enough to make looking at the handsome demon very fun, and the way his jeans hugged his hips should have been illegal.

"I've taken the information Sabian gave to me to the police. They're working on finding new leads. If there's anything you can help them with, I'll be in touch."

I didn't bother to point out that I hadn't offered to help further, Sabian had. Darius knew if he asked, I'd come.

Darius stayed for a little while longer before heading back to his church, leaving a now clothed Sabian and I alone. I kind of didn't want to take him to work with me. I kind of did. I never took guys I was dating or just sleeping with to the pizza shop and if they showed up there, they were summarily kicked out and told not to return. If they really wanted pizza, I'd get them take out. I was not sleeping with or dating Sabian, but it felt the same.

Oh well, I wasn't about to leave him on his own, at least not yet, and I had a few things to do, including teaching Billy how to do payroll.

I leaned against the frame of the sliding glass door, arms crossed. My father had stood that way many times in the past and I'd taken up the habit at some point. The doors faced west, and we got some spectacular views of the desert as the sun set.

Sabian came over behind me and put his hand on my shoulder. I stiffened for a moment before relaxing into his touch. Unlike Mal's, his hand was quite warm.

When I didn't pull away, he dragged his fingers lightly down my bicep and across my forearm until he could tuck his hand around mine. Sabian fitted himself against my back, put his other arm around my waist, and stood there, holding me.

Eventually I remembered to breathe again, though my heart sped at his proximity. After I relaxed a little, Sabian tightened the arm around my waist, rubbing my hip gently. I leaned back against his chest, stomach tightening with need, heart racing again. What was I doing? Mal hadn't minded Sabian feeding off us, but surely he would mind if the minute he was out of my sight, I jumped the demon.

As if sensing my hesitation, Sabian stilled his hand, just holding me, while I tried to get my racing heart under control again. I finally calmed down, though now I ached for release. Damn him, anyway. Having an incubus around was going to be really interesting if he affected me like that constantly.

Still, it was a few more minutes before I reluctantly pulled away from his warm embrace.

"Probably ought to show up at the shop for a few. Guess you can come along," I grumbled.

Sabian didn't say anything, simply followed behind as we went from the air-conditioned house out into the hot evening air. He watched me closely as I got in the car and put on my seatbelt, before doing the same on the passenger side.

Once he was secure, I pulled out of the driveway and headed into town.

We didn't speak, though I was completely aware of his presence. It was like sitting next to a lightning bolt. My skin prickled, sending jolts all the way down to my core. Having actually been on the other end of him using his power, I didn't think he was actively trying to do something to me, he was just being him. Unfortunately, my body was reacting strongly to his presence and it was a touch uncomfortable.

I wasn't ready to call Malak yet. We'd just parted ways, and I thought a little distance between the two of us might not be a terrible thing. Maybe I'd just have to have a solo party with my vibrator tonight.

Thinking of that got me even more bothered and I gritted my teeth.

I managed to make it to the pizza shop without pulling over and jumping Sabian on the side of the road, and once we were out of the car and I was able to breathe in a bit of the dry, dusty desert air, I managed to calm down some.

He never said a word, just followed me from the air-conditioned car through the blast of heat, and into the air-conditioned pizza shop.

I inhaled the overwhelming scent of garlic and sauce, hoping it would chase the memory of Mal's spicy scent away. It didn't.

Sabian followed close behind me until I noticed I was getting curious looks from my staff. At least a few of them had been present for me throwing over ambitious lovers out of my restaurant and knew my personal rule about not bringing anyone else by.

I glanced at the hostess, pointed at Sabian and mouthed 'table.'

She held up two fingers and I led the demon over to table two. I couldn't help but notice how everyone's gaze followed the incubus and I doubted it was pure curiosity that motivated that.

"What do you like?"

"What do you mean?" Sabian was looking around, studying the décor and he turned his attention back to me.

"To eat."

"Besides sex?" He grinned at me.

I groaned. "Yeah. Cause that's not on the menu here."

He faked a pout before answering. "I don't know. I'll try your favorite. You need dinner, too."

Sabian had a point, so when Stacy came over, I ordered my favorite, all the cheese, and then extra cheese, mushrooms, and pepperoni, and a couple of ginger beers.

"Stay here and be nice to Stacy. I need to go do some paperwork." Maybe I should have defined nice, because the expression she directed toward Sabian was a bit more than just friendly. I wondered if he could tone his power down a bit more, but it wasn't the best time to ask with other people around.

He pushed his lip out in another pout.

"I'll be back before the pizza gets cold."

Sabian turned his adorable, pouty lips up into a bright smile and I kind of wanted to suck his lip into my mouth so

I could taste it. There were other things I wanted to put in my mouth, too. I cleared my throat when Sabian's smile slid into the seductive range and jerked my attention away from those kissable lips and practically fled to my office.

Billy came in a few minutes later and I gestured for him to take my place. "You've done payrolls before, right?"

"Yes."

"Okay, let's get started."

He raised his eyebrows and I realized I had neglected to tell him he was taking on that responsibility.

"Yeah, think it's time I handed that over to you."

"Sure, boss. No problem. Who's your friend?" He slid into my vacated seat.

"Just a friend." I sighed.

"Sure." He didn't press, though his curiosity was palpable.

Shortly, I had him reviewing time records and since he was already familiar with the payroll system, I doubted it would be long before he was better at it than I was.

"I'm going to go eat. Let me know if you have any questions. Otherwise, I'm probably going to take off early. There's not much else to do on the paperwork end and I need to get a few other things done."

"That's fine, Chris. It should be a quiet night."

I chuckled. "You just jinxed yourself."

"Ugh, let's hope not."

"Yeah, mate. Okay. Holler if you need me." I clapped him on the shoulder before leaving the office and heading back out to the dining area.

The pizza had arrived by the time I got there, but Sabian had waited for me.

"Go on." I slid into the booth.

He stared at the pizza and I understood he actually wasn't sure how to start.

"Okay, like this."

Demonstrating the finer points of successfully eating a ridiculously cheesy pizza kept us occupied for another hour.

"So, pizza going to do it for you tonight? Or do you need more?"

Sabian eyed the empty tray before turning his gem-like amber eyes on me. Things inside tightened and I really should not have been considering dragging him back to my office, kicking Billy out, and locking the door.

"I will be okay for a while," he allowed. "It's a lot easier if I just feed every night."

"Noted. Um, where do you want to go?"

He studied me for a few minutes before shrugging. "Someplace where sexual energy is high. That would be best."

"There's a seedy strip joint out in the desert a way," I offered hesitantly. "Only place I know around here. Closer than going all the way to a big city."

"That would probably do it."

"Great. Well, let's go then. You tell me when you're full though so we can leave. I don't mind the girls, it's the clientele that bothers me."

Stacy walked up just then, because of course she did. She gave me a quizzical look but was too polite to ask if she'd heard what she thought she had.

"Need anything else, Chris?"

"Naw, thanks, mate."

She nodded and headed to another table. I threw down a twenty as a tip and slid out of the booth. Sabian followed.

The sun was considerably lower in the sky when we left the pizza shop. I slid into the car and let the air conditioner run while I thought. I didn't mind taking him out tonight, but while I had money, taking him to the strip joint every night would get expensive. Not to mention I really didn't want to spend that much time there.

"You could call Mal instead," Sabian offered.

I sighed. "I'll let him think about things for a day or two before I call him. Make sure he doesn't want to change his mind or something."

"There are also other options," he offered softly.

I glanced at him, expecting a sly smile or something, not the hesitance I found in his expression.

"Eh, we'll get you good and full tonight and then I'll see what me and my vibrator can accomplish tomorrow. How's that?"

A smile flickered briefly across his lips and my panties tried to melt again. "Okay."

"My biggest hesitation is that I know the owner from before."

"Is that bad?"

"Eh, it's not the best. It's also not the end of the world. Haven't seen her in years, though."

"Before what?"

"Oh, yeah. Before I quit being an exorcist." I pulled out of the parking lot and headed for the desert.

"You quit?"

"Yeah, five years ago." Mostly, anyway.

"Then how?" He waved his hand at himself to finish the question.

"How'd I end up with you? Darius didn't think to cast a reveal spell, or you might have been stuck with him instead."

Sabian's eyes glittered with lust when I glanced at him. "I'm glad I'm stuck with you."

I cleared my throat and tried to focus on the road.

Sabian studied me while I drove, and I did my best to ignore him and the heat settling in my belly that his intense gaze caused. I was practically squirming by the time we made it to the strip joint.

Darius was really going to owe me.

I dug out my wallet and tried to hand all the cash I had over to Sabian. "You do know how a strip club works, yes?"

He nodded. "This is one thing that I have kept up on, places for incubi to feed when on Earth, and how they work. Just in case I ended up here. It wasn't necessarily my plan, but now that I'm here I'm glad I paid attention."

He waved away the money and held up his hand, revealing a whole bunch of cash.

"They need real money."

Sabian grinned. "It's real. Call it a demonic power."

"Where'd you get it?"

"We lust demons have our ways."

"Okay, I probably don't want to know, anyway."

We climbed out of the car and he bounced on his toes, reminding me of an over excited kid.

It was a weekday and a little early, so hopefully there would be enough going on to feed the demon. There were a few other cars in the parking lot and the neon sign flashed open. Maybe I would get lucky and Andi wouldn't be in. She was a former dancer. She started the place after winning a harassment lawsuit from her previous employer. I assumed she was still doing well but I hadn't heard from her in quite some time.

I went over to the door and pushed it open, Sabian on my heels. Loud music, the smell of cheap booze, and the musk of sweat assaulted my senses as I blinked, trying to get my eyes to adjust to the darker interior.

A bored looking bouncer with forearms as big around as my thighs was perched on a bench inside. He raised his eyebrows when he saw me–probably didn't get many female patrons–but gestured for us to come in.

"ID's?"

I hoped Sabian had that under control, too. I dug my wallet out of my jacket pocket and handed over my ID.

Somehow Sabian also had an ID and after the bouncer carefully studied both, he gestured for us to enter.

The narrow hallway turned a corner and entered into the main room. It was a small club, bar along the back wall, three stages, chairs scattered around the stages and a few private tables. I knew there were a few back rooms here, too. I'd been in a couple of times way back in the day when Andi had first bought the place. I called it seedy, and it was to some degree, but Andi ran a tight ship. Her girls had talent, they did draw in crowds, and she did not tolerate shenanigans from her patrons. Her bouncers had long memories and if you messed up more than once, you never got back in.

This early in the night, there weren't many patrons yet, and only one stage had a dancer. She was a light skinned red head, currently getting frisky with the pole and, despite the light crowd, she really was killing it.

Sabian rumbled softly, pleased. I tried not to moan as the sound washed through me. This demon was going to wreck me. Probably in a good way, but still.

I gestured for him to go have fun while I headed to the bar. If I was going to lurk in the background, at least I could get a drink.

Sabian went up to the stage and took an empty seat. I ignored him for the time being, asking the bar tender, a relatively attractive blond man that could have doubled as a bouncer, for a whisky sour.

"What brings a lady like you to a place like this?" the bartender asked as he mixed my drink.

I didn't answer for a minute, vaguely annoyed by the cliché line before shrugging.

"Mate needed a night out." I gestured vaguely toward Sabian.

"So you're the wingman?"

"Something like that," I allowed. I knew bartenders were supposed to be friendly and all, and normally I would have appreciated it. Unfortunately, tonight I just wanted to sulk in a corner, and I wasn't even sure why. I refused to be rude to servers though, so I forced myself to answer his questions with as little annoyance as possible coloring my voice.

"Where are you from, anyway?"

I tilted my head, wondering what to say. If I said Santa Fe, which was the actual truth, he was definitely calling bullshit on my mostly adopted accent. I'd traveled enough that I'd picked up phrases from here and there, and the cadence I'd added to my speech was the bastard child of my father's British accent and growing up in the South West. The more my mother had tried to correct my speech, the more I'd embraced it until she had finally given up. I'd taken one day to prove to her that I could speak what she considered normally if I really wanted to, then gone back to doing what I damn well pleased with the way I spoke.

"Here and there," I finally gave my standard answer.

"Twenty bucks says here and there is actually just down the way," a very familiar voice said.

I turned and, surprisingly, didn't have to force a smile. Andi hadn't changed a whole lot since I'd seen her last. She still wore pants I could only define as trousers, suspenders holding them up over a white button up shirt with rolled up sleeves, and a vest. Today it was blue. Her short, spiky hair was currently a bright teal. She did have more of a tan to her pale skin than I was used to, but maybe she'd finally taken up gardening or something. She'd always wanted a garden in the past.

"May be the case," I allowed and wrapped my old friend in a tight hug.

"You driving?"

I nodded.

69

"Too bad. You still owe me a dance." Andi winked.

I widened my eyes in mock horror. "I'd have to be pretty drunk for that, mate." She was right, though. If she really called me on it, I'd made a stupid claim once and had yet to make good on it.

"Precisely," she grinned in reply. "I'll let you off the hook this time. What brings you this way?"

The bartender handed me a drink and Andi waved me off when I tried to pay for it, so I tipped the guy and let her lead me back to one of the private tables before I answered.

"Eh, friend needed a night out."

"I haven't seen you for five years, and you bring him here?" Her eyes darted over to the stage where Sabian was now the dancer's very favorite. Fortunately, he'd used his incubus charm on everyone, and the guys seemed accepting and even happy about the arrangement, too. Hopefully, he was getting what he needed.

"Price?"

I jerked my attention away from the yummy incubus and back to my friend. I tried to remember what she'd said, rewinding the last few minutes in my mind until I recaptured the thread of our conversation.

"Yeah, long story, that."

She gave me a lazy smile. "I'll bet. Never thought I'd see the day Chris would have to bring a guy to a strip club to keep him happy." She jabbed at me a little, obviously not content with my evasive answer.

I jerked my attention back to Andi and raised my eyebrows. Leaning back in the booth, I sipped my drink before replying. "I'm not sleeping with him."

She grinned. "Why not?"

Sighing, I shook my head. "Also a long story."

"Now I'm really intrigued. Another man?"

She was closer than she knew but I denied that, too.

"What is he, some sort of incubus?"

I barely managed to not choke on the whiskey as I nearly inhaled it. "What?" I wheezed.

"Well, he's certainly popular with Sherry, and you can't keep your eyes off of him. And you know how you and demons are."

I shook my head while I got my breathing under control. "Exorcist...I banish demons. Remember?"

"You're not usually this closed lipped, Chris. What's going on?"

I shrugged. "You know me well enough to know that if I don't want to talk about it, might be safer you didn't actually know."

Her eyes tightened for a moment before she nodded. "Okay."

Fortunately, she shifted the topic of discussion to more neutral affairs, the state of her business, the state of mine, she promised to come by for pizza some time and I declined to promise to come by for a lap dance, which had her holding her sides with laughter.

"No objection," I protested when she accused me of being a prude. "Just not my scene."

"Was once," she teased.

"Eh, not quite. Still, got a friend out of the experience, didn't I?"

She nodded.

We'd met when I'd drunkenly accepted a dare to get a lap dance at a club. I actually had enjoyed myself and somehow Andi and I had ended up friends after. Still, I preferred to get my kicks other ways and Andi knew it.

I was about to see if Sabian was ready to leave when he came over to the table and scooted into the booth next to me, his expression pinched.

"Problem?" Andi asked sounding slightly annoyed.

Sabian shouldn't look worried after all the attention he'd gotten from her girl.

71

"Chris, that guy who just came in." He pointed and my attention zeroed in immediately on who he meant.

"Mother fucker," I snarled. It was one of the humans using the demons.

"Friend of yours?" Andi now sounded worried. Wise of her.

"No, not in the least."

"That one's barely subdued," Sabian offered after a moment.

"Any idea what kind it is?" I muttered as I watched the possessed human stalk up to the stage, eyes glued to Sherry.

"Shit, demons, really, Price?" Andi groaned.

I turned my attention to her and arched an eyebrow.

"Chris, the only thing that gets you more excited than watching your not-boyfriend here is the idea of fighting a demon."

"Not so," I objected.

"She's right," Sabian the non-helpful, replied.

"Wait, what?" I turned my attention fully to Sabian for a moment.

He grinned suggestively at me. Right, he could apparently sense more emotions than just lust.

"Wait, he actually is an incubus," Andi exclaimed, staring at Sabian.

The demon's eyes widened slightly before he glanced at me.

I sighed. "Told you, long story. He's relatively harmless, though, so no worries there."

"Thought you quit." She crossed her arms, though she kept most of her attention on Sabian for the moment.

"Blame Darius."

"To answer your other question, a very unfriendly and pissed off demon," Sabian continued when Andi didn't reply.

"Andi, call the sheriff. Tell them one of Deputy McClellan's delinquents showed up at your place. You can tell them I'm here which is how you know to ask for her if they question you. We'll keep an eye on him. If he behaves, we'll leave him alone until the cops show. If he causes a problem, well, I'll see what I can do about it."

Andi eyed me before nodding and getting up from the table and heading toward the back.

For now, the human acted content to watch the woman who had replaced Sabian's dancer. The mood had certainly shifted, though. Unlike before with Sabian's presence where everything had been light and friendly, the audience shifted restlessly, and though the woman was good, it just wasn't enough for them. Nothing about that energy was normal and I could tell the dancer was uncomfortable.

"Should you do something?" Sabian's voice was full of worry.

"Me? You're the demon."

"I'm a lover, not a fighter." He held up his hands.

"Can you counter that energy at all?"

"I could try, but I think it would start a fight sooner rather than later."

"Great, mate. Leave it to the puny human to handle the big bad demon."

"I could incite an orgy."

"I can't tell if you're being serious or not. Probably not the best time for it, though."

He shrugged. "Think Mal can get here in time? He's actually a warrior."

I tilted my head. "He is?"

Sabian gave me an exasperated look.

"Okay, yeah, I noticed the scars," I conceded. "And the muscles, and everything else." I might have had to wipe a bit of drool away and this time it wasn't Sabian's fault.

While I was contemplating if I should call the vampire or not, the demon surged to his feet.

One of the bouncers charged forward and then went sailing through the air as the demon tossed him as if he weighed nothing.

Yeah, little old me wasn't going to do shit against that guy in a fist fight. A magical fight on the other hand... I raced forward, hopped onto a vacant chair, and leapt onto the stage, putting myself between the dancer and the demon.

He glared at me, human eyes rimmed in red as the chained demon worked its way through the cracks in the binding spell. That might prove to be in my favor since I didn't have a crystal to destroy so I could unbind the demon before exorcising it, and there was no way in hell I was touching that focus necklace.

Best guess, the human had wanted to come to the strip club. The demon was using the human's distraction to work further into his system and now he just wanted to cause problems.

"You're blocking the view," the demon hissed.

"I am the view, asshole," I snarled back and called out the first line of the Latin exorcism ritual I knew best.

His eyes widened and he turned to bolt. Sabian blocked the doorway, and the demon twisted around, picking up a chair as he went and swung it at my head.

I dove out of the way, rolling across the stage and nearly sliding off the far edge. I caught myself in time and scrambled back to my feet, hoping the normal humans had taken the hint and left. The dancer was gone, at least.

I started over. "*Exorcizamus te, omins immundus spiritus...*" I chanted, lending that extra power I had to my voice, the power that made me just a little bit better than your average exorcist. Something innate. Something that commanded demons, even when they didn't want to be commanded.

Wow, I really hoped I didn't get a two for one here and send Sabian back to hell on accident.

The man screamed, spit spraying from his mouth as his back bowed and the demon fought. I suspected it had full control of the body now, but it was caught up in my incantation.

"*Ab insidiis diaboli...*" I shouted, focused on expelling the demonic presence that polluted the atmosphere in the club.

"More are coming, Price! We'll get you!" it shouted as I yelled the last words of the rite and commanded the demon back to hell where it belonged.

The human collapsed as the demon was sucked away.

"Chris!" I glanced at Sabian, the panic in his voice tugging at me. He had sunk to his knees and was grasping the doorframe as if his life depended on it.

"Sabian! Stay!" I shouted, not sure what else to do. I'd never tried to command a demon to do anything but leave before.

Fortunately, I had his true name and that and my simple order was to be enough. He sagged in relief.

Well, shit. No exorcisms with the incubus present.

I leaned back against the pole on the stage and sighed, suddenly exhausted.

No one moved for a minute, then the human groaned, rolling over.

A couple of people pushed past Sabian and I made myself focus on them. Deputy McClellan and another cop quickly handcuffed the now mellow and bewildered looking human.

McClellan studied me while the other deputy handled the arrest. "That was something to see," she marveled.

Uncomfortable, I shifted my gaze away from hers and shrugged. "Yeah, can get ugly. That was an easy one."

She continued to stare at me before her attention flicked over to Sabian. "That the one you pulled out of the other charm?"

I ran my hand through my hair and sighed. So much for not telling anyone Sabian was a demon.

"Yeah, mate. He's all right. Helping us." Maybe Darius had told her.

She didn't ask what we were doing here, so my suspicion that Darius had spilled the beans intensified.

Rolling my shoulders to ease stiff muscles, I straightened off the stripper pole that had been holding me up.

Wide-eyed expressions from the remaining normal folk in the bar followed me as I headed toward the edge of the stage. Sabian met me, a grateful look on his face as he helped me get off the stage more or less gracefully.

He massaged my shoulders while I stared at Deputy McClellan. "You need anything else? Cause I need to get home."

She shook her head. "No. Thank you for saving us quite a lot of trouble." She gestured to the mostly intact bar. The bouncer that the demon had tossed was on his feet and looking pissed as hell. Andi stood next to him, probably explaining what had happened.

"Great, later." I headed for the door. "Andi, call me, or come by for pizza soon. Thanks for a good night."

"I'd flip you off, Price, but you kinda saved our butts, so I guess you get a pass tonight." She grinned at me.

I waved and Sabian followed me out into the cooler evening air. The sun had set. I hadn't realized how long I'd actually been in there.

Exhaustion tugged at my feet and I trudged back to the car.

Sabian helped me in the driver seat before getting in. "Think you can make it home?"

"Yeah, mate. Had worse."

He grinned. "I'll help keep you awake."

My entire reproductive system nearly orgasmed with the seduction in his voice.

"You're going to wreck me," I groaned.

"As long as you don't wreck the car in the process."

"Fuck."

His chuckle ripped through me and I shuddered, back arching, eyes rolling back in my head as my body exploded with pleasure. If nothing else, I was no longer tired. No. I was wide awake and desperate for more.

Dakota Brown

Chapter 7

Price

Sabian's little voice trick in the car did get me home, but now I was so keyed up, I practically fled into my bedroom and dove for my vibrator.

It was not going to be enough, but unless I was fucking a demon or calling a vampire, it would have to do. Why was I not fucking the demon? I seriously had to ask myself that as I yanked my clothing off. Why was I not calling Mal? Oh, right, because I didn't want to be that desperate. Surely, he would understand...I was living with an incubus. No. I could literally take care of myself. I didn't need anyone else.

I collapsed onto my bed, aching for release.

I killed the battery on my vibrator before I even managed to feel satiated. Damn Sabian, anyway. I mean, I was grateful for getting home safely, but did he have to key me up this badly?

Still, I wasn't about to explode anymore and that was something. A quick shower and I crawled into bed. I wasn't even sure where Sabian was, but he was a big boy. He could take care of himself.

Fuck, my brain latched onto that thought and I was nearly back to pre-vibrator horniness levels in an instant. I buried my face in my pillow, and my fingers in my pussy, and finally managed to get myself off enough that I could at least get some sleep.

∞ ∞ ∞

"Price," the voice crawled through my mind, slipping through my veins like sludge, crawling into my heart, clenching.

I clutched at my chest, crying out, sinking to my knees.

"No! What did you do?" I crawled forward, grasping.

"Honey, what's wrong?" My mother turned to look at me, an ancient tome in one hand. How had she gotten that?

"Chris, get up," my father demanded.

I tried to do what he told me, but when my mom went back to chanting the words from the book, my body stopped cooperating. I screamed as my heart tried to stop.

"Chris! Wake up!"

I tried to do what my father said, but the demon had crawled inside me and I was losing the fight.

"Chris!"

A sharp sting on my face made me bolt upright, fist connecting with something solid.

I looked around, drenched in sweat, heart racing, but I was just in my room. It was a dream. The same dream that had plagued me off and on for years. Though my mind had twisted things from how they'd actually happened, the dream captured enough of the real events that had killed my parents.

Wiping tears away, I glanced up at Sabian, who knelt straddling my legs. Moonlight filtered in through the open curtains, showing concern creasing his brow. I wanted to sink into those glowing amber eyes and lose myself for a while.

I almost reached for him.

He brushed his thumb along my cheek. "Are you okay?"

"Yeah, just a nightmare. Thanks." I collapsed back onto the bed. I'd expected them to hit after sparking the memories by going into my parents' room, but that didn't make it any easier.

"Do you want to talk about it?" He shifted until he was next to me. Sabian laid down, and before I could say anything, he'd gathered me against his chest. I snuggled into his warmth, feeling protected.

"Naw, thanks."

He held me tight, not pressing me to talk, just comforting me.

I really could get used to this. I shouldn't be thinking that, but damn it was nice to be held. I thought about Mal, and the way he had held me. I missed him. I wanted to see him again and that scared me. When you depended on others, they left. Didn't they? It was better to be on my own.

Sabian tightened his arms around me.

"Neither of us want to leave you, Chris," Sabian whispered, apparently reading my thoughts.

"What's in it for you, then?"

He kissed my neck, and my pulse quickened again.

"You. We both want you."

I whimpered. The intensity of his answer scared me. What could I possibly offer to Sabian? He was an incubus, after all. Surely, he could get whoever and whatever he wanted now that he was here on Earth. We hadn't banished him. Truth be told, probably wouldn't banish him. He'd given us his name, and therefore we had power over him should he choose to misbehave. He was growing on me as a companion, too. So help me, I liked having him around and he'd only been here a short time, but I couldn't imagine why he would want me. And why would Mal possibly be interested in me as more than a momentarily interesting diversion? Sabian was right about a lot of things, but this couldn't be one of them.

He sighed. "Chris, why wouldn't we want you?"

I didn't answer. Couldn't answer. He probably sensed the dark turn my thoughts took, anyway.

"Get some rest. I'll guard your dreams."

My eyelids dropped and before I could protest, I'd drifted back into a deep, dreamless sleep.

∞ ∞ ∞

"You should call him," Sabian insisted.

I glared at my computer, trying to ignore the demon and the unsatisfied ache between my legs. I hadn't seen Mal in a week and I'd literally broken my damn vibrator two days ago. Traitor.

"Whoever 'he' is, you should definitely call him," Billy agreed, coming into the office. "Because you're going to scare off your new team members if you're not careful."

I turned my glare on Billy. He grinned back at me, unperturbed. He'd gotten used to Sabian's presence, though, like just about everyone else, his eyes lingered on the sexy demon longer than normal.

Sabian followed me everywhere. To be fair, I hadn't told him not to. He was sweet. Helpful when he could be, grabbing a door for me now and again, carrying things for me when I needed an extra hand. The only awkward thing about having him around, other than the staff giving me curious looks all the time, was the low level arousal being around him caused. Well, sometimes it wasn't low level at all, but being out doing stuff during the day helped. It was evenings when I had more time that it got really uncomfortable. He claimed he was keeping it under wraps as best as he could.

We did have two new members of the wait staff. I'd met both of them a few days ago and they seemed nice. Billy had a talent for hiring good people. The two they had replaced were moving on to college in other states. We did not have a high turnover at Price's Pizza Parlor. I took care of my people.

I was about to reply when Rebecca, one of our new team members ran in. She was a younger Native girl whose family had just moved to the area, and her eyes were wide with fear.

"Billy!" She avoided looking at me. "A man just ran into the bar demanding the exorcist." She blurted something in Navajo that I didn't quite catch but the word Skinwalker stood out to me.

I shot to my feet.

"I'm sorry, Ms. Price. I just...he scared me." Unshed tears made her eyes shine.

Shit, if she was that scared of me, I must be in some kind of mood.

I felt a blast of energy and flinched as the lights flickered. Sabian glanced at me, uneasy.

"Sabian, why don't you *stay* here, just in case," I said to the demon, putting a bit of extra power behind my words just in case I had to do something drastic. I didn't want to lose the incubus on accident.

He nodded.

"Rebecca, you don't ever need to worry about being afraid of someone in the store. We've got your back. We'll take care of it." I patted the girl on the shoulder as I stalked past.

Billy and Rebecca followed me out of the office. The kitchen was a disaster. Sauce had splattered everywhere. The dough had virtually exploded. The cooks looked shell shocked and just kind of stared around at the mess.

They turned their wide eyes to me when I stormed through the kitchen.

"Don't worry about it, mates, not your fault," I shouted as I jogged out into the dining area.

The man, or should I say demon, causing all the ruckus was not someone I'd ever seen before. He was decent looking if you overlooked the red rimmed eyes of full demonic possession, and the torn and blood splattered shirt barely concealing a scarred chest. A few poorly done tats circled his biceps. His blond hair stood on end, but I doubted that was its normal state.

"Bring me the exorcist!" he shouted.

Patrons were scattering from their tables as he stomped toward the back of the restaurant.

"Hey, what the hell do you think you are doing?" I shouted, hoping to get his attention before anything else exploded. This mess was going to be hard enough to clean up as it was.

The guy turned, eyes narrowing, focusing on me. "You!"

"Yeah, I'm the owner and we're calling the cops. What the hell, dude?"

"I will have the exorcist!"

"Yeah, there's a Catholic church down the way with a qualified priest. Maybe you should go there."

"No." He hissed.

Fuck.

I jumped up on a clean table. "Everyone out! Sorry for the mess! Come back next week, tell the waiter discount code *demon* and you'll get fifty percent off your order. Anything you managed to eat today before this jerk showed up is on the house."

That was all it took for the restaurant to clear out while the demon stared at me.

Billy came up next to me. "Discount code demon?"

"Um, well, uh, yeah. Just, uh, make sure it gets honored, okay?" I should have picked a better discount code. "And maybe get..."

"You will come with me!" The demon pointed at me.

"Go fuck yourself."

It howled in anger and all of the pitchers of liquid exploded upward. My poor staff. The ones who hadn't already been covered in pizza sauce were now soaked with pop or water.

"Listen, asshole. There's no exorcist here, though clearly you need one. The cops are on their way, and you're going to jail if you don't get out of here now," I yelled, jabbing my finger at him. I fished around in my jacket pocket, grateful I'd left it on. My dedication to the look, despite the temperature, was paying off because I still had a small squirt bottle full of holy water tucked in there. I stalked across the table so I was closer to the possessed human.

A moment before he raised the energy, I saw him focus his attention on my vintage movie posters.

"Oh, hell no!" I whipped the bottle out and squirted him full in the face.

He screamed, clutching at his eyes.

"Price," the demon hissed. "You will help us."

"You come in here and destroy my shop, attack my staff, and expect me to help you? Hah!" I squirted him again, enjoying his agonized scream a little too much.

"What the hell is that?" Billy asked, voice tight.

"Holy water," I grumbled.

"Wait, really?"

"Yeah. Fucking demons. I don't help demons, you asshole. I banish them, now get the fuck out of my restaurant!"

He picked up a chair, probably intending to toss it at me. For someone who said he wanted my help, he was really bad at acting like he actually wanted it.

"*Exorcizamus te,*" I started.

He howled, dropping the chair, and doubling over in pain. "You must release us!"

"Trying, mate. *Omnis immundus...*"

The demon screamed in fury, but whatever he was now howling at me was in a language I didn't speak. It grated on my ears and I shouted the exorcism rite over the top of his cries of rage.

This one wasn't nearly as easy to release as the one at the stripper bar had been. He was clearly trying to get a message to me, but I wasn't having any of it. No one got to destroy my pizza shop and get my help. Also, I was pissed and horny, and I really wanted to kick the shit out of something.

In the end, the demon really had no chance. I was so fired up about everything, it simply didn't have the power to resist as I shouted out the last of the exorcism.

The human collapsed to the ground and I winced as his head smacked the bare floor. That wasn't going to feel good when he woke up. Of course, he probably wouldn't notice over the rest of his aches and pains.

"Go back to hell and fucking stay there!" I shouted as the demon was sucked back into the abyss.

Sucking in breath, chest heaving, I glared at the unconscious human, daring the demon to try and come back.

Nothing.

Exhaustion washed over me, but I was angry enough that I pushed the weariness away.

"Um, Chris?"

I jumped. I'd forgotten about Billy and the others for a moment.

"Yeah, Billy?" I asked trying for innocent nonchalance as I hopped off the table.

"What the hell just happened?"

"You know, just dealing with unruly customers." I shrugged.

He gaped at me.

I ran my hand through my hair. "Yeah, so, uh, let's just not talk about that ever again, huh?"

"Did you just exorcise a demon?" Mandy rushed over.

Sabian and Rebecca came out of the kitchen, surveying the mess. I breathed a sigh of relief when I saw the incubus.

"No, that's ridiculous," I protested weakly.

"You saved us from the skinwalker," Rebecca whispered.

I gave in. There was no covering this up from the staff. "Demon, mate. Not a real skinwalker. Not sure I have the chops to take on one of those."

She simply stared back at me.

"Yeah. Okay, so, um, we're closed for the rest of the day," I raised my voice so everyone who wasn't right here could hear me.

"If you want to leave, you can. There's a big bonus in it for anyone who sticks around and cleans this place up. Also, you'll get your normal wages, so, uh, yeah, thanks and all." I clenched my jaw. "If you could keep quiet on all this, that'd be great."

The door chimed before any of them could answer. Deputy McClellan and another cop came in.

"This is becoming a habit," she declared.

"Hey, if I gotta do your job for you..." I grinned to take any sting out of the words. There was no way they could handle the demons normally.

She smiled back. "We appreciate it. What's the story with this one?"

"Uh, came looking for..." I glanced around at my staff before sighing. "Came looking for me. Wanted help with something. Unfortunately, demon picked a bad day to ask me a favor and, well, went about getting my attention the wrong way."

She raised her eyebrows as her gaze swept the disaster that was the restaurant. "If you figure out what it wanted, please let me know."

"Will do."

They took the guy into custody and left me with my bewildered staff.

"Yeah, like I said. Let's just not talk about that. And, uh, get this place clean. I'll make sure this doesn't happen again."

"For real?" Stacy stared at everything before turning her attention back to me.

"Yeah. I got a friend who's good at warding places. I'll get him to hook us up with some great demon preventatives." I grinned, trying to ease their fears.

"You're an exorcist," Stacy stated.

"Yeah, I guess." I cleared my throat.

"That's so cool," she breathed.

"Uh..." I had no reply to that. Why were they not freaking out more? Maybe they were in shock.

Sabian came up and put his arm around me. "It is kinda cool."

His heat lit me up and I groaned, leaning into him for a moment. Fucking incubus.

"Yeah, so, you heard the boss. Let's get you all cleaned up, and then get this place cleaned up." Billy clapped his hands together.

That got them moving with a chorus of agreement.

I cocked my finger at Billy, gesturing for him to follow me back to the office.

"That's going to take forever." I groaned as I viewed the destruction in the kitchen.

"Yeah. We'll get it done."

"Great, mate. So, pay everyone... twenty an hour to clean this mess up. Yourself included, on top of whatever they normally would have made. And... is five hundred enough of a bonus to keep mouths shut and keep people from quitting?"

His eyes widened. "Yeah, that's really generous. Hell, we'd probably do it if you just threw us all one of the jean jackets." He referred to one of the merch items we sold occasionally. We had shirts and jean jackets with the pizza logo on the back.

I raised my eyebrows. "Yeah, you all can have one of those, too. Get one for everyone, even if they weren't here."

"So, you're really an exorcist," Billy said.

"Yeah. I was. Had given all that up. Events are chasing me back into it, though."

"So, demons are actually real."

"Yeah."

He paled a little. "That's going to take some getting used to."

"Try not to think about it. Not something you want to get caught up in," I cautioned.

"Right. So, what do you think that was all about?"

Clearly not taking my advice.

"Probably related to the events trying to drag me back into the occult. Best to leave it at that. Hate to leave you with all of this, but I need to go check some stuff out. Call me if you need anything."

"Sure, Chris. I know you hate to clean."

I laughed. "Yep. Also, I really do need to check into a few things. Probably urgently."

Billy smiled and followed Sabian and me back out into the dining area where the team was hard at work cleaning everything up. Wide eyed stares followed me as I headed toward the exit.

I hurried outside into the afternoon heat. My car was parked in a small degree of shade, but it was still going to be hotter than hell in there. Still, the leather jacket would protect me from burns, so I left it on despite the sweat that beaded my brow and trickled down my back.

Sabian and I got in my car and dropped the windows while the AC cranked away. I still couldn't touch the steering wheel without it burning my hands, but I needed to get out of there. I needed to call Mal. Damn it. At least this time I had an excuse other than that I wanted to get laid. Felt a little less desperate, though the thought of running my hands over those firm muscles of his was making me pretty happy. Was it just Sabian's influence? Or was there something else there that was drawing me to the vampire?

The trip home didn't take too long. I shed my boots at the doorway in case I had sauce on them that I didn't know about and hung my jacket on the hook.

Sabian did the same with his shoes and followed close on my heels. I was practically vibrating, and I really needed some release. His presence behind me was like an electric charge and I wanted to throw myself against him.

I pulled out my phone and stared at Mal's name in the contacts before taking a deep breath and hitting call.

He answered quickly.

"Chris, how are you?"

Lord help me, he sounded really happy to hear from me.

"Oh, all right, I suppose. Hey, so we had a demon show up at the pizza shop. I was wondering if you might be willing to help me with some wards later?"

"Of course. Is everything okay?"

"Great, and yeah, I got it taken care of." I clenched my fist. I really needed him now. I did not want to beg.

"Was there something else?"

Sabian grabbed the phone out of my hand. "You should come over now," he ordered before I snatched it back, glaring at him as I put the phone back to my ear.

"Should I?" He sounded amused. "Is your incubus hungry?"

"Maybe."

"She's hungrier," Sabian shouted, a grin on his face.

My cheeks heated, and I continued to glare at the demon.

"Oh? Sabian not enough to keep up with you?" He sounded genuinely surprised.

"Wait, what? I'm not sleeping with Sabian," I protested.

"Why not?"

"I didn't..." I trailed off, dumbfounded.

"Chris, I wouldn't leave anyone alone with an incubus and expect them to keep their hands off him. How have you managed?" The amusement was back.

"Not well. Broke the damn vibrator. It's been two days." Now I sounded desperate.

"I imagine Sabian feels about as desperate as you do."

Sabian hadn't complained about being hungry the last couple of days. He'd acted content with feeding off the energy I generated with my solo party times, but Mal was probably right about how Sabian felt. I glanced at the demon. He glanced away, as if not wanting me to feel bad about it. So we both needed Mal. Damn it. After the demon incident at the strip club, I hadn't taken him back, afraid to push my luck with Andi.

"Are you not going to come over?" I about cried.

He chuckled and I groaned, crossing my legs before collapsing onto the couch.

"Of course, I will," he purred. "I am tied up at the shop for about another hour."

I might have whimpered at the thought of him all tied up. Or me all tied up. Maybe Sabian should be the one tied up. I bet he liked that sort of thing.

As if sensing where my thoughts had gone, Mal laughed. "Chris, why don't you and Sabian enjoy yourselves. I'll join you as soon as I can."

"Are you sure?"

"That I'll join you soon? Of course, I'm sure. I've missed you."

"You have?" My chest clenched and I wasn't sure if the thought of Mal missing me had me in a panic or if that was the feeling of melting from affection.

"Yes."

"Oh, but, Sabian?"

"Ahh, I see. Chris, I don't own you. I'm perfectly happy to share your affection with our incubus friend, if that's what you needed to hear."

I swear Sabian just sighed in relief, but by the time I twisted around to look at him, he had a neutral expression on his face, and I couldn't tell if he had actually overheard the vampire or not.

"So, like, you come over in an hour and we're in bed, you're not going to be mad?"

"No. Of course not."

"That's...unusual."

I could almost see him shrug. "As I said, I do not own you. Also, I would certainly have to make some sort of allowance for his nature if I were going to be possessive of you. And truly we have not discussed any aspect of our relationship beyond that I hoped you would call me. Why would I expect you not to sleep with Sabian?"

I didn't have an answer to that.

"Perhaps you should stop torturing yourself, and when I arrive we can see how you feel. If you're up for more, I'll join you. If not, we'll discuss the new aspect of your demon problem."

"Join us?" I squeaked and I swear my ovaries might have done a happy dance right then.

He laughed. "Sure, why not."

I literally couldn't speak for a moment. "Yeah, that sounds great," I gasped out. "I'll leave the door unlocked for you."

"I'll see you soon." Mal's voice was full of promise and I sort of melted into the couch.

"Good."

The phone went dead, and I stared at it before glancing over at Sabian.

"You get all that?"

He winked.

I was not used to being such a slave to my hormones, and I knew Sabian's presence had something to do with it, but damn it, I was getting myself a demon and a vampire today.

Before I could say anything, Sabian came over to me and picked me up off the couch. Holy crap, he was strong.

"If you hadn't told Billy you were available by phone, I'd steal that away from you," Sabian said.

He was such an interesting mix of serious and child-like enthusiasm. Right now, he was leaning more toward the serious side.

I'd been considering leaving the phone in the living room, so I was grateful for the reminder. Instead, I clutched it as Sabian carried me toward my bedroom. His light amber eyes glowed faintly in the dim light.

"Mmm, your desire is delicious," he purred, his voice full of sexy, panty melting lust.

I groaned, squirming in his grasp.

"We're almost there," he chided me gently.

Once we were inside, I dropped the phone on my nightstand as soon as Sabian set me down on the bed.

He didn't waste any time, pulling off his T-shirt. I wiped away a little drool as I took in his defined muscles. And there went his pants, and I certainly needed a change of clothing as my ovaries wept in joy.

Sabian walked over to me and I got up on my knees on the bed, pulling my shirt off and unhooking my bra while he presented himself to me as if for inspection. Or maybe he was just reading my mind, because holy crap I wanted to suck him off badly.

I grabbed his hips and pulled him close before running my fingers down his large cock.

He purred as I teased him a little before taking him into my mouth. There was no way I could fit all of him, but I did my best. He tangled his fingers in my hair and I worked my mouth down his hard length, tongue flicking at the tip, tasting salt. He thrust gently as I really got to work on his magnificent dick. Sabian's reactions to my attention were perfect, amping me up even more as he rumbled in pleasure, fingers tightening in my hair, thrusting more urgently.

"Chris," he gasped my name.

"Mmm," I managed around his cock.

He shuddered and stiffened, spilling into my mouth with an ecstasy filled groan. I swallowed him down. Once he stilled, I leaned back, grinning up at him. He was still hard, and I figured he probably had similar stamina to the vampire.

Sabian's contented and lazy grin went straight to my core and I fumbled at the button on my jeans. He helped me undress the rest of the way, but before he could dive in with his tongue, I grabbed his shoulders and pulled him to me.

"Just fuck me. We can get to the rest later."

Sabian grinned. "Anything you want, Chris."

He obliged, pressing into me.

It occurred to me that we hadn't discussed condoms or anything, but at this point I didn't care, and I guessed I was probably safe. The implant would save me from accidental pregnancies if that was even possible.

"Same as Mal," Sabian whispered, having read my surface thoughts as he did sometimes. "No diseases, and breeding takes special circumstances."

"Oh, good." Well, that was handy.

I tilted my hips and wrapped my legs around him while he slowly entered me, stretching, filling, making me see stars and I hadn't even gotten off yet.

Sabian got in as deeply as he could and pulled back out. I was nearly crying at the slow pace he set, but when I tugged on his hips, he refused to speed up, a mischievous grin on his face. He tortured me for a few more slow thrusts before picking up speed. I cried out as my entire body trembled with the need for release. Pressure built in my core and I clawed at Sabian's back, gasping out his name. He rumbled in pleasure.

When he finally took me over the edge, my life flashed before my eyes as I crashed into a powerful orgasm.

Sabian rode me through it, enhancing the pleasure as he came right after I did, dragging me into another orgasm. I suspected demonic powers because it was just as strong as the first one. That took my breath away, and when I finally caught it again, Sabian held me tightly against his chest, both of us laying on our sides, much as Mal had. I tangled my fingers in Sabian's short brown hair and kissed him.

Speaking of, the vampire leaned in the doorway, arms crossed, lust filling his liquid brown eyes as he stared at us.

He'd said it was okay with him, but I still felt uncomfortable, like I'd done something I shouldn't have.

Well, I mean, there was a pretty strong school of thought that you shouldn't have sex with demons, but I felt I got a pass. It was a priest that had left him with me, after all.

Malak sauntered forward, a hand straying to the button on his shirt. He tilted his head slightly, questioningly. I nodded and his lips curled into a smile. I wasn't even sure I saw him get undressed, because the next thing I knew, he was pushing me back into Sabian's broad chest, lips pressed to mine. I opened for him and he took my breath away with his kiss.

This time, as I slipped my tongue into his mouth, I felt sharpened fangs. A little less in control of himself this time, then. Good. I might get bit, but I didn't think he would hurt me. It occurred to me that he might have been watching for a while, though we'd gone pretty fast, so I suspected he'd left work earlier than he had intended.

He kissed and nipped along my jaw.

Sabian cupped my breasts, rolling my nipples between his fingers. He trapped one of my legs with his, and I could feel him, still erect, pressing against my ass.

"Chris," Mal whispered between kisses.

"Yes?" I managed to gasp out.

"I would very much like to taste your blood tonight," he breathed softly, tongue flicking along my neck.

My heart skipped a beat, and I froze for a moment.

"You'll enjoy it," he murmured as he nibbled his way down to the curve of my shoulder.

"Any, uh, lasting consequences I should be aware of?"

"No, not from me just taking some of your blood."

I rocked my head back against Sabian's chest, exposing as much of my neck as I could. "Okay." I both could and couldn't believe I'd agreed. I'd never been one to turn away from a good time.

He rumbled in pleasure before nipping at my neck, sending all sorts of tingles through me, all the way to my toes.

"Soon," he promised.

Sabian, possibly reading Malak's intentions, slid one hand down my side, over my hip, until he could slide his fingers between my thighs and pull my leg up, exposing my soaked pussy to Mal's tongue.

Mal, who obviously didn't care that I'd just had sex with Sabian, dove in with enthusiasm, quickly driving any thoughts out of my head other than the warm presence against my back and his attention to my clit.

Pretty soon I was crying out wordlessly. Sabian held one of my legs and Malak had the other trapped against the bed. I squirmed, not really trying to get free but because the pleasure was so intense, I almost couldn't handle it. Except, I had no choice unless I asked them to let me go. No amount of intention on my part would ever be strong enough to overpower those two.

My body shattered.

I came down from that high pressed between the demon and the vampire, and I was really happy to be there.

Malak kissed me softly, nipping at my lower lip, biting gently at my jaw. I gave him my neck, but he didn't take what I offered yet, instead glancing at Sabian, still holding me pressed against his chest. The demon loosened his hold on me, but before I could wonder what they were up to, Malak rolled me so I was facing the demon. Sabian took my leg and hooked it over his hip and Mal entered me from behind. The new angle had him filling me in all sorts of interesting ways and I found myself moaning in pleasure as he thrust into me.

Mal wrapped his hand around my neck, squeezing gently. Not enough to actually cut off my air, just enough to get my attention. My heart raced, and I leaned back into him.

He lowered his lips to my neck, tilting my head back with his hand. The briefest flash of pain, then pleasure rocketed through me and I came hard as Mal tasted my blood. The orgasm kept going as he drank my blood, sending me to heights of pleasure I never thought possible.

Sabian lowered his lips to mine, as if he were drinking my small cries of pleasure, which was about all I could manage as the two of them wrecked me completely.

It was a while before I managed to see straight after that, and I didn't even try to move from where I was cradled between them. Sabian was like a furnace, warming me. Mal was cooler, but no less comforting.

97

"How was that?" Mal finally asked.

"Yeah, we can do that again some time," I breathed out.

He caressed my shoulder, and Sabian did the same to my hip.

"Good."

I really just wanted to go to sleep, but we needed to talk wards and I wanted to see if Sabian had any insight into the other demon's words before I'd banished his ass.

"How are you, Sabian?" I inquired, voice a little steadier now.

"Never better," he purred.

Both Mal and I groaned softly as his power washed over us.

"Mal?" I felt I should check in with the vampire, too.

"Certainly one of the better days I've had in a while," he replied, kissing me on my shoulder. "Perhaps we should clean up."

"Sure."

Mal scooted off the bed, and I managed to do the same, but then my knees gave out on me. Fortunately, vampire reflexes saved me from crashing to the floor. Mal kissed my temple as he cradled me in his arms.

"Sabian, I guess we get to bathe our goddess." Mal glanced at the demon, who's eyes lit up with delight.

That man said the damndest things.

Chapter 8

Price

I found myself curled up on the couch later, content, and cradling a cup of tea while Mal and Sabian both gave coffee some attention. I was leaning against Sabian's strong shoulder and Mal sat across from us in one of the chairs.

"Tell me what happened today," Mal suggested.

"Well, we were at the restaurant and some asshole came in and started blowing the place up all poltergeist style. To make a long story short, I sent his ass back to hell, but not before he poorly tried to ask for my help. He wanted me to go with him, and when I refused, he tried to go after all the vintage posters and shit. I lost my temper pretty fast."

Mal chuckled. "Imagine that."

"Hey!"

He shrugged.

Sabian put his arm around me and squeezed. "It's part of your immense charm."

"Now I know you're full of shit."

The demon laughed. "Okay, tell him about the strip club."

Malak's eyebrows shot up.

"Well, he needed something to eat. You know what happens when the incubus gets hungry."

Mal let his eyes travel over my body, lingering suggestively. "Yes, it's quite enjoyable."

I shook my head in feigned annoyance, though I couldn't disagree.

"So, anyway, we were doing fine, and then a human with a poorly contained demon, kind of like the one at the restaurant, showed up looking for a good time. The demon managed to get control and was, understandably, pissed, so I sent his ass back to hell, too. But he did manage to get out that more were coming. I'm not quite sure what that was all about."

"Sabian, any insight you can lend us?"

Sabian nodded. "Yes. The plane of hell is not quite as the human religions envision it, of course. I'll tell you more later, but there is a hierarchy of demons. I'm sure you've figured that part out. Some of it is related to what kind of demon you are, some of it to how much power you have, though that can be gained or lost, and some of it is related to your level of ambition. I've done well for myself in the past and am relatively powerful for an incubus. I'm also not terribly ambitious. For example, I've built myself up to a state where I don't get hassled, but not so much that I get noticed by the princes. I'm not interested in being their pawn."

"So, you're here on Earth hanging out avoiding notice?" I asked.

Sabian shrugged. "I have a feeling my position here on Earth is going to make me very interesting to whoever sent that message asking for your help. I'm actually here on Earth hanging out, as you say, because you caught my interest."

I cleared my throat and looked away from the intensity in his gaze.

"Sabian, do you have a way of communicating with demons still in hell?" Mal leaned forward, staring at Sabian.

He nodded in response, perking up at having been given a task.

"Perhaps we should find out what they want. It's not that I'm advocating that we work with them, so much as this trend of binding demons and using them is troubling. Especially since it seems like not all the bindings were done well. It's possible this demon trying to send Chris a message could give us enough information to stop things before they get out of control."

"Hey, mate, if the demon trying to contact me is named Lott tell him to fuck off, there ain't no way. Otherwise, I'll listen to what he has to say."

Sabian studied me. "You know Lott."

"Unfortunately."

"He was a crossroad demon and is now a prince, elevated relatively recently," Sabian explained.

"Fucker."

"He is certainly not my favorite demon." Sabian hunched his shoulders.

"Sabian, do you owe any allegiance to princes we should know about?" Mal asked.

"I'm very loosely associated with a demon prince that goes by the name of Ezra. Obviously, this is not his true name. I actually suspect that this prince is the one trying to contact us. I believe most of the demons bound belong to him."

"Oh, well, good. At least it's not the other asshole." I sighed. I couldn't believe we were actually doing this. It was like the opposite of my normal activities.

Sabian chuckled. "I wouldn't say any of us are exactly good, but we're not all terrible creatures, either."

"Can't believe I'm saying this, mate, but I kind of like you."

Sabian gave me the most adorable puppy dog eyes that I about died.

"Seriously?"

He grinned and my heart melted a little more.

"Okay, what do you have to do to contact your prince?"

"Actually, just give me a minute. I really don't have to do much." His expression turned inward before his eyes widened in alarm and he stiffened.

"Wait! We should probably go downstairs first," I barked.

Too late. Fuck. What had we just done?

His entire expression changed, and I scooted to the end of the couch, having an idea of what might have just happened. I'd fight to get him back, but that might not be necessary. Of course, I might have just invited a demonic prince into my house. I exchanged a quick, worried glance with Mal while a probably possessed Sabian surveyed the living room.

"This is not exactly how I would expect the living area of a notorious exorcist to look." Not-Sabian turned his attention to me. His normal amber eyes were rimmed in red. Definitely possessed. Damn it.

"You're going to give him back, right? Otherwise, this is going to get ugly fast." I tried not to swell in pride at him calling me notorious, though. That was pretty badass.

"Yes, Price. I'll give your demon back. For now."

"For good mate, he's mine," I surprised myself by saying. Huh, I'd really meant that. How had Sabian worked his way into my heart that quickly?

The demon sighed. "Sabian is practically dancing with glee at the moment. It's giving me a headache." He pinched the bridge of his nose.

"I take it you're not here to destroy my house or be an utter shit?"

"No, Price, I want your help to free my demons."

"Did you send that jerk to my restaurant?" I crossed my arms and glared.

The demon inhabiting Sabian shook his head. "I apologize for his behavior. He will be informed of the proper way of addressing you in the future."

I got the impression the demon prince was not used to apologizing. Especially to mortals.

"Naw, don't ever send a minion again. You want to talk to me, you gotta talk to me straight." *Shit, really Price, that was the dumbest thing you've ever said. You do not want to deal with a demon prince on the regular, or ever.* I tried to keep my alarm at what I'd just done out of my expression.

"Very well, if that's what you require for your assistance."

"Naw, mate, that's just what I require to be willing to listen to you."

Sabian smiled coolly, but the expression was so foreign to his normal cheerful attitude that it sent chills through me.

"Very well. What do you require for your assistance?"

"What are we talking about here? What's going on?" I was seriously bargaining with a demon? I'd really gone and lost my mind.

"Let me say it this way, what would you do to prevent a bound demon prince from being in the possession of your unsavory human friends?"

I raised my eyebrows. "They're going after a prince?"

He nodded.

"We want the same thing, Price. The demons want to be released back to hell. I want whoever is summoning them to burn in the deepest pits of my realm for eternity. You want us not on Earth. I'm asking you to actively look into this problem. I doubt the priest has what it takes to prevent what's coming."

"What is coming?"

Not-Sabian's brow furrowed. "There is much to this scheme I don't yet understand. I suspect it is a power bid in hell spilling over into your realm."

"So, you want me to help you. I'm getting that right? You've come to me, an exorcist, to help you."

Though he looked pained, he nodded. "I need someone who can work on this plane. I do not wish to be summoned myself. My days of bargaining for souls are long behind me and I wish it to remain that way."

My chest clenched and icy tendrils of fear laced their way through my spine. Fuck. Sabian had failed to mention his prince was also a crossroads demon.

"What do you wish in exchange for your service?"

"'Kay, get this straight. I look into this. I'm not working for you. I'm doing you a favor. You don't get to order me around. You don't get to act like you own me. And you will owe me a favor in the future. No strings attached. No trying to find ways around what I'm asking. I ask you for the return favor straight up, you give me straight up help in return. For example, I ask you for a puppy, you ask me what kind."

He tilted his head as if considering. "Would you like a hell hound? I could arrange that. One might even be useful for you in this coming battle."

"That's not my favor!"

"I understand. Price, you must know this. If things were not dire, I would not make this bargain, but I believe they are. I agree to your terms."

"Okay," I replied slowly after shooting a desperate look at Malak. He looked about as shell shocked as I felt.

"I do not know enough now to be useful, but I am close to discovering some information on my end." He hesitated. "It would be most useful if I could communicate through this one."

I took that to mean Sabian.

"Up to Sabian."

The demon's expression turned inward for a moment before he nodded. "He agrees. I will reward him suitably when this is over."

I figured I'd leave those arrangements to the demons. Sabian would know what would be best for him.

"Good day," the demon said.

Sabian gasped and clutched at his chest.

"Holy crap," I exclaimed.

"Yeah, you can say that again," Sabian murmured.

Not sure what to say, but not wanting us to delve into a weird silence we had no way to work out of, I forged on with running my mouth a little. "So, what do you think the chances are we're going to have a hellhound show up in the very near future?"

Both Mal and Sabian focused on me, before they cracked smiles, Sabian's seductive, Mal's a bit more ironic.

"I hope you don't mind hair on the furniture." Mal laughed.

I sighed. "So, that just happened, right? It's not some post-sex hallucination?"

Sabian reached out and pulled me back over to him. I tucked in under his shoulder and snuggled against him.

"I never thought I'd be working with the supernatural." I was feeling out of my depth, and I didn't like that. I was used to being at the top of my game, but what I knew was exorcism and the occult. Minor spells and such. Getting involved in demonic power plays was far outside of anything I was even remotely comfortable with.

Mal chuckled and shot me a suggestive look. Sabian tightened his arm around me.

"Yeah, right, or fucking them." I groaned.

"Regrets?" Sabian sounded worried.

"Mate, did I not just claim you in front of a demon prince?"

"Yes, but I can see you doing that just to be contrary." Sabian really did sound worried now, and clearly he was figuring me out quickly.

I sighed. "Well, that's true. No, Sabian, so far, no regrets. Not sure how I ended up with the two of you, but I'll happily keep you around."

The incubus purred happily, and I nearly had an orgasm as the sound vibrated through me down to my very core. I squirmed. "Yeah, that's not something you should do in public."

He laughed.

Mal shifted in his chair and I glanced at him. He had a slightly pained expression on his face. "Yes, not in public, thanks."

"You sure you want to stick around, Mal? Could get pretty dangerous. We could end up entangled pretty deeply with demons other than Sabian here." Now I sounded worried. I didn't want to lose the vampire this fast. How I'd gone from, 'I'm good with my vibrator' to desperately needing the two men in my living room to stay in my life, I wasn't sure. Yeah, they were hot, and interesting, and sweet, and seemed to like me. Okay, those were pretty good reasons to keep someone around. Two someones in fact. The feelings were a touch uncomfortable, but I felt I had to own up to them. It wasn't fair to them otherwise.

"I'm no stranger to dangerous times. I'm happy to stand by your side, and Sabian's. If nothing else, it'll make things interesting for a while. We need to stop this occultist before the idea of binding demons spreads, and before they get more involved in the other aspects of crime that your priest is worried about. Besides, I like you, Chris Price and you might need me to watch your back."

I raised an eyebrow. "Just my back?"

His grin turned suggestive. "And the rest of you."

I took a deep breath. "Okay, right. So, we have a few more hours to kill before I suspect the staff will be done cleaning up the restaurant. What do you want to do?"

Mal grinned.

And that was how I ended up playing a drunken dwarf in a dungeon crawl for my very first tabletop roleplaying adventure. Sabian played a celestial paladin, and Mal told us all what to do.

∞ ∞ ∞

We showed up at the restaurant at about ten pm. Everyone was still there, eating pizza and drinking beer. The place was as clean as I had ever seen it, and I fully approved of the pizza party.

Billy grinned when we came inside. He knew me well enough to know I'd be okay with the party and no trace of worry crossed his features.

The smell of fresh pizza also made me realize how hungry I was. Had I eaten?

"Everyone, this is Mal, and you know Sabian. They're going to help us keep the riff raff out." I hoped if I could avoid mentioning demons long enough, they would forget. It was a vain hope, but I could pretend.

The guys responded to all of the greetings while I snagged a piece of pizza.

"So, what exactly are you going to do to keep the demons out?" Billy put a foot on the chair he stood next to and leaned his elbow on his knee, studying the guys.

Mal glanced around. "First, probably a cleansing ritual. You've done a fantastic job with the physical cleaning. We will have to clean the traces of that demon away. Then we will put up wards that should keep most demons out."

"Not all?" Billy frowned.

The others stared at Mal with rapt attention.

"I'm not sure anything can keep every demon out. Some are simply too powerful. However, it's unlikely that we will encounter any demons that could breach the wards, uninvited."

"Why would someone invite a demon in?" Mandy glanced around as if expecting one to pop out of the woodwork, as it were.

Mal shrugged, obviously not going give the real answer. "I can't foresee every possibility, of course. Simply that there may be a time when we need to invite a demon in. Obviously, it would be under strict orders to behave itself."

"Can you order a demon around like that?" Mandy's eyes went wide.

"Depends on the demon," Sabian answered. "And what the arrangement with the demon is."

"So, we're supposed to be forgetting that demons exist, right mates?" I clapped my hands together after I finished my slice of pizza.

They all looked at me with similar 'seriously?' expressions on their faces.

Why were they not freaking out more?

Sabian leaned over and whispered in my ear, "I might be keeping them from losing their shit too badly. I didn't think you needed the drama."

I sighed, not prepared to deal with that tidbit of information. Sabian's revelation was a bit unsettling, but I'd deal with that later. "Just do me a favor. You don't want to get caught up in any of that shenanigans if you can avoid it."

"How'd you get involved?" Stacy asked quietly.

I clenched my jaw, before shrugging. "Darius dragged me in when I was young and impressionable."

"You're hardly old," Mal stated.

I shrugged. "Thirty-five isn't old, sure, but I'm much more jaded." I grinned at him.

He conceded my point with a quick nod of his head and a mischievous smile.

"The priest?" Billy raised his eyebrows in disbelief.

"Yeah, wasn't always a priest. Anyway, we grew up together. He got me involved. Then he dragged me back in the other day. So, misspent youth and all that. Not real interesting."

The look everyone gave me let me know they thought I was full of shit. I shrugged.

"So, how many demons have you sent back to hell?" Stacy clasped her hands together in delight.

"Not sure. Look, it's getting late. Um, lot of unhappy memories and all." I ran my hand through my hair and thought maybe I should style it up again into the short mohawk I'd been neglecting for a while. Maybe having a boss with crazy hair would distract them from the demons. Probably not.

"Sorry, Boss," Billy said. "It's simply not something we ever thought we'd hear anything about. It's like stuff you see in movies or on TV."

I nodded. "Yeah, some shows are closer to the truth than others. Mostly it's just saving people from bad choices. Sometimes you can't save them, but you can at least make sure the demon isn't loose on Earth."

They nodded soberly.

"What other kinds of supernaturals are there?" Mandy grinned, eyes lighting up.

I'd have bet anyone a hundred bucks right then that she was into vampire romances. I managed to avoid looking at Mal, though I could practically sense the amusement rolling off of him and Sabian.

"Don't know, mate. Mostly just dealt with demons. I suspect there's all sorts of things out there we don't want to know about, though."

Mandy looked a little disappointed. Hopefully, she wouldn't go looking for trouble. I finally glanced at Mal, but he didn't look alarmed. Maybe he was the only vampire in the area. Come to think of it, I didn't know how their society worked at all. I made a mental note to ask him later.

"Okay, get this cleaned up and get out of here. We need to get this place buttoned down and I need to get some real sleep." Lord and Lady, I hoped Mal was planning on staying the night. I wanted some more of him and Sabian once I'd had a chance to get some rest.

It didn't take long before my team had cleaned up after their dinner and headed out for the night. I wandered around, inspecting their efforts.

"I don't think this place has been this clean in years. They really did a good job."

Mal had pulled all the blinds closed, even the ones on the door, and locked us in. I checked the back door just in case it was still open while I was in the kitchen. We were as safe from observation as we could be.

"Can I use this table?" Mal asked once I rejoined them in the dining area.

"Yeah."

He pulled a few things out of his backpack, including a smudge stick for each of us, a few canisters of salt, and some chalk.

"First a cleansing ritual," Mal declared.

"Yeah, let's sage this place," Sabian agreed enthusiastically.

I wasn't sure if I should laugh at Sabian or sigh. Mal ignored the incubus as much as anyone could ignore someone who basically exuded sex.

Obediently, I lit my smudge stick with a lighter and watched it burn until I could put out the flames and let it smolder instead.

Sabian and Mal did the same, then we moved through the shop, spreading the sage smoke through the air.

Mal spoke a few words once we were done and the air instantly felt lighter, as if it were fresh and new.

"This next part is going to take a while, since I need to draw the wards. I'll go as quickly as I can, but I think it will

110

still take me about an hour." Mal picked up the package of chalk from the table.

"Chalk permanent enough?" I asked.

"Once I'm done, it will be."

"Great."

"Have a seat."

Sabian and I grabbed chairs and kicked back to watch. Well, I relaxed. Sabian leaned forward and watched intently.

Mal pulled a chair over to the wall and stood on it while he drew an intricate symbol. It took nearly ten minutes for him to get it the way he wanted it, and I couldn't imagine he'd be done in an hour at that speed. It turned out I underestimated the vampire's speed. Once he had the shape worked out, he moved considerably faster, though as he had guessed, it still took him about an hour to cover the shop with the wards.

After he finished drawing, he spilled salt across every exterior doorway and window.

Well, the place had been clean. I didn't say anything.

"You may consider having me add to the warding on your home," Mal suggested when he joined us at the table.

"Yeah, you're welcome to." I stared at the chalk marks all over my restaurant and hoped he had a plan for that, as well. I trusted him, though. As surprising as that was to me.

Mal nodded. "Okay, now we need to activate these. I don't really need your help for this, however, since you own the place, and Sabian will be here frequently, I thought it best to include your energies in the warding. Sit around the table. Let me light a few candles, and then join hands."

Once Mal was ready, I slid one of my hands into his cool one, and my other into Sabian's warm hand. I could feel the energy Mal pulled from himself and the environment, and my innate energies responded to his, melding into the shape he formed his energy into.

"Chris," Mal said softly. "Did you know your eyes go almost black like a vampire's when you use magic?"

"Uh, it's been mentioned, though not with that comparison." I shifted uncomfortably in my seat.

"You do realize you have some innate magical ability, yes?" He caressed the back of my hand with his thumb.

I stared at the table. "It's the running theory on why I'm so naturally good at exorcisms," I choked out.

He brought my hand to his lips and kissed my knuckles. "Nothing wrong with having abilities," he tried to reassure me. "Maybe you'll let me help you explore them later."

"Maybe," I whispered. I nearly sighed in relief when he turned his attention away from me and back to energy he'd gathered. I couldn't quite see it, but I could feel it crackling between us. Sometimes I could see energy, and it was possible if I opened myself more, I'd be able to see this. Still, I imagined that Mal shaped it into a form that looked like the sigil he'd chalked on my walls. He chanted softly under his breath, and I could feel the moment when he released the spell, or warding, or whatever it was actually called. The energy plowed through us and slammed into the walls.

I gasped as there was an audible pop and suddenly I felt like we were completely cut off from the outside world. Holy crap.

"Black abyss," Sabian swore. "That's powerful. You weren't joking, Mal. A demon strong enough to break through those wards isn't likely to ever bother with a place like this."

A small, pleased smile curled his lips before he shrugged. "I've had quite a lot of practice, but thank you."

He released our hands and I stood. A wave of exhaustion crashed over me.

"Fuck," I muttered, grabbing at the chair so I didn't fall.

"We should be done here," Mal said. "Let's get back to your place. Mind if I stay the night?"

"I was hoping you would," I admitted before looking around. The wards had turned invisible and the salt lines had vanished, but I could feel the energy thrumming through the air. Neat trick.

Mal gathered his things and put them back in his backpack while Sabian offered me his arm. I was tired enough that I took it, letting him support me as we left the pizza shop. I locked up behind us and we all climbed into my tank of a car. The trip back to my place was something of a blur, and I was only marginally alert as I stumbled to my front door.

Therefore, it took me a moment to notice something staring back at me.

"What the hell is that?" I blurted out.

Dakota Brown

Chapter 9

Sabian

We all stared at the creature perched on Chris's doorstep. It was small, fluffy, yellowish in color, and clearly demonic as it wrinkled its lips at us before wagging its small, fluffy tail. What the hell was that thing?

And then I realized that hell was the right word. That was the earthly form the hellhound sent by my prince had chosen. What in the black abyss was it?

I traded a look with the vampire while Chris continued to stare, dumbfounded.

Mal tilted his head in a question and I nodded. He burst out laughing.

"Seriously?"

I shrugged. "They can choose whatever canine form they like on this plane. Once they choose, they're generally stuck with it, however."

"That's a Pomeranian," Chris sputtered.

"It's a hellhound," I offered.

"No." She shook her head vehemently. "Just...No. I'm not having a...a... purse..." She couldn't even seem to get the words out.

I wasn't sure what she was trying to say, but the horrified disbelief on her face made me chuckle.

I wasn't sure how I'd actually fallen in love with a human, but there was no denying that's what I felt for my exorcist. While my kind typically dealt in lust and fed off of feelings like love, they didn't usually fall themselves, but I surely had. I didn't even mind.

"A purse dog!" she finally gasped out.

The pom-hellhound growled at her.

"No!"

It pranced forward on its tiny feet and lifted its leg. By the time I figured out what the damn thing was doing, it was too late. It, well, clearly a he, peed on Chris' leg.

"What!"

Mal grabbed her before she could punt the tiny dog.

"You will not come in the house if you can not behave!" She was still nearly shrieking. As much as a woman like Chris would ever shriek.

At least she'd gone from no, to you have to behave to come inside. The hellhound would have to agree to her commands to start the bond a hellhound had with his owner.

"Chris, he was marking his territory. He won't do it again, but he did have to get his scent on you."

"By peeing on me?" She glared at the tiny creature.

The pom-hellhound sat, not even trying to look contrite.

"Okay, do all Pomeranians have red in their eyes, or is it just this one?" Chris asked.

"While I believe they are all truly demonic in nature," Mal said with a laugh. "I think ours is probably the only one that is truly a demon in disguise. They normally only have red eyes when the light hits them right."

Chris groaned and leaned her forehead against Mal's shoulder.

"How is something this tiny supposed to help us?" Probably her last-ditch effort to send it away.

"It will have a hellhound shape that is much more formidable," I supplied, trying, and probably failing, to keep my amusement out of my voice.

"Why couldn't it have been a German Shepherd?" She sounded defeated. I almost felt bad for her, but I suspected it was because she was exhausted.

"Your leg would be a lot wetter if it had been," Mal stated gently.

Chris just sighed. "If you're coming in the house, you have to behave yourself. No peeing on things or crapping inside. No eating anything but actual food inside, or outside. I do not need vet bills. Do hellhounds have vet bills? Don't get on the table, or things like that. You're welcome on the couch, of course. And, uh, no excessive barking."

The pom-hellhound wagged its tail as if in agreement.

"Am I forgetting anything?"

"Act like a housebroke, trained, well-mannered dog," I supplied.

The pom-hellhound turned its reddish gaze on me in a condescending glare.

"Yes, everything Sabian just said."

The creature huffed in annoyance, but finally wagged its tail again.

"Fine, if you agree to all that, you can come in." Chris trudged into the house, dumped her coat, kicked off her shoes, and went toward the living area.

Mal picked up her jacket from the floor and hung it for her.

The pom-hellhound trotted into the living area behind Chris and by the time I got there, he had curled up on her lap on the couch.

She had basically collapsed onto the couch, staring at the ceiling. "Fuck," she muttered.

I sat down on one side of her, and Mal took the other. For a while we all just sat there, but finally Chris sighed.

"I really should get some sleep. I want the two of you for breakfast, and I won't have any energy if I don't get a few hours of rest."

Her nonchalant way of telling us she wanted us in the morning sent a jolt through me, and I could sense that she'd both surprised and aroused the vampire, too.

"And then, maybe real breakfast." She looked hopefully at Mal who laughed in reply.

"Whatever you desire, my dear exorcist."

She grinned. "Bed, right now. Well, a shower, then bed. Maybe some cuddles. Sleep, sex, food. Repeat over and over again."

I laughed. "I like the sound of that." How had I gotten so lucky as to be rescued by this delicious human, and then also desired by her, as well. Really desired, not just because of what I was. I could tell the different flavors of desire from anyone I fed from, and hers was the purest of true desire, not simple lust. Potent, and addictive.

Mal stood and offered her a hand. I watched how he treated her, determined to offer her the same respect and courtesy. He likely knew far more about how to treat a woman when in an actual relationship, and I was eager to learn. I hoped one day that I could have that with Chris, too. I knew Mal and Chris were still figuring out their own relationship, but hopefully there was room for both of us in her heart.

The creature on Chris's lap hopped to the ground and followed as Mal led Chris to her bedroom.

There was more to the hellhound than Chris and Mal knew, but as long as he didn't get overly possessive, at least where Mal and I were concerned, I wasn't going to let it bother me.

I had no idea what the creature's feelings on being here were. Did it want to be here? Or was it simply under orders? That would certainly affect his attitude toward Chris, but I had no doubt that he would do his job. He even acted friendly enough, at least toward her. I did wonder why he had chosen the earthly form he'd taken. It was a bit strange. Most of them went for something much more impressive than a small, what had Chris called it? Purse dog? Still, I knew what hellhounds looked like in their natural form and his other shape would take Chris's breath away.

∞ ∞ ∞

I didn't think I'd ever get tired of waking up with Chris curled up in my arms. The vampire hadn't minded sharing the bed with me, and we had sandwiched our exorcist between us. There wasn't a lot of extra room, but we made it work. The pom-hellhound had curled up behind her knees, though he had done his best to not touch me in the process.

Though neither the vampire nor I needed as much sleep as our human, I didn't think either of us would want to get up before her. Her chest rose slowly, though I could tell she was slowly returning to consciousness.

Mal was laying on his back, an arm wrapped around her while she lay with her head on his chest. He stared at the ceiling, lost in thought, though he glanced over at me and smiled when I turned my attention to him.

Chris took a deep breath and her eyes fluttered open. Mal and I both tightened our grips on her, and she sighed contentedly.

"Could get used to this," she murmured into Mal's chest.

"Me, too," the vampire replied.

She shifted around slightly before sitting up. "I'm going to go to the bathroom real quick, and then I'm going to come back and start shit." She grinned. "If that's all right by you two."

We both shifted to make it easier for her to crawl out from between the two of us and she left the room.

119

The pom-hellhound moved so that he could curl up on her pillow while we waited for her to come back.

"Okay, so what do we call you?" Mal asked, probably perceiving that a hellhound was far more than an earthly dog.

The creature looked at Mal, almost seemed to shrug, then tucked its tiny button nose into his fur and shut his eyes.

Mal looked at me for clarification.

"We have to choose a name for him," I translated. "Or Chris does, anyway."

The vampire nodded and lay back on the bed.

Chris came back into the bedroom, bleached blond hair still mussed, a sleepy glaze to her deep brown eyes. Her old T-shirt barely covered her ass, and her lean, muscular legs captured my attention. She got back on the bed and crawled toward us. My breath caught, and her movements made the ink that painted her arms seem to come alive in the low morning light.

She noticed my attention, and had fixed her gaze on me. Mal had gone still and watched her, the predator observing his prey.

A small smile tugged at her lips, though her gaze did flick over to the pom-hellhound sleeping on her pillow, before she turned her attention back to me and Mal. She acted resigned to the creature's presence at this point.

Mal reached for her and she let him draw her close. I sighed as the energy from their lust washed through me, revitalizing and feeding me.

Not wanting to be left out, after the initial wave of pleasure filled me, I rolled onto my side, and paid some attention to Chris' thighs, while Mal's hands roamed over her back as they kissed.

I was about to pull her panties down so I could give her another type of kiss when her phone rang.

120

We all froze, and then she cursed. "That's Darius and I don't think he'd call this early if it wasn't important."

I wasn't starving, so I didn't press her to ignore the call knowing she would be just as frustrated about the interruption as we were. Mal took it with good grace, too, reaching over and snagging Chris' phone for her. She sat up, straddling Mal in the process. He groaned softly as she shifted around, rubbing against his cock and teasing him a bit as she answered the phone.

"Yeah, mate?"

Mal grabbed her hips and stopped her from squirming. She grinned, amused, before the expression on her face hardened into something akin to resigned annoyance.

"Yeah, sure. We'll be right down." She dropped her phone on the bed and frowned.

Mal also looked concerned. Obviously, his hearing was far better than my own, or I'd been fixating on Chris' ass and what she was doing to Mal with it. Chris shifted to get off Mal, but he didn't release her hips, a wicked grin forming on his lips.

"We have a minute," he stated.

Chris raised her eyebrows. "Darius urgently needs us at the jail for another exorcism."

Mal's grin deepened and he shifted his hand until he was brushing the front of her pussy with his thumb.

Chris groaned and the wave of lust hit me. I flopped back on the bed, drinking it in, sighing with pleasure.

The pom-hellhound grunted and shifted out of the way when Chris let Mal lay her back on the bed and pull down her panties.

Mal glanced at me. "Want in on any of this?"

"If I get involved, we're going to be here longer than the few minutes it'll take you to get her off," I replied a little drunkenly.

He chuckled and went to work on Chris.

Shortly he had our exorcist squirming on the bed, crying out in pleasure. I couldn't help adding tiny moans of my own as I drank in their ecstasy. No, I certainly wasn't going to be hungry today.

Mal was clearly talented, even though he got her off quickly, she still came hard, panting out his name as he worked her through her orgasm.

After we took a moment to enjoy her release, we all reluctantly got up and got ready to go meet Darius and his newest problem. I yet again thanked whatever deity, from above or below, that had let me fall into this woman's life.

Chapter 10

Price

While I'd gotten some satisfaction this morning, I was still grumpy at the interruption, and police stations of any sort were never going to be my favorite places.

"Sabian," I started as I pulled into a parking spot.

He purred at my use of his name and I groaned as his power hit me and Mal.

"Public, mate."

He chuckled and though the sound did things to me I'd rather not think about while in a police station parking lot, he kept his power in check.

I arched an eyebrow and gave him a look.

He smiled back, all sorts of innocence on his face.

Mal laughed, and I tried to hide the smile that was trying to break through my frown.

"As I was saying," I continued once I'd turned off the car. "Why don't you stay out here. I don't want to exorcise you."

"That would be unfortunate," Sabian agreed.

"Or, if it's too warm you could wait in the lobby." I wasn't sure what sort of disturbance Sabian's inability to not ooze sex would have in there, but it might be amusing.

"While the demonic plane is not exactly as humans have pictured it, it's certainly a great deal harsher than the human landscapes. This level of heat will not bother me. I'll wait outside."

"Okay. You coming, Mal?"

He nodded.

When we got out of the car, the Pomeranian shaped hellhound followed.

"Um, mate, think you probably have to stay here, too. Unless you want me to explain you to the cops?"

The dog huffed but trotted over to Sabian's side.

We left Sabian and the hellhound with the car and headed inside. A couple of other people waited in a line by a window where they might have been paying tickets. I headed over to the desk where a male deputy sat typing away at a computer. He was clearly busy, but had taken the time to examine us when we came in. When we came over, he checked us in and called for Deputy McClellan. She came to claim us after an uncomfortable minute standing in the lobby.

"Where's your other, uh, friend?" She gestured for us to follow her through the door she opened with her keycard.

"Sabian is waiting in the car. Seems exorcisms don't agree with him very well," I said.

Deputy McClellan gave me a disbelieving look.

I shrugged. "He's helping. He promised to behave, and he actually does the dishes, so, guess he's an alright house guest."

Her eyes widened before she glanced at Mal. "I don't believe we've been introduced."

"Malak Naji." The vampire offered his hand and Deputy McClellan shook it after giving him her name.

"What is your role in all of this?" she asked.

"I'm a little muscle and some occult backup if needed," Mal replied. "This is getting a lot deeper and I thought Chris could use some backup."

"The..." she shook her head. "Demon isn't enough muscle?"

I laughed. "Sabian is a lover, not a fighter."

She choked.

"His words, not mine. He can hold his own against humans. I'm not sure how he'd fare in a fight against another demon. Probably depend on who he was up against. But while he's got powers, he's not an occultist," I added.

Deputy McClellan gave Mal another searching look before she led us into the same holding cell as before.

The containment spell drew my eyes. It was stronger than the last one Darius had done, though now that I had seen Mal's work, it looked a little less professional, though it would certainly hold the demon contained within.

The woman cuffed to the heavy metal chair was taller, muscular, and drenched in sweat, as if she'd been fighting something. Her head lolled back, as if she were staring at the ceiling, though her eyes were shut. The gray tank top clung to her, and her cargo pants were damp with sweat. Her dark hair hung lank on her head and when she finally did muster the energy to look at us, her eyes were rimmed red with possession.

Darius had set up the spell to release a demon from a charm, along with the general stuff we used in our exorcisms, but clearly it wasn't going well or he wouldn't have called me.

"So, what's the story?" I glanced at Darius.

"I don't know. The demon is fighting me far more than I feel like it should be able to, but it's yelling at me in demonic and I have no idea what it's saying."

I swore and glanced at Mal. "Could you go get Sabian?"

Mal and Deputy McClellan left the room and came back a few minutes later with our incubus, the hellhound perched on his shoulder.

I hoped if I ignored the dog, everyone else would, too.

Sabian looked around the room curiously before settling his attention on the bound demon.

We all stared at it expectantly and it stared back.

"What's up?" I prompted.

"Maybe toss some of that holy water on it?" Sabian suggested. "Perhaps the demon needs some sort of disruption on its host to break through the compulsions."

Darius complied and we all winced as the woman screamed in agony, but her red rimmed eyes blackened as the demon took greater control. The voice coming out of the woman's mouth was far deeper than you would ever expect from a human, and the sound of it grated against my ears. I couldn't understand any of the words, but Sabian's expression went from pensive to alarmed. The incubus' expression turned inward much as it had when he had contacted his prince. Once he refocused on me, he shook his head eyes tight with worry.

"The demon bound in that charm cleverly figured out that they hadn't forbidden him to speak in the demonic tongue. Of course, no one speaks it but another demon, so it's a good thing you have me." He winked at me.

My lips twitched, but I managed not to smile.

"They figured out the police had found an exorcist and upped their timetable. They're attempting to summon the demon prince now. We have to go."

"Do you know where?" I turned toward the door.

"I think so," Sabian replied.

"Let's go." I headed for the door.

"Price, what about this one?" Darius protested.

"Darius they're trying to summon a demon prince. This is something we do not want to happen. If they could actually bind one into service, it would be worse than if the creature was loose on its own. There's no telling what the humans would do with a demon prince to command."

Darius paled a bit and nodded.

"Besides, I don't think this one will fight you as much now."

The demon shook the woman's head like a puppet, and I shuddered. I never wanted a demon in control of my body. Ever. At least not like that. I pulled my thoughts away from the things I wouldn't mind Sabian doing to me. This was really not the time to lose focus.

The four of us, counting the hellhound, rushed out of the station and into the furnace that was my car after sitting in the sun.

I rolled the windows down, and Sabian gave me some general directions. While I drove, Mal questioned him further on where we were going, and by the time I needed more specific information, we thought we knew where we were headed.

Strangely enough, we weren't headed to some out of the way warehouse, or abandoned building. We were heading to a suburb outside of Santa Fe. It was a nicer area that you wouldn't expect someone from a crime syndicate to live. Of course, my main experiences with those sorts of people were more from movies than anything. Despite my minor lawbreaking as a youth, the most contact I'd had with real criminals was low key drug dealers working the streets where I'd roamed. Of all the things I'd never tried, hard drugs were high on the list. Your mind had to be clear to safely perform an exorcism, and about the only drug I'd ever allowed myself was alcohol and a little weed and it had been years since I'd done anything but drink.

Maybe the occultist lived in the suburb?

I supposed we'd find out soon enough.

Driving as fast as I could without overly risking getting pulled over, I wound through Santa Fe, grateful it wasn't rush hour or high tourist season. Traffic wasn't as bad as some places, but it could get pretty intense sometimes. We finally entered the subdivision and Sabian pointed out a couple of turns.

"You okay?"

I glanced at the incubus before turning my attention back to the road. Sweat glistened on his forehead despite the AC being on high. He'd already told us that the desert heat in the summer didn't bother him, so something was clearly going on.

"I can feel the summoning. It's actually pulling on me, as well. Perhaps because it is our prince that is being called."

"How'd they get that specific? Do they have his name?"

Sabian shook his head. "Probably the political maneuverings he mentioned when you actually spoke with him. I wasn't able to reach him directly when I tried at the jail. The ensnared demon gave me all of the directions."

"Great," I muttered. The tires squealed as I took the last turn and screeched to a halt in front of a perfectly ordinary suburban house.

"I feel like this should be happening someplace really creepy," I grumbled as I killed the engine and threw my door open.

Mal beat us to the front door and had it open by the time Sabian, the hellhound, and I caught up.

I could feel the pressure of wards around the front door as I went inside, but they didn't stop Mal from entering. He did something and a moment later Sabian and the hellhound–really needed to name that thing–were charging down the hallway after me.

I didn't need directions now. Even I could feel the energies of the summoning.

"Damn it, they didn't even have the decency to do this in a proper basement," I complained as I burst into what essentially looked like a large office, or a library, by the bookshelves lining the walls.

I took a brief moment to survey the scene. A black man was bound to a chair, shirtless, and I caught sight of some strange white tattoos on his biceps and pecs that I didn't take time to study. Blood ran down his chest, but he was currently still alive, eyes wide and staring at me. A tall, light skinned woman, with blond hair, high cheekbones, and a very startled expression on her face paused in the middle of an incantation to stare at us.

That could be a real mistake depending on the timing. She wore normal everyday clothing, jeans and a T-shirt, but she had on a white stole embroidered with very familiar symbols draped over her shoulders and a tome of a book cradled in one hand. The other held a crystal of some sort.

One other person was in the room. Now *he* looked like a thug. A well-dressed thug, in a pressed shirt and khakis, but the expression on his pale face was further darkened by the shock of red hair that framed it. Crazy Irish thug? I liked crazy Irish folks, at least until they were trying to kill me or summon demons.

The thug was currently reaching for a gun. Mal blurred and I trusted the vampire to intercept. I hoped we were in time to disrupt the ritual, and charged forward, tackling the occultist before she could do anything, and hoped that if we were too late, the summoned prince would take into account I was at least loosely allied with him. We crashed into the table she'd set for the ritual, breaking the line of sigils that had created the containment circle and scattering implements everywhere.

Candles went flying and I hoped they went out instead of catching everything on fire.

I heard Sabian yelp and I spared a glance, but he was only shaking his hand and acted okay. It looked like he had tried to release the bound man and come up against some sort of barrier that caused him pain.

The woman I'd landed on screeched in anger and punched me in the face.

"Hey!" I elbowed her in the gut.

Yeah, that was going to leave a mark. Ouch.

Someone went flying across the room and crashed into one of the bookshelves.

The woman pushed me off of her and I rolled, then went still, all my attention focused on the gun now pointed at my face.

Turns out the crazy red head's eyes were rimed in red and I was willing to bet he had surprised the vampire. If we survived this, I was so giving Mal a whole bunch of crap about that later.

Sirens blared in the distance and the bad guys traded a glance before the woman grabbed her book and headed out the door. The red head backed up, gun still pointed at me, until they were clear of the door. They slammed it shut behind them, then I felt something pop as if we were being cut off from the outside.

I struggled to my feet and hit the door hard, but the handle wouldn't budge.

Fuck.

The other thing I should have noticed sooner was the flames licking up the curtains and spreading across the floor from the downed candles.

"Chris, come untie him," Mal shouted.

I turned. Both Sabian and Mal were staring at the black man with surprised expressions on their faces.

"What's wrong with your fingers?" I grumbled as hurried over there, head aching from the punch.

"We can't touch him," Sabian replied.

"What?"

The guy looked just as confused.

I pulled out one of my many blades and hacked away at the thick ropes binding him.

The smoke was starting to get heavy and I coughed. "Why don't you two see if you can get us out of here," I ordered. "Where's the dog?"

They went over to the door, but I didn't see the hellhound anywhere. Hoping the creature could take care of itself, and putting it out of my mind, I worked to cut the guy free.

"What's your name, mate?" I coughed as the smoke thickened.

"Aaron Reed," the man answered. And oh boy was his voice rich, deep, and contained just the right amount of gravely notes. I could listen to this man lecture about physics and I'd probably enjoy it. "Who are you?"

"Chris Price. Friends are Sabian and Mal."

I finished slicing through the rope binding his arms and moved in front of him so I could work on his legs. Dude had some serious muscle. It was either focus on that or start to panic about the smoke filling the room and the fact that we couldn't get out.

Looking up for a moment, I saw Mal smash a chair against the one window despite the flames. The chair shattered against the wardings. He swore in what was probably Arabic and shied away as the flames reached for him.

I went back to work on the bindings. It was the only thing I could do.

Both Mal and Sabian threw themselves at the door and bounced off it. Damn, those were some serious wards. I bet Mal could get around them if he had time, but there wasn't much left. I was starting to feel woozy, and Aaron was coughing.

My knife slid through the last of the bindings and Aaron threw himself out of the chair and to the ground where the air was marginally clearer.

Mal and Sabian tried again, and this time they crashed through the door, and slammed into the wall on the other side.

I grabbed Aaron's hand and tugged. He perked up enough to follow me out into the fresher air, though the draft had lent life to the flames inside the office and flames chased us out.

Mal grabbed my arm and pulled on me while Sabian ran ahead, probably to check the front door. I kept my grip on Aaron's hand.

Was that a flash of yellow? Had the hellhound escaped ahead of us?

Either way, we needed to get out of the house now. Fortunately, Sabian had the front door open and we all burst out into the bright sunlight and clear air just as fire trucks screamed to a halt in front of the house. How they'd known about the fire already was anyone's guess, but I suspected they had scared off the bad guys and probably saved at least my life.

The firefighters ran up to us. "Anyone else home?" One shouted.

"No," Aaron gasped out. "I was the only one home."

Oh, it was his house. That explained a lot, except why the bad guys had targeted him. Maybe the strange tattoos had something to do with it. Now that I wasn't in danger of dying, I studied them more closely. They looked like eyes on his pecs and biceps. Something like stylized wings draped down his back. The white against his dark skin was pretty awesome, but the eyes were seriously creepy, and I wondered why he had chosen them.

Mal and Sabian, and yeah, the hellhound, kind of faded into the background as the paramedics rushed up to me and Aaron.

The next little bit was a blur as they checked me out, treated me for minor smoke inhalation, and the firefighters tackled the fire. I watched as the house burned, resisting all attempts to put it out. That was clearly a supernatural fire, though I wasn't about to say anything.

The cops questioned Aaron, and finally came over to me.

"What caused you to come here?" the one officer asked. "Mr. Reed says he's never seen you before you saved him."

I smiled tiredly at the young man's earnest expression. Those bright blue eyes, if they'd belonged to someone a bit older, might have grabbed me for a night or two of fun before I moved on.

"I'm working with Deputy McClellan on one of her cases. We got a tip and hurried over. Guess it was a good thing. I'm not sure how much I can say since it's an active investigation." That was true enough.

The officer questioning me nodded. "I'll get in touch with her. Thank you."

"Sure." I leaned against the side of the ambulance and watched the controlled chaos of the scene until Aaron, now with a blanket draped over his broad shoulders, came over to me.

"So, you going to tell me how you knew to show up and save my ass? Not that I'm not grateful, it's just a bit convenient."

I sighed in pleasure as his voice vibrated through me. Maybe I was still suffering from smoke inhalation? Now that he was standing upright, I was struck by how tall he was. Sabian wasn't short, and I felt like Aaron had several inches on the incubus. He was quite a bit taller than Mal, and he would tower over me once I was standing.

"It's a long story. I'll tell you once we're alone."

Mal and Sabian joined us, staying clear of Aaron. Their reaction to the man was strange and I really wanted to hear their explanation.

Aaron eyed them uneasily.

After the house was mostly destroyed, it started behaving like a normal fire probably should, and they started making some headway on putting it out.

We watched it burn in silence. There wasn't much I could say to make the situation any better, and I didn't know Aaron at all, so I had no idea what sort of words he might appreciate.

The sun had sunk low in the sky by the time the fire was out and most of the people had cleared the scene. Aaron talked with a few more police officers before coming back over to us.

"I get the idea we need to talk."

"Yeah, mate," I agreed.

"Well, my car was in the garage, and I think I'm lucky to have had my wallet in my pocket. Mind giving me a lift to a store so I can grab a few things, and then a hotel?"

He was handling the destruction of his house fairly well. Either that, or it simply hadn't sunk in yet.

"We can do that," I agreed and gestured toward the car.

Sabian, Mal, and the hellhound got in the back while we took the front. Aaron kept the blanket around himself to protect his skin from the hot car.

"Then maybe some food and we can talk," I suggested when I started the car.

"I know this really great pizza place," Aaron replied tiredly.

Ahh, hell, if he said Tony's...we were going to have to have words. They were the other dedicated pizza joint in town. They were good enough, but nowhere near the quality of what I put out. "Yeah, mate?" I prompted.

"Price's. It's the best pizza in town."

"Damn straight," I agreed.

Sabian and Mal chuckled.

"I know the owner," I said. "I bet I can get us a good deal."

Aaron glanced at me and frowned. "Oh, hell, I thought you looked familiar."

I shrugged. "Just glad for the honest review. Let's get you some essentials, and then we'll get the best pizza in town and we can trade tales. Got a lot to talk about. Where do you want to go to get some clothes?"

He named one of the nicer department stores in the less touristy part of town. I raised my eyebrows but headed that direction. We'd have to find some place to wash up on the way to get the soot off. The smoky smell would linger, but we could take care of that at home.

Dakota Brown

Chapter 11

Aaron

Getting a few essentials proved a touch more difficult since I didn't have a shirt in the first place. Mal–I could sense a hint of a lie when they told me his name. Not so much that I thought they were outright hiding who he was, more so that it might be a shortening of his full name–ended up running inside and getting me a shirt. Then he and I went in together. I wasn't sure why the other man joined me, but I had a feeling he was protecting me. If so, I was grateful. Though the man was quite a bit shorter than me, he moved a lot like some of my friends who were really into martial arts. He probably knew how to handle himself.

Still, that didn't explain why he found it painful to touch me, and I was looking forward to their explanation later over dinner.

Chris Price was an interesting character. I'd seen her once or twice in her restaurant, and she was fairly distinctive, but I figured I had a pass on not recognizing her right away. What with the fire and all.

That really pissed me off. I had liked that house quite a bit, and I got along with my neighbors really well. I guess the land was still mine, and I could rebuild. It would just take a while. I'd have to deal with insurance. Aww, hell, my work laptop had gone up in the fire. Everything important was backed up on the network, but I might have lost a few notes. Still, I was alive, and the rest was an inconvenience compared to that.

Who had those people been, and what were they after?

Armed with a bag of clothing, toiletries, and a new phone, I felt at least a little better able to face the next few hours. After that, well, I would probably need a stiff drink or two. I suspected what my new friends would have to tell me was going to be harder to handle than the fire itself.

Chris pulled into the parking lot for the pizza parlor and we all climbed out. My stomach was really growling by then, and I was glad we had opted for food during our discussion.

I studied the sign to the shop as we approached. Something was different.

"Did you rebrand?" I asked.

"What? No, mate," Chris answered tiredly. She stopped and looked at the sign. "Son of a bitch," she muttered.

Sabian burst out laughing and Mal chuckled.

"It's a good touch," Mal said.

"But…we're supposed to be forgetting about demons," she exclaimed, and I could hear the exasperation in her voice.

That was what was different. There was a pentagram now gracing the pizza pie in her sign, the point of the star facing the ground. And what was this about demons? The marks that looked like eyes on my biceps and chest tingled and I rubbed my hands together to try and chase the unpleasant sensation away.

She smacked her forehead. "I don't know if I should be upset or not."

The small dog that trotted after her woofed and wagged its tail as if it were amused, too. No one had paid much attention to the dog. I thought it was a Pomeranian. I wondered what was going on with that.

"Just own it, Chris," Mal suggested.

The woman took a deep breath and pushed through the double doors into the cool, air-conditioned building. We all followed, even the dog that everyone was ignoring.

I ate here often enough that the changes to the decoration were obvious. Whoever had done the sign out front, had hit the inside, as well. They'd spent some time adding the upside down pizza pentagram to the signs. Obviously, by Price's reaction, it was new. I wondered if what had prompted that change was related to the earlier events.

The staff looked up and kind of froze when they saw Price.

She tilted her head and put her hands on her hips.

The woman at the hostess station twisted her hands and smiled hopefully. "Did you want a table, Chris?"

Price raised her eyebrows and tilted her head, pointing at the addition to the sign.

She shrugged. "It was Billy's idea."

"Yeah, sure, blame it on me," Billy said as he came into the dining room. Someone must have grabbed him.

Chris turned her attention on him.

"If you don't like it, we can fix it. It's temporary. We've got some suggestions for the menu and a few other things. I've got a sign priced out."

"What, exactly, prompted this?" Chris asked, voice neutral. She glanced back at the woman at the hostess station. "Table?"

The woman held up three fingers and Chris gestured for us to follow.

There weren't many patrons right now, but a few glanced at us as we headed to a large table in the back of the dining area.

The garlic smell made my stomach grumble constantly and I hoped we got around to ordering soon. Not that I wasn't interested in the pizza shop drama, but I was also interested in food.

Another woman, with dark hair and high cheekbones and a hesitant smile, came over once we were seated. "Do you want me to let you yell at Billy first, or do you want to order?"

Price glanced at the woman, eyebrows raised, before she burst out laughing. "We'll order really quickly, Rebecca. It's been a hell of a day and I think we're all hungry. My normal, large, and whatever he wants." She gestured toward me.

I ordered a pizza with all the meat and water to drink.

Rebecca headed off to put our order in and Billy pulled up a chair, spun it around and sat in it backward. "So, yes or no?" He gestured at the nearest pizza pentagram.

"Keep it," Sabian urged.

Price turned her attention to Mal. He looked like he was trying to fight off a grin, and he nodded his agreement with Sabian.

Price sighed and turned to Billy. "Why me?"

Her manager grinned. "We hoped you would like it."

"Guess it's all right," Price allowed.

"Do you want to see our menu suggestions?"

She buried her face in her hands. "No, just run with it. Have fun. Try not to summon any actual demons."

Billy laughed, got up, and put his chair back at the other table. As if that were the signal, Rebecca brought over our drinks.

Once we were alone, Price ran her hand through the long part of her hair and sighed again. "Right, where were we?"

"You were going to tell me how you knew to show up and save my ass," I prompted. "And maybe explain what the hell is going on?"

She nodded. "That's right. Okay, so, I got no idea why they wanted you, mate. Anything special about you?"

Yeah, but I didn't know them well enough to tell them my secrets yet. I shrugged.

Price smiled, as if reading into that and accepting that I probably had an idea of what she was referring to, but didn't want to say it.

"Right. So, I'm an exorcist. The staff found out last week. That's where all the," she gestured at the décor, "extra touches came from."

I raised my eyebrows. "Really?"

"Yeah. Anyway, friend of mine came to me not long ago and asked if I could help him with a tricky case. Long story short, we're now entangled in some sort of demonic power play that is leaking into our world. These drug runner folks seem to have figured out how to bind demons into charms and are using them to up the power on their minions. They're also trying to summon a demon prince and bind him. I think that's what they were doing at your place." Price studied me while I took in her words.

I couldn't deny that I was having a hard time processing what she said and believing her, but everything rang with truth. She wasn't lying. And, considering my own abilities, I had to accept that there was more out there than was generally acknowledged. Still...a demonic power play spilling into our world?

She gave me a sympathetic smile. "Trust me, I get it, and I already believed in demons. Just never thought I'd be helping them instead of fighting them."

"You're helping them?" That certainly made me uneasy.

"Common goals, mate. They don't want to be here, at least in this context, and I don't want them here."

Anything else was interrupted by the arrival of our pizza.

We spent the next few minutes scarfing pizza, though I did pause long enough to notice that Mal didn't eat any. He did drink the ginger beer Price had ordered for him, though.

141

Interesting. Sabian's attention was glued to Price while she ate her pizza with obvious bliss on her face.

There weren't any leftovers by the time the three of us who were actually eating were done with the pizza, and Price leaned back in her chair, looking content.

"Okay, so demons. That still doesn't answer how you knew to come save me."

"Oh, yeah, right. Well, those demons who are being somewhat helpful because they're not real excited about what's happening to them, tipped us off and we raced to the rescue."

I nearly choked on my water. "Wait, seriously? I owe my life to some demons?"

"Yeah, I wouldn't let them in on that idea. They're still demons. They might let it go to their heads." Price looked a touch uneasy at that idea.

The cold chill in the pit of my stomach echoed her unease.

"You're just filling me with all sorts of warm fuzzies." I took a breath and tried to center myself. When I got freaked out too badly, that's when strange things happened. When my… abilities, if I wanted to call them that, came out. I still wasn't sure why I hadn't been able to get out of those bonds. It shouldn't have been difficult. Maybe some of the magic that woman had been using had prevented me?

"Okay, so why can't you two touch me?" I pointed at the other two men.

Sabian and Mal traded a confused look before they both shrugged.

"We don't know," Sabian answered.

His voice made me think of velvety chocolate and I didn't typically think of men in those sorts of terms. He just oozed sex, even to me. It was a touch uncomfortable when he turned his attention fully on me.

I tried not to squirm while he studied me.

Mal also stared. From him, I got a predatory feel, as if he might consider eating me and not in any way that might even be remotely fun.

"Maybe it has something to do with those abilities you don't want to tell us about," Price added. "No worries, mate. We all got secrets. Though, I guess you know mine." She rolled her eyes and gestured at the signs. "Everyone does, apparently."

That broke the tension and I chuckled. "Well, being able to send demons back to hell is kinda cool."

She shrugged. "Yeah, I guess. Okay, so you got a place in mind to stay, mate?"

I really couldn't place her accent. I thought it was at least partially British, but whatever it was, it fit Price in a way that was kind of uncanny.

"No. Guess any decent hotel would be fine for now."

"You should stay with Chris," Mal said slowly. "I have a feeling you're not entirely safe yet."

"And I'm safe with you?" I leveled a look at him.

Mal chuckled. "Safer with us than you are with the people summoning demons, anyway."

His statement rang with truth, though I found his phrasing very interesting.

"I don't want to impose. I can find a hotel. It'll be okay, now that I know someone is after me."

"Naw, I have a guest room. If Mal thinks you should stay with us, he's probably right." Chris downed the last of her ginger beer and stood. "Unless you really want to argue, let's get back to my place so we can relax and finish cleaning up. Mal, maybe you want to beef up the wards?"

He nodded, and I gave in. The situation felt right, and I also thought I might learn more once we were no longer in public. Maybe I'd even tell them my secrets. It would be interesting to know if they could shed some light on my abilities, because I had no idea what to make of them. I'd

143

learned to trust my instincts, and they said I would be safe with these three. Not to mention, Chris Price was very intriguing.

Chapter 12

Price

I wasn't sure if it was Sabian's influence or something about Aaron, but I was really having a hard time keeping my mind off of all the interesting things we could be doing in the bedroom as I studied him while he wandered around my living room. Damn Sabian and his pull on my ovaries, anyway. If I was going to keep him around, I'd have to get used to the constant arousal, but did it have to hit me with Aaron, too?

As soon as we had gotten back to my place I'd shown Aaron the guest bathroom and then we'd all cleaned up. Then I'd collapsed on the couch. Sabian and Mal were currently working on the wards, and Aaron had sat down for a few minutes, but then he'd gotten up and started to pace.

"You know, if you want to make some phone calls, or anything, feel free. I can give you some privacy. Figure there's a few things you need to take care of."

Aaron stopped pacing and turned to look at me. "No. Sorry. I'll take care of all of that in the morning. I already sent a message to my boss and he gave me a few days to manage stuff. They've got to build a new laptop for me, anyway."

I frowned. "Where do you work?"

"Over at Los Alamos."

I raised my eyebrows. "What do you do there?"

"Particle physics research."

"Holy shit, that's intense." I supposed I might enjoy listening to a physics lecture if he was the one giving it. Damn his voice was fine.

Aaron smiled and shrugged. "I enjoy it. I also coach soccer clubs for part of the year. I'm pretty vanilla and boring, really."

"Apparently not, mate, or the bad guys wouldn't be after you." I grinned at him.

He shook his head and crossed his arms over his chest as if hugging himself before folding himself back into the loveseat. He was really damn tall, and muscular, but he managed himself gracefully. I suspected he played a lot of sports by the lean but well defined muscles. He probably kept very active.

"You want to talk about it?" I prompted, hoping he would open up a little.

I felt the atmosphere in the house… tighten, was really the only way I could describe it. It had been sealed before, but whatever Mal had just done to my wards had blocked us off solidly from any outside influence.

Aaron looked around, frowning.

"Mal just tightened the wards. I'm good, but he's way better."

"Wards?" Aaron enunciated the word as if he wasn't familiar with it.

"Protections on the house against the supernatural," I explained.

"Ahh. I guess I don't know a lot about the supernatural world. I wasn't even completely sure it existed." Aaron hunched his shoulders and stared at his hands.

"Well, it does. Tell you what. It's been a crazy day and I'm sure we're all tired. Why don't you get some sleep, and we can talk more in the morning?" I stood and Aaron did the same.

I wasn't especially tall, but I didn't normally feel short. Aaron made me feel short. Really short. Next to him, I didn't hate the feeling. I kind of wanted to wrap him around me and... Head out of the gutter, Price. You've got two guys already.

Aaron followed me down the hallway to my parents' room. The guest room was across from theirs. My room was on the other end of the house, which, was good because I didn't intend to be celibate while we had a visitor, and I didn't want him to hear us. I didn't typically mind an audience, but he might not want to hear it. Not to mention, I hadn't exactly mentioned I was shacking up with both of them. Figured if he wanted to know he could ask. Otherwise, wasn't his business.

Why was I even worried about what Aaron thought? I'd never cared in the past. This was a new and uncomfortable feeling.

"Here you go, mate. Make yourself at home. Might be here for a little while if you can stand us."

Aaron smiled. "Thank you, Chris."

"Yeah, no problem."

He went into the room and I took a breath and headed for mine. I shed my clothing once I was inside and headed for the shower. I'd just rinsed off before with three of us sharing this shower. I wanted to stand in the hot water for a few minutes and really wash my hair. The little dog that I was ignoring as best I could followed.

"So, what do you get out of all this?" I glanced at the tiny puff ball hellhound.

He woofed at me.

"Yeah, that's what I thought." Whatever that all meant. At some point I was going to have to name him. I had no idea what to call a hellhound shaped like a poof, though.

I turned on the tap, waited until the water was steaming, and then got in. Freaking hell, I was tired. And my face hurt from getting hit by that crazy bitch. No one had said anything, but I was certain I had a bruise. I wasn't ready to look in the mirror, however.

My phone chimed, interrupting my shower. Damn it. Though I was tempted to ignore the intrusive piece of technology, it was probably Darius and I suspected he and his sheriff's deputy would want to talk to Aaron. If I could keep him from swinging by until the morning, that'd be great.

I dried off my hands, dripping all over the floor, and grabbed my phone.

Darius: *You have eyes on that guy from the fire?*

Nice of him to ask how I was doing. I jumped a little when I felt something touch my leg.

The hellhound woofed, and as soon as I stopped moving, went back to licking the water off my leg. Dogs. I shook my head and typed out a quick reply.

Price: *Yeah, he's staying in the guest room.*

Darius: *We'll be by in the morning.*

I assumed that meant him and the cops. Great.

Price: *See you then. Don't come too early.*

He didn't reply, which I didn't take as a good sign for my ability to sleep in tomorrow. Aaron was probably a morning person, anyway. I groaned, put down the phone and finished drying off.

"Thanks," I muttered to the hellhound, who had gotten most of the water off one calf.

He wagged his tail and pranced out of the bathroom ahead of me. So far, I wasn't sure what good he was, but he was behaving himself around the house and didn't require a lot of attention. Speaking of, I hadn't actually fed him, either. Maybe Sabian was taking care of it?

"You hungry?" Speaking of hungry, I needed to have a discussion with Sabian about this lust problem I was having. I wondered if he could tone it down some more.

The creature hopped up on the bed, which was a significant jump for a dog that size, and curled up on my pillow. I took that as a no.

Mal and Sabian came into the room before I could decide if I was getting dressed for bed or not. They both let their gazes travel over my mostly exposed body. A predatory smile curled Mal's lips. Sabian's was more playful.

Before I could figure out something to say, Mal pulled his shirt off and everything fled from my mind except the exquisite view of my vampire shirtless. I almost didn't notice as I dropped the towel to the floor and stepped forward, reaching out to touch those defined muscles. I traced my fingers along the scar across his stomach and my brain short circuited when I tried to decide if I wanted to drag my hand higher, or lower.

"You two are completely wrecking me," I managed to get out, voice low.

Mal ran his hands up my sides, tracing my ribs, then gently running his hands over my breasts, making me shiver in anticipation. "Complaining?" he teased.

"No. Just not used to this." I was scared to admit how much I was coming to need them in my life.

Mal curled his fingers around the back of my neck and slid his other hand behind my back, pulling me close, hugging me to him. Nothing demanding, just offering comfort. He was so damn perceptive it was creepy.

I relaxed into his embrace, tucking my head under his chin.

"Would you let me worship you tonight, Chris Price?" he whispered, his voice vibrating through me.

"That sounds amazing," I replied, gasping a little at the thrill of emotion his words sent through me.

It occurred to me that Mal might be just as stressed out about almost dying as I was. Sabian probably would have survived, but Mal and I would have been toast if they hadn't been able to get the door open. Aaron, too, I imagined.

I melted into Mal's embrace, letting him devour my lips, sensing an urgency in him that made me think I was right. We both wanted to feel alive right then. He pushed me back, until my legs pressed against the bed, then gently lowered me onto my worn unicorn comforter. He slid out of his pants then leaned over me.

Mal's lips consumed me, working their way from my mouth, down my neck, pausing there, before he paid attention to my collarbone, and then further south over my breast. He traced some of the lines of one of my tattoos with his tongue before nibbling at my stomach. Then he went lower, teasing me, making me squirm, until finally he buried his face between my legs.

I cried out wordlessly, moaning as he worked on my clit, bringing me right to the edge, then backing off, building me slowly, torturously.

It was almost a surprise when Mal finally let me tumble over the edge, a powerful orgasm spiraling through me and taking my breath away.

He held me while I rode that high, head swimming with the intensity. Once I could somewhat think again, I pushed on his shoulder until Mal was on his back. I straddled him, groaning as I pushed myself down onto him, still sensitive from my orgasm.

Mal grinned, grabbing my hips and holding me while I moved. I was pleased to see he'd lost enough of his control that his eyes had gone fully black with desire, and his fangs were out. He was likely hungry. I was willing to donate. First, I wanted to get him off.

He was close already, and his eyes fluttered shut. He clenched his jaw, fingers digging into my hips, groaning as he went rigid with his release.

I leaned forward, pressing my lips to his, and he kissed me with a fierce possessiveness I didn't feel I deserved. He clutched me against him as if he would never let go.

"You're really going to make me think about keeping you around if you keep that up, mate," I whispered.

"I do hope so," he replied.

"Hungry?"

"Do you mind?"

"Mmmm, not one bit," I answered.

"Thank you."

Mal cradled the back of my neck with his hand, tilting my chin, kissing me softly before burying his fangs in my neck.

I might have passed out with how powerfully my body responded to his bite. When I was able to focus on more than the sensations rippling through me, I found myself cradled in Mal's arms. He kissed my cheek when I turned a sleepy eye on him.

"Let's get you cleaned up," he said, "and then get some rest. Today was far more exhausting than it should have been."

"Yeah, near death experiences will do that."

Mal nodded, squishing me against him. "Yes. Not something I'm particularly used to these days. I do not approve."

I chuckled. "Yeah, me neither."

He helped me back to the bathroom. We took a quick shower together, and by the time we headed toward my bed for actual sleep, Sabian and the hellhound were there. I was sure Sabian felt fine after that, and I still had no idea what the hellhound was doing for food, but at that point I didn't care. Curled up between a hellhound, an incubus, and a vampire, I fell fast asleep, feeling safer than I ever had in my entire life. Which, admittedly, was a little messed up, but hey, that was par for the course of my life.

∞ ∞ ∞

Barking woke me the next morning. I jolted upright, heart racing.

Sabian put a comforting hand on my back. I didn't see Mal and I hoped he was both making breakfast, and taking care of whatever had set the dog off, though I guessed it was Darius.

I grumbled in annoyance, turned and gave Sabian a kiss, which he turned into something with a bit more heat than I had intended. Pleasure tingled along my spine and I shivered.

"Do we have to get up?"

"Yep," Sabian said, sounding far too cheerful for whatever time it was in the morning. "Company and all. Your house, they probably want to see you."

I flopped back onto the bed and Sabian traced his fingers along my bare stomach. I hadn't bothered with a night shirt after showering with Mal last night.

"You're not helping, mate."

"I know." Sabian chuckled and my stomach tightened with need. "But we really do need to get up. At least for a while."

"Tease." I glared at him.

He simply smiled back.

Sticking out my tongue, I rolled out of bed.

Speaking of teasing... "Is there any way you can tone down the lust thing any more? Being constantly hot after the two of you is one thing, but now my poor ovaries have set their sights on Aaron and I don't even know the man. Not to mention I have the two of you."

Sabian grinned. "It's not entirely me, Chris. Something about him is calling to you. See how it goes."

"That wasn't an answer."

The incubus grinned. "I've got my powers under as much control as I can manage. You will note, you're not attracted to everyone who walks in your door."

I glared at him. "It has to be your fault."

He shrugged, not denying it, but also not accepting the blame.

I grumbled and headed to the bathroom.

By the time I wandered into the living room, Mal had gone back to cooking breakfast. Thank the heavens. Even better, he was still shirtless, though I suspected that would change as soon as he was done cooking. Damn having company, anyway. I hoped I wasn't drooling as I went over and accepted the cup of tea he held out when I came into the room. Sabian got coffee and sank down onto the loveseat.

Darius sat on the couch and the fluffy hellhound was standing on the coffee table, staring at the priest. Darius looked confused by the little creature.

Aaron sat across from Darius in the chair and Deputy McClellan leaned against the doorframe of the patio door, much like I often did.

"Price, when did you get a dog?" Darius inquired by way of greeting.

"Nice to see you, too, Darius. We're all fine, by the way. Didn't nearly get burned down in a supernatural house fire or anything." I perched on one of the stools, and resisted the urge to draw attention to the light bruising on my cheek from the fight.

He tore his eyes away from the dog and turned to look at me.

"Sorry, you're right. But...when did you get a Pomeranian?"

Clearly, he couldn't get over the small dog.

"Hellhound, mate."

"Yes, I know little dogs are basically all demonic, but why do you have one?"

153

"No, literal hellhound. No idea why it looks like a purse dog."

"Wait, seriously?" Darius jerked his gaze back to the creature.

Deputy McClellan chuckled. "You're getting quite the collection of demons, Price."

I shook my head. At least they didn't know about the vampire in the kitchen. "Yeah. It's your fault, Darius."

He blinked a few times before leaning back against the couch and sighing. "I suppose it is."

He took that accusation a lot harder than I had intended, but he had been the one to drag me into everything, and it seemed he still blamed himself for a lot of the bad things that had happened since.

"It's okay. He's house broke." I shrugged. "So, what's up now?"

"We came to talk to Mr. Reed here, and see if he could shed any light on our situation, or why they might have been after him as a sacrifice," Deputy McClellan explained.

"Unfortunately," Aaron said, his deep voice enriching the conversation just by speaking. "I don't really have an answer."

"Chris," Mal said from the kitchen. "When you came to my shop, what led you there?"

I squirmed on the barstool before sighing. "Used a spell to find what I needed at that moment. Hoped it would lead me to an unbinding spell, and it did."

Darius leveled a look at me I knew all too well. "This might be the first time that spell hasn't backfired on you," he said, voice dark.

"Yeah, well, got me Mal and Sabian and the spell I needed, so there." I took a sip of my tea to quell the urge to stick my tongue out at him. I could have some decorum in front of the cop.

"And a hellhound, and what else?" Darius crossed his arms.

"Eh, I think it was just trying to lead me to Mal, to be honest." I winked at the vampire who looked surprised. "Just lucky he also had what I needed to unbind demons."

Aaron was also staring at the hellhound, though he hadn't joined in that part of the conversation. It occurred to me that he had no idea Sabian was an incubus, either. We probably needed to fill him in before he found out the hard way. Wasn't sure what to do about Mal, though. I'd let the vampire decide. So much for not telling anyone what Sabian was. Seemed we pretty much had told everyone but my employees. They really didn't need to find out.

"My point with the question was this. Perhaps they did the same thing to find Aaron?" Mal put a stack of plates on the counter, followed by a stack of pancakes that he put a towel over to help keep the heat in. Syrup followed. Real syrup. Where had that come from?

"Possible," I replied. "Maybe even likely. It's not a hard spell. It's simply fickle."

"I have to go to the shop for a while, Chris. I'll be back in the evening," Mal said.

I went over and he brushed his fingers along my temple before giving me a quick kiss.

"I'll see you later."

He smiled, glanced at Sabian, and gave a quick wave before he headed back toward my room.

I may have drooled a little bit watching him leave.

"He's one of the fittest nerds I've ever met," Darius observed once Mal was out of normal human earshot.

I fought a grin, knowing Mal could hear anything that happened in the house. "I'm enjoying it." Though my tone was light and innocent, Darius' eyes widened, and I swear he blushed.

Sabian chuckled.

Not wanting to let the vampire's excellent cooking skills go to waste, I grabbed a plate and helped myself.

"Anyone else want food, help yourselves."

Sabian, able to tell what other people desired even if they were going to deny themselves, ended up serving everyone else.

Turns out hellhounds eat pancakes. Good to know.

I settled onto the loveseat with Sabian, and once I'd finished stuffing my face, Sabian put his arm around me. Not really thinking about it, I snuggled against him and waited for everyone else to finish their pancakes.

Darius, the most used to me, raised an eyebrow before shaking his head and going back to his food.

Aaron openly gaped and Deputy McClellan tried to hide her surprise.

The hellhound hopped into my lap and settled in for a post breakfast nap. I put my feet up on the coffee table and ignored everyone's looks. They were just going to have to get used to it.

"Thanks for breakfast," Darius said once they'd finished.

"Thank Mal next time you see him. I don't even know where the real syrup came from," I replied.

"Mal," Sabian clarified.

"Figures. So, what else do you all need?" I glanced at Darius.

He traded a look with Deputy McClellan before shrugging. "We're trying to put the pieces together so we can find these guys and stop them before they try again. If Mr. Reed truly doesn't know why they were after him, then we'll just have to keep looking."

"I really have no idea how they would have found me, except I suppose by magic," Aaron said slowly. "I've never encountered anyone like that woman before and that guy was extremely strong."

Something occurred to me. Sabian and Mal had both reacted strongly to something about Aaron when they had touched him trying to free him. I wondered if the guy with the demon riding along had the same problem. I wasn't sure I should ask in front of the other two, however. That might clue them in to Mal's not quite human nature which would bring other awkward questions.

"Well, I suppose we should go then. If there's anything else you can think of, Mr. Reed, please let us know." Darius stood and Aaron did as well, offering the priest his hand.

They shook and I reluctantly moved from Sabian's comfortable embrace so I could see them out.

Aaron also shook hands with Deputy McClellan and then I walked everyone to the door.

We all watched as they got into the deputy's car and pulled out of the driveway before Aaron turned to me.

"What other demons have you collected?"

"What?" I frowned, confused.

"Deputy McClellan said you were getting a collection of demons. One hellhound isn't a collection."

"Oh. Uh." I glanced at Sabian who shrugged, looking unconcerned so I pointed at him. "Incubus."

I could feel the force of Aaron's stare between my shoulder blades as I headed back toward the living room. Sabian went ahead of me and started cleaning up. I really could get used to this.

"I truly don't know how I feel about that," Aaron said when he joined us a minute later. I'd almost thought he was going to go hide in his room.

"Yeah, well, Mal's a vampire," Sabian declared from the kitchen. "He's way more dangerous than I am."

Aaron, who'd just put his coffee mug to his mouth, choked.

I glanced at Sabian, raising my eyebrows.

"He said I could tell Aaron."

157

"Ahh." Well, that was good at least. "If it wasn't clear, you gotta keep that under wraps. We tried to keep the whole Sabian's a demon thing on the down low, but that didn't work out so well."

"Yeah, not going to tell anyone," Aaron wheezed as he tried to catch his breath. "They'd lock me up, if nothing else."

"So, something about you is apparently painful for demons to touch."

"More felt like an electric shock. Surprised me," Sabian explained. "But I think now that I am expecting it, I wouldn't have as much of a problem. Mal probably had the same reaction."

Aaron hunched his shoulders and folded himself into the chair.

"You okay, mate?"

"It's a lot to take in."

"So, that super strong guy, did he have any issues grabbing you?"

"Now that I think about it, he did react surprised the first time he grabbed my arm, but the woman did something and then he didn't have any problems. I...uh...wasn't able to get away, or..." He clenched his hands together and stared at them. "I guess I know your secrets. I do have some sort of weird ability." He shrugged. "I don't know anything about it. No one else in my family does. I can tell when people are lying, and some other stuff."

"Guess it's a good thing I'm a shite liar," I replied, hoping to set him at ease, and wondering what the 'other stuff' was. He could tell us when he was more comfortable, though. It probably wasn't immediately relevant.

He smiled. "I had noticed you haven't even tried."

"Life's not exactly an open book, but, well, there's not that much to hide. I'm an exorcist, and apparently now I help demons instead of banishing them. Took a strange turn, is all. Still, not about to go out and sell my soul or any of that crap. What more do you want to know?"

"Probably none of my business, but..." He glanced at Sabian, gestured helplessly, and shrugged. "Both of them?"

"Mate, Sabian is an incubus. I challenge you to keep your hands off him if he doesn't want you to."

Aaron blinked a few times.

"Never fear, I could pick a form far more appealing to you," Sabian joked from the kitchen.

"I... what?"

"Incubi are apparently shape shifters," I replied with a grin.

Aaron squirmed in his chair. "I'm good, thanks, Sabian."

The demon chuckled and I groaned. He really needed to stop doing that when I couldn't tackle him to the ground and have my way with him.

Aaron looked pained and hunched over again.

"He has a few bad habits," I explained.

Sabian laughed, but this time he kept his power in check.

"Anyway, fortunately, Mal is pretty open minded when it comes to Sabian."

"For his background, Mal is extremely open minded about a lot of things," Sabian added.

"Yeah, I guess that's probably true, isn't it?" I hadn't actually thought too much about it, but Sabian was right. The vampire was positively liberal as far as I could tell.

"Okay, so you're shacking up with a demon and a vampire and you're helping me out because the demons have you doing the same thing Father Darius and Deputy McClellan are, except you're not giving the humans all the information you have? That about right?"

I laughed. "Yeah, mate. Darius can't handle all of this. It's safer if I keep him out of it as much as I can."

"Okay," Aaron agreed. "And you have a hellhound."

"Yeah. Not sure why, but he's here."

The creature appeared from wherever he had been and wagged his tail. I pet him on his fluffy head.

"Okay. I need to process all of this. I also need to get a car. Can you give me a ride? I'm sorry to impose."

"Naw, mate, it's no problem. I gotta head over to the shop for a bit and maybe I'll swing by Mal's and say hi. We should probably get some more crystals if we're going to unbind any more demons, if nothing else."

"Great. I really appreciate you helping me out," Aaron said.

"Happy to. Sabian, you coming?"

"If Aaron has no objection, I'll stick with him today. We probably shouldn't leave him alone in case they make another attempt to grab him."

I glanced at Aaron. He took a deep breath as if steeling himself before nodding. "Yes, thank you."

"Great. Let's go."

Chapter 13

Price

I dropped Aaron and Sabian off at a car dealership and headed for the restaurant. I just wanted to stop in for a minute and then I was going to go bug Mal at his shop. I had a thought that we might want to see if we could figure out anything about Aaron's crazy eye tattoos. I needed to ask him about those, but it hadn't been the time earlier.

The air conditioning of my restaurant welcomed me out of the hot desert air, and I stood under the vent for a moment. I could not wear the leather jacket in the summer. It was a lighter one, but still, it was hot. Yet, I couldn't bring myself to give up on my dedication to the punk look. Also, the jacket had actually saved my ass on more than one occasion. Even if it was just because I usually kept holy water in a squirt bottle in one of the pockets.

The hellhound followed on my heels and it was too hot to tell the creature to stay outside. Besides, most people didn't seem to notice him, anyway.

Wiping some sweat away from my brow, I headed the rest of the way into the restaurant. The staff members that weren't busy greeted me. A few of them sported the jean jackets I'd told Billy to give everyone.

"So, we need new shirts, too," Billy said by way of greeting when I walked into my office. He was sitting at my desk working on one of the projects I'd handed over to him.

I collapsed into one of the spare chairs. The hound settled by my feet.

"Whatever you want, mate." I didn't have the energy to argue about it, and it probably was time for an update.

"Seriously?" He stopped what he was doing and looked at me.

"Yeah, sure. The guys like it. You all like it. Isn't hurting me any." I shrugged.

"Okay. I'll get to work on some designs. And designs on the official signs and all. Once I get it put together, I can run it by you?"

"Yeah, great."

"You okay, Chris?"

I nodded. "It's just been a very trying few days. I'd never expected to be involved with any of this again and now I'm neck deep in it."

"So, you mentioned the guys. Both of them?" Billy gave me a sly look.

I realized what I'd done, sighed, and gave Billy a 'look.'

He grinned in reply.

"I gotta go. Everything going okay here? Anything I need to know about?"

"No, boss. It's all good here. No demons that I know of. Customers have been relatively under control. We've got this while you deal with whatever that priest has dragged you into."

"Thank you, Billy."

"Yep, see you later, boss."

I got up and left, knowing he'd take care of everything, waved at a few folks while I made my way through the restaurant, and got back into my oven-like car. As I'd suspected, no one noticed the dog.

I'd go see Mal for a few minutes, ask him about the tattoos, and then head back to my place.

The trip to the touristy town square didn't take long and I found a parking spot relatively quickly, though I hesitated getting out of the car once I'd turned it off until it got uncomfortable from the heat outside. Why was I suddenly uncomfortable? I doubted Mal would mind me swinging by, especially since I wanted to ask about occult stuff. Was I nervous? Okay, this was getting dumb. The hellhound woofed softly, possibly in agreement. I doubted he was too hot.

I got out of the damn car, let the dog out, and slammed the door in frustration. Chris Price did not get nervous about men. Even sexy, dangerous, nerdy, fangy men. It just didn't happen.

Despite the pep talk I still dragged my feet a little as I headed toward the store. Even with my hesitation, it didn't take long before I was pushing the door open to the shop and getting smacked in the face by the heavily incensed air.

Mal glanced up from a computer, a smile lighting up his face when I came inside.

"Chris, hello."

"Hey, Mal."

His brow furrowed. "Is something wrong?"

"No. Sorry." I shrugged and came over to the counter. "I actually just was hoping I wasn't bothering you by stopping by. I thought it might be wise to see if we could figure anything out about Aaron's strange tattoos," I said in a rush.

Mal's lips twitched and I thought he was trying not to smile. He reached across the counter and brushed his fingers along my cheek. I leaned into his touch a little.

"Malak, that had better be your girlfriend."

We both jumped and Mal looked a little sheepish.

"Olivia, this is Chris."

A tall, wonderfully curvy black woman came out from the back of the store. She hit every stereotype of a new age

163

shop owner that Mal did not. Pink T-shirt with a black cat on it. Witch hat dangly earrings. Capris and sandals. Well, the last were more Santa Fe in the summer than new age. She was grinning at me, and I liked her instantly.

"Hi." I forced myself to talk normally, though I still felt really awkward. I did not like feeling awkward. It was not a normal experience for me.

"Hello. I've been trying to get Mal to bring his mystery girl by. So glad you are here."

I glanced at him and he shrugged, looking a touch embarrassed.

"Yeah, it's been a busy few days. First chance I got. Nice place you have here."

"I'd press you for details, and trust me, I want to know everything." She paused, wrinkling her brow for a moment before laughing. "Maybe not everything, but I've got to run next door for a few minutes. I'll be back. My apologies for meeting you and running out."

She was out the door before I could say it wasn't a problem, so I turned my attention back to Mal and arched an eyebrow.

"She made assumptions," he said hesitantly. "We haven't really had a chance to talk about our relationship."

"Right." I could not explain the sinking feeling in my gut. What the hell was wrong with me? "It's fine. I did just come by to see if you had any thoughts on Aaron."

Mal studied me for a few moments. "Chris. I do want a relationship. We just haven't had a minute to talk. Between the demons and everything else." He threw in a smile probably to lighten his statement a bit. "You have said you want to keep me around."

"Yeah, I did, didn't I." I stopped myself from saying any of my normal stupid lines. I did not want to fuck this up, though I had no idea what actually to say. I never talked about relationships. I just had a little fun and eventually moved on. Usually fairly quickly. This might have been only the second time in my life I'd found someone I wanted to stick around. Two someones even. Three, a small voice whispered, and I told it to shut up. I could barely handle the feelings the vampire and the incubus were bombarding me with. Aaron probably wanted someone that would fit nicely into his white picket fence life. An eighties throwback punk was not that person. Especially one that was an exorcist.

"You're thinking awfully hard, Chris," Mal said.

"Sorry, not good at any of this relationship stuff." I shoved my hands into my pockets.

"Well, it hasn't exactly been normal circumstances, either."

"Probably just as well for me." I laughed, some of the tension easing out of my shoulders. "My normal usually doesn't turn out well. You heard Darius. He thought a demon would be better for me than my normal types."

Mal chuckled. "Sabian is trying very hard to be good for you. He likes you a lot. So do I."

I shifted uncomfortably.

"Tell you what. Let's deal with this demon problem and if you're still speaking to me by the end of it, we'll discuss where we're going from here."

"Sounds good, mate." The idea of a future discussion made me uneasy, but I felt it was probably just because the entire situation was uncertain.

Fortunately, Mal changed the subject. "I'm sure it won't surprise you to know I was also curious about his tattoos. I've done a few searches in between other tasks. The only thing that really seems to match up is a rather old description of biblical style angels. There are plenty of other mythologies that deal with eye imagery of course, but in combination with the wings, and the style, well, it was the only thing that seemed even close. Aaron doesn't seem the religious type, especially for ancient religions, so it is a very confusing choice. Honestly, I think we'll have to ask him." Mal slid a book over to me and I looked at the picture.

"Well, that's terrifying." I studied the picture. It was of a creature with six wings, three on each side, and a set of some sort of crossed rings in between the wings, all covered in eyes. The center was depicted as a fierce glow, also covered in eyes.

"Vaguely," Mal agreed. "If he does have some celestial blood, and the tattoos are actually markings instead of choices on his part. That might explain why Sabian and I had a hard time touching him." Mal frowned. "Though I never really did go for the idea that vampires were damned. Perhaps it's simply something contradictory in our natures that causes the pain."

"He did admit to having some powers after Darius and McClellan left. He can sense if someone is lying or not. He now knows about you and Sabian."

Mal nodded, as if he had expected that. "That also lends to this theory. Interesting. I suppose sacrificing someone with angelic blood would be diabolical enough to summon a demon prince who did not wish to be summoned."

I shuddered. "We've got to stop them. Maybe it's time to get Sabian to contact the prince again and see if we can get more information."

"I agree." Mal took the book and slid it under the counter. "I've got to be here for another hour. Where is Sabian, anyway?"

"He's guarding Aaron while our new friend picks out a replacement vehicle."

"Why don't you stay here until Olivia gets back. Then we can leave together. My car is at home."

"Yeah, sounds good. Where do you live?"

"Just down the way." He told me his address. "I'll take you by sometime soon."

"Sounds good."

166

"I have a question," Mal said and I tensed slightly. Why was I having these strange reactions? I did not get worried about what men thought of me. Or anyone, for that matter.

"Yeah, mate?"

"You're an exorcist and an occultist. Surely you've got your own library?"

"Oh! Yeah, when I quit, I kind of really quit. Buried all that fuckery up in some chests on family land in the mountains."

Mal raised his eyebrows. "Really?"

"Dude, it was a bad time leading up to me getting out. Really bad time."

"I understand. If you ever want to talk about it..."

I shuddered. "Maybe someday."

He nodded his understanding. I supposed he'd seen his fair share of bad things. Probably far worse than what I'd experienced.

"Someday I want to hear your stories, too."

Mal smiled and ducked his head a little, as if embarrassed. "Sure. Sometime. Though it might be far less interesting than you're expecting. I've spent a lot of time with my nose buried in books."

"Fair enough."

The door chimed and Mal glanced over toward the customer who had just come in.

"Hey, you got anything interesting to read while I wait?" I glanced around and noticed a few comfortable looking chairs by the window.

Mal nodded and handed back the book he'd shown me. I took it and curled up in one of the chairs, wondering if maybe I should unbury the past. Literally. There were a lot of things in that stash that would have been very handy to have at the moment. It was probably time to get into a deep occult discussion with Mal, too. Pick his brain and all. Maybe he had some of the things I was missing.

167

Of course, if I could finish this task, maybe I could get out again.

The hellhound jumped up on my lap and made himself comfortable.

Point taken. There was no way I was going to get out again. Oddly enough, the thought did not make me sad. My heart picked up its pace a little, and I felt truly excited for the first time in years. Of course, I'd made some fairly epic mistakes right after feeling like this, so maybe it wasn't so good. Still...it would be better to be prepared moving forward, than to continue hiding. First things first, see what kind of book Mal had given me to read, and then head home and ask Aaron about his tattoos. After that, well, we had a really messed up occultist to stop. Then Mal and I would have a relationship talk. I was way more stressed out about that talk then any of the rest. How messed up was that?

∞ ∞ ∞

"You come back when you have a minute to talk, Chris. Mal is so quiet about his personal life. I want details." Olivia waved as we left the shop.

I didn't promise to blab anything, but I also wanted her to not hate me, so I did agree to return as soon as I could.

Mal chuckled.

"She know anything?"

"Some. I'll fill you in later."

"Fair enough."

He put his hand on the small of my back, and stayed close while we threaded our way around a handful of tourists.

"Fuck," Mal hissed.

I glanced over from the window I'd been shopping through just in time to see the thug from Aaron's house point something at me.

Mal shoved me out of the way, jerked, and crumpled to the ground.

"Mal!"

He didn't answer and I tried to ignore the rising panic tightening my chest.

The thug lowered a fucking crossbow of all things.

I looked around, but no one else noticed our struggle. The street was full of people, but we were completely ignored. Mal and I had both been blindsided.

When I glanced back at the thug, he now had a gun pointed at my chest.

There was nothing I could do. I held up my hands and hoped that the hellhound, who had vanished, could get help somehow.

"So nice to see you again," a familiar female voice said behind me.

"Naw, it's shite."

She laughed. "Oh, I think I'd like you if you were going to be around long enough for me to get to know you. Tell me, how did you get out of my wards? They shouldn't have been breakable. Even for your friend here." She kicked Mal, hard. The vampire didn't react.

I really hoped he wasn't dead, and not just because I wanted him to rescue me. The thought of losing Mal made my heart clench, though I tried not to show my reaction.

Something must have come through because she sniffed.

"Don't worry, you'll be gone before we wake him up."

Well, that answered one question. Two really. Apparently, they were going to kill me. Great. At least Mal wasn't dead. I was only slightly relieved.

"Still, since you apparently are something of an escape artist, and we can't have that, I'll have to knock you out, too. Nice body wards, by the way. You do know how dangerous those are, don't you?" She said the last in a bit of a sing-song voice before she touched my back.

Whatever she did, the wards deflected. Normally, that would have been enough to give me time to get away, but with the demon possessed thug over there pointing a gun at my head, I couldn't do anything but take it as she blasted me again, and again, until my vision blackened as my protections sapped my strength. I staggered, trying to keep my feet as long as I could. Not wanting to give them any satisfaction.

I thought I heard her snap orders at the thug, but I couldn't make out what she said. I really hoped they caught me before I cracked my head on the cement as my legs gave way and I passed out.

∞ ∞ ∞

Slowly, ever so slowly, I fought my way back to consciousness. As soon as I made it, I wished I hadn't bothered. Pain more extreme than the worst hangover I'd ever had–and I'd sported some doozies–blasted through my head. I cracked my eyes open to slits and all I could see was flashing lights, and I was fairly certain it had nothing to do with what was actually in the room with me.

Slowly my vision returned, followed by sound.

Chanting.

Yeah, should have expected that. Fuck. I took away their first sacrifice, guess they were going to use me. Wondered if whatever magic ran through my blood was enough to summon a demon prince. Hopefully, I wouldn't find out.

I was laying on my back. I could tell that now, too.

As my energy slowly returned, the urgency of my situation hit, and a jolt of adrenalin surged through me. Better than drugs, that stuff. The headache fled to the background, my vision cleared, and I got enough juice back to lift my head.

Just in time to see a flash of silver descending toward me.

I didn't even have time to flinch before the knife plunged into my stomach.

Yep, this hurt worse than waking up had.

I screamed as white hot fire radiated out from my abdomen.

She jerked the knife back out, twisting a little on the way.

Help was probably too distant to save me. I doubted Mal was even conscious, and the others had no idea where I was. Apparently, I was going to find out where chaotic exorcists went when they died a lot sooner than I had planned.

Well, damn it, I wasn't going down without fucking up as much of their plans as I could.

Pulling on what little of that extra power that flowed through me I could grasp–Mal called it magic–I shoved it into my gut. It wouldn't save me, but it might stabilize me long enough to cause a last bit of chaos before I died.

I turned my head. Fuck that hurt. We were inside a containment circle and the asshole twat that had stabbed me was dripping something, likely my blood, into a bowl. Today she was dressed a bit more ritualistically. Flowing robes and all that shit. Candles flickered everywhere. This floor was stone, or concrete, and it had the feel of a more permanent ritual space, as opposed to hijacking Aaron's study.

Though my vision was a bit blurry and pain radiated through me, I tried to focus. I thought I made out one of the pendants they had been binding demons into on the table surrounded by candles and other implements of the trade.

I wasn't sure what I could do, but maybe I could pull the same stunt I had before and just crash into everything. At the very least, it would piss them off.

My vision blacked out and pain seared through me when I tried to move.

Crap.

More magic. More reserves. I needed them. It was my last stand, and I wasn't going down without being a giant pain in the ass. I drew on everything I had, pulling it to that spot of agony where my life was leaking out of me far faster than I'd prefer.

There. I could move.

By the time I looked back at the ritual space, the twat had left the circle.

Damn.

Light flared on the table, some sort of magical fireworks I'd mostly missed, and the flames on the candles shot upward, growing to nearly a foot of flame each.

"Huh, cool," I grumbled, and forced myself to move. I nearly blacked out, but I did it.

"I offer you this life in return for your presence!" I heard the twat shout and then rage like I'd never before experienced filled the space.

Well, the prince was here. Hope he didn't mind damaged goods.

I made it to my feet, holding back a scream by sheer force of will. I did not want to attract attention if she hadn't noticed me yet. Maybe I could disrupt the circle before she contained him in the pendant.

The prince howled something in demonic, but amazingly didn't outright attack me. Great, score one for the nearly dead exorcist.

"Huh," the twat said.

Sometimes those were famous last words.

Unfortunately, in this case, she didn't really need my life. The demon was here, and she wasn't bargaining with him.

She yelled out another enchantment, one I wasn't familiar with, and couldn't concentrate on enough to even try to understand.

I staggered forward. My legs gave out. I crashed into the table, sending everything flying. Maybe if I could get my hands on the amulet long enough to fuck with her spell...

I had no idea where it went, and my time was up. I didn't even feel the concrete as I slammed into the ground. Hopefully whoever came to collect my soul had a twisted sense of humor, because boy did I have some fucked up stories to tell.

Chapter 14

Sabian

Time stopped, and what passed for a heart for an incubus nearly shriveled up and died as I watched Chris fall into the table then crash to the ground.

"No! Chris!" This couldn't be happening. I'd just found her.

A flash of silver very near her hand caught my attention, jerking me out of my momentary paralysis. I was certain it was no accident I noticed the pendant. I could feel the pull of my connection to the prince. We had to get that before the others did.

Acting on instinct, I shouted at Aaron and pointed. "Grab that!"

Guided by the tiny hellhound, Aaron dashed forward.

Darius fired at the demon possessed men who had belatedly realized we had arrived to ruin their party. The bullets hit, and they must have been blessed, because they slowed the men down enough that they ran instead of staying to fight.

The occultist had split as soon as Aaron had broken the circle. Probably wise, though the prince was still contained. Darius chased after her.

I hadn't been lying when I told Mal I was a lover, not a fighter. I could take a few hits, but against someone who knew what they were doing I'd get my ass kicked, so I didn't try to stop any of the possessed humans as they ran.

Chris was not moving, and the pool of blood spreading around her was not promising. I could sense she wasn't quite gone, but she certainly wasn't going to survive unless we could intervene. I couldn't lose her now. I just couldn't. I needed her.

Where was Mal? I thought they had been together.

I couldn't enter the circle like Aaron or the hellhound could, so I watched anxiously from outside the ring as Aaron snatched the charm up, held it for a moment, then bellowed in pain.

Bingo. He had angelic blood. I thought those eye tattoos were more than tattoos. The wing markings on the guy's back were the giveaway, though.

In this case, it was going to save Chris' life. Hopefully. I curled my hands into fists and tried to fight off the rising panic that we were too late. I just couldn't lose her.

Silver dripped through Aaron's fingers as the charm melted. He flung it away from him as light flared around the guy, consuming him. I swear I saw the outline of wings, six of them, and eyes freaking everywhere, as Aaron backed out of the circle. He collapsed to his knees, looking a lot more normal, though drenched in sweat, on the other side of the containment ring.

The hellhound licked at Chris' face. She really needed to name that thing to complete the bond. I'd actually thought she already had, until he'd come to find us once she'd been taken.

A lot of this could have been prevented if the hellhound had fully manifested into their bond. I cursed myself for assuming she'd done what most humans did and immediately named a pet that came into their lives. If this didn't work, I'd never forgive myself. Of course, if it did, she might not forgive me.

"Sabian, break the circle," the prince, now free of the charm, stood and stared at me in his close to human aspect. Relatively short, dark hair, dark eyes, the hint of horns peeking out from the curls, dusky skin, a suit. Why did the princes always wear suits?

"Save her." I winced as I realized I'd basically given my prince an order.

"You know how it works, Sabian. I can't save her unless I get something in return. She won't want to sell her soul, nor is she in any position to sign a contract. It's the rule and magic binds me. I can't break it." He actually sounded unhappy about it.

"You still owe me something for my service in this. Save her. Quickly." This time I left the honorific off on purpose.

"I was prepared to reward you extremely handsomely. You would give up everything I'd offer for a mortal's life?"

"All I need is her."

He raised his eyebrows before turning to look at Chris, prone on the ground, more blood outside than in at this point. She was quite dead, but not yet gone. We had only moments, though.

"I'll have to possess her."

"Fortunately, I know a couple of good exorcists. They might even be gentle with you if you save her life."

The prince barked laughter before he nodded. "Very well. Your reward then."

I sighed in relief. He hadn't told me it was too late. We'd save her.

Darius came back in at that moment and shouted something inarticulate as he saw the demon swirl into black mist before it soaked into the prone exorcist.

"What did you do?" He grabbed my shoulder and jerked me around to look at him.

"Saved her life, Darius," I replied quietly. I really hoped he would understand.

"Possession isn't life," the Priest snarled back, and I swore he was about to send my ass back to hell.

Fortunately, Aaron was likely more team Sabian than he was team priest, and I could probably get him to stop Darius long enough for me to explain if he tried it. Chris was worth the risk.

Aaron had managed to get back to his feet and had approached us warily.

"Darius," I pleaded. "He'll leave. Willingly. He owed me and there is no debt that Chris will have to pay. She was dead. They killed her." I wiped a few tears from my eyes, startled at their appearance.

The priest glared at me.

Aaron's eyes were wide as they darted between me, the priest, and Chris, who was still dead on the floor.

I could sense the energy the prince used to repair her body and how he held her spirit. Thank the abyss, she would wake up before long. Prince Ezra was using a lot of energy. I hadn't realized how much this would cost him. He must really have felt he owed me. Or perhaps he felt it absolved some of his debt to Chris, though he would still owe her the favor he had promised.

"Where is Mal?" Aaron asked when Darius didn't reply.

Darius frowned and glanced around the room, before his eyes widened. "That's kind of fucked up."

None of us had noticed the vampire bound to a chair in the corner. He was slumped over, a shaft of something shoved through his chest. That's how they'd done it. They must have seriously gotten the drop on Chris and Mal to have managed to stake him. I took a step toward Mal, then hesitated, turning toward Chris. I wanted to go to both of them, but I couldn't help either at the moment. At least I wouldn't have to tell either one of them that the other was dead.

"Chris is going to be pissed." Darius sighed. "She really liked him."

I was really starting to get a sense of why Chris didn't fully trust Darius anymore. He seemed to have forgotten some of his humanity. I was more affected by the idea of Chris losing Mal than he was, and I was a damn demon, *and* I knew Mal would be okay once we could figure out how to safely wake him up.

The hellhound whined and I turned my attention back to the circle. Chris groaned, fingers twitching. She climbed to her hands and knees, resting as if getting used to her body again.

I really hoped she wouldn't send me back to hell for this.

"Mother fucker," she blurted as her eyes snapped open and they zeroed in on me.

My heart sank.

Dakota Brown

Chapter 15

Price

Price... The familiar voice hissed through me, both filling me with warmth and grating on my ears.

I turned to see a man standing before me. He was handsome, dusky skin, dark eyes that seemed to contain the universe, though twin horns curved up through his wavy black hair.

"Yeah, mate?" Well, shit. Not exactly what I had hoped for, but probably what I deserved.

The demon chuckled. "I'm not here to claim your soul, Price," he said. "I'm here to save your life. If you'll let me."

Ahh, that's why I recognized his voice. It carried the same intonations as the demon who had spoken through Sabian. This was our prince. Ezra. The one I had thought they'd bound.

Some of my confusion must have shown through.

"Sabian and your friends showed up in time to thwart the other humans. We do not have much time, however. Sabian has requested I save your life as the reward I had offered him. You must still choose, and you must do it quickly." He held out his hand.

A warm, comforting *something* tugged at me, summoning me, promising me peace, but I didn't turn. I'd never had much use for peace anyway. At least not that kind.

181

And I still had shit to do. Yet, I hesitated. Would this choice cost me in the future? I imagined if I asked, the prince wouldn't answer. Could almost feel that the question was beyond his knowledge. I could have peace. Or I could continue to live.

I supposed it wasn't really a choice, after all.

"This going to cost me anything?" I slid my hand into the demon's. His hand was shockingly warm, and I had to keep myself from pulling away as his power burned into me.

"Sabian paid the price. He gave up...quite a bit. Though, I suppose I can see your appeal."

I raised my eyebrows but didn't know how to reply. I still felt like I was slipping away, even with the prince's strong hand gripping mine.

Ezra quirked a smile. "Sorry about this."

I didn't have time to ask what he meant before he jerked me forward into his arms and pressed his lips to mine. I was no longer slipping away. No, now I was melting firmly into his embrace. His heat filled me, and pain seared through me as I was pulled back into my body, though his kiss distracted me from most of it. Were all demons amazing kissers? I wasn't going to make this a habit, but for now I opened for him when he pressed with his tongue, and let him explore my mouth, before doing the same when he retreated for a moment. His hands roamed my body, spreading heat and fire, pulling me back together, repairing flesh, and shielding me from the pain with the intense pleasure of his touch.

"Fuck me," I whispered when he released me from his kiss.

The demon prince chuckled.

"You can wake whenever you're ready." Ezra stepped back and faded from my awareness until it was just me in my head.

I groaned as I became aware of the cold concrete beneath me. I gave my hands an experimental twitch, then climbed to my hands and knees.

Wait.

Why can I still sense you?

The only way to save you was to possess you.

The one thing I'd hoped to avoid. It had been one thing when Sabian had been riding along. He'd still been in the charm, so it wasn't a true possession. This...the prince had saved my life, but eventually he would still consume me, and I'd felt his power. I wasn't sure Darius could get him out if the prince didn't want to go. I could have, but I wasn't sure if I could do an exorcism on myself.

"Mother fucker," I snarled in reaction, snapping my eyes open and glaring at Sabian. I could sense him pretty clearly, probably from the connection he had to his prince.

Sabian flinched, though he didn't look away.

I will be staying for now, but you will not have to fight me when it's time for me to leave. I promise.

No, you need to leave now.

You're not completely healed yet, Price. Also, there's the matter of waking up your vampire. I'm giving you a free hint here. If you pull the stake out of him now, while I'm still healing you, I can continue to heal you while he tries to drain you dry at no additional debt accumulated.

I looked around until my gaze fell on Mal. He was slumped over in the chair, not moving. At least he was still here to save, though seeing him like that made my heart clench.

If you wait, or you cast me out, you're going to have to get creative to save him. So, unless you want to find a random human to sacrifice to your vampire, you'll accept my presence without a fight. And I will fight you.

Why?

I will explain later.

183

His presence faded and I got some idea that he might be conserving his strength. If I took his suggestion and woke Mal up, he'd probably need it. I could only guess based on what the demon had said and what I knew of vampires–which wasn't a whole lot–that Mal needed a lot of blood to recover from what they'd done.

I sighed and climbed the rest of the way to my feet. Mal had saved my life, is what he'd done. The least I could do was make it so that he didn't kill anyone because of it.

Now that I was somewhat recovered from dying, I noticed Darius and Aaron standing next to Sabian. My hellhound was at my feet.

I was not happy about seeing Darius.

He's not particularly happy, either, the prince supplied.

I almost laughed.

Knowing what would happen, I put my hands out and leaned against the invisible barrier that held me in.

"Someone want to let me out?"

"Chris, you're possessed by a demon," Darius replied.

"No shit, Sherlock. And right before that I was very dead. He promised to be a good house guest, so let me out."

"Of course, he did. That's what demons do." Darius crossed his arms, seeming to forget he was standing next to an incubus.

Sabian looked incredulous.

My hellhound growled.

It occurred to me that both Sabian and the hellhound had also promised to be good houseguests and had completely made good on that promise.

Aaron looked like he wanted to run away.

I flipped Darius off.

He pulled out a bottle of holy water and I felt the prince flinch inside of me.

It would be best...

Yeah, I got this, I cut him off.

"Sabian, do me a favor and punch Darius in the face until he stops being an asshole."

Darius blanched, as if just remembering what Sabian was. I suspected Sabian could take more hits of holy water than I could at the moment, and the incubus didn't look worried when he turned to confront the priest.

"Look, I need to help Mal. I'm probably the only one who safely can right now. Let me out."

"Chris, Mal..." Darius trailed off, looking back at the vampire before his eyebrows rose. His gaze darted back to me. "Seriously?"

I put my hands on my hips and tapped my foot. "You were right, they've both treated me way better than any of the humans I've dated."

Darius flinched. He'd been my first, long before he'd joined the priesthood.

"I deserve that."

"Yeah, you do. Now stop being a dick. I think we've got the demon situation under control. If this one wasn't friendly, I'd let you send his ass back to hell. He's got a vested interest in helping us stop these twatwaffles, and he promised to leave quietly as soon as he could. I'm still healing, so he can't leave yet." Didn't need to bring up the rest of it.

"So how are you going to help Mal?" Darius asked warily.

"Pull the stake out and let him drink as much of my blood as he wants. The demon will keep healing me. Probably need to eat a whole cow's worth of steaks later, but it'll be fine."

"Jesus, Chris, you're really in deep."

"And who's fucking fault is that?"

Darius threw up his hands before he turned and headed to the door. "Fine, but you'll have to find yourself a different exorcist when you can't get free of all this."

"Yeah, typical, leave when it gets tough," I shouted after him.

"The cops will be here soon, Price. Someone's got to hold them off unless you want them to know about Mal," he shouted. Somewhere a door slammed, and I sensed he was gone.

"Fucker," I muttered.

"Aaron." Sabian broke the thick silence that settled in after Darius left. "I can break the circle, but it would be easier if you did it."

"Yeah, sure. What do I do?" Aaron rubbed his hands together and I could smell his fear.

"Just put your foot over it."

"You can't do that?" Despite his question, Aaron walked forward and slid his foot over the runes etched into the floor.

The circle popped and I practically leapt out of it, the hellhound on my heels.

"No, not this one, anyway. Some, yes. I'd have had to figure something else out. Chris, are you sure you can handle Mal?"

I glared at Sabian, but after the tirade I'd just thrown at Darius, my anger was spent and anything I could have said would just be petty. Sabian had saved me, which was far more than Darius would have done.

"Yeah." I softened my expression and Sabian relaxed. "It's just one more thing the prince has to heal. Since he's still trying to put me back together, he assured me that it was all included."

I went over to Mal and tugged at the ropes that bound him. It looked like they'd simply tied him into the chair to keep him upright, not with any real intent at restraint. The ropes came away easily and I took a deep breath before I put my hand on the bolt of wood through Mal's heart.

Price, let me distract you. This is going to hurt. A lot.
Why are you so concerned?

If you want to experience what it's like to nearly die again, I'll leave you two alone, the demon replied sharply.

I hesitated. I did not want to get in any deeper with this demon, as Darius had put it, but I was also not keen on another near death experience.

I will keep you alive, but it's not going to be fun if you don't let me distract you.

It usually feels good when he bites me.

He's not in control of himself right now, and won't be for a bit.

Sounds like you've some experience with this.

I could almost feel the demon shrug, as if something under my skin rippled. That definitely creeped me out.

What exactly are we talking about here, mate?

Invisible fingers trailed up my spine, sending a thrill of pleasure through me.

Oh.

A distraction only. Nothing more. Believe it or not, this is not my first choice, either.

Okay. Just this once.

I'm just engaging your mind, he explained. *It will keep you from feeling what getting drained by a vampire actually does to a person without the helpful endorphins they usually use to pacify their prey.*

Just...do whatever it is you're going to do.

Pull the stake out.

Taking a breath, I grabbed the shaft of wood and yanked. I was surprised at how easily it came free, though the barbs on the end must have done some damage on the way back out.

Mal's eyes snapped open, and if the demon hadn't been somewhat in control of my body, I would have flinched away at the empty look in his fully black eyes. He grabbed me, jerking me forward and going for my neck.

His teeth broke skin and for the barest moment I felt pain before the demon prince intervened and my system flooded with endorphins.

For a moment, I wondered what he had been fussing about. If that was all he had to do...but then my attention returned to what Mal was actually doing to me. That very brief moment made me extremely glad when I suddenly found myself standing in front of the prince again.

He looked tired, lips drawn, dusky skin unnaturally pale, some wrinkles I hadn't noticed before at the corners of his eyes.

"You are quite a lot of trouble, you know that, Price?"

"It's why everyone loves me." I gave him a cocky grin.

"It may be the clue to your charm. I don't know you that well yet." He held out his hand.

Still making me choose. I guess that was fair. The yet on the end of his statement worried me though, and I tried not to think too much about it as I placed my hand in his. I didn't really want him to know me well at all. Despite that, I didn't resist when he pulled me forward. He was gentle, putting an arm around me, hand cupping my hip. He threaded the fingers of his other hand through the longer part of my hair and tilted my head. He wasn't tall, but he was still taller than I was, and he leaned over to press his lips to mine.

Though he'd professed some reluctance earlier, he pressed me against him now, and devoured my lips as if they were a lifeline. My heart raced, and I hoped it was from what the demon prince was doing to me, not impending cardiac arrest from blood loss.

After a moment lost in his embrace, I slid my hands around him, under his suit jacket, his warmth nearly overwhelming through the dress shirt he wore.

It took a great deal of restraint to keep my hands from wandering, though I did grip his shirt, pulling him against me, trying to ignore my ovaries that were demanding I get naked, get him naked and satisfy all of those urges that were racing through me.

He was helping me survive Mal without getting a complex, that was it. He didn't want anything more. Really.

Ezra shifted against me, rumbling in pleasure as he tightened his hold on my body.

I had no idea where he had learned to kiss, but damn, I could get lost in this so easily and come back for more.

Holy crap something was seriously wrong with me. Lusting after Aaron, and now the prince? I had a pretty good excuse to make out with the demon prince right now, but not wanting more later. Yes, he was probably the best kisser ever, but still...

You are living with an incubus, he pointed out without breaking off from consuming me.

So, it's Sabian's fault?

No. Just trying to give you an excuse. Though, his presence isn't helping.

The prince nibbled at my lip, and I groaned, letting him lean my head back, gasping as he kissed along my jaw before biting gently at my neck.

I couldn't even think anymore. My body was putty in his hands, and the only thing keeping me from collapsing to the ground was his arms around me. I needed more, but he didn't lower me to the ground, didn't pull my clothing from my body and bring me to even greater heights of pleasure.

No, instead he leaned back, breathing just as heavily as I was, his eyes shining with lust.

"You should wake up now," he ordered, though I swore I heard a hint of disappointment in his voice.

"Chris!"

I jerked my eyes open, waking up to a frantic vampire.

"Mal, you're okay," I managed to get out before he crushed me against him.

"Can't breathe," I mumbled against his chest.

189

"Sorry. I'm so sorry. Are you okay?"

"Yeah, mate," I slurred. "Mmm, fine."

"You should be dead, as much of your blood as I took." His voice broke and I wasn't sure if I was about to see if a vampire could actually cry or not. Apparently, no one had the time to bring him up to speed.

"Yeah, I already did that once today. Wasn't about to do it again."

"What?"

"Long story. Look, I think we need to get out of here and I need some rest. Sabian can fill you in."

The world tilted, and suddenly I was cradled in Mal's arms. I lost track of what was going on after that, drifting in and out of consciousness until I woke in my own bed, still curled up in Mal's arms. He was asleep and it was dark outside. Sabian's absence was strange, but I didn't have the energy to be truly alarmed. Mal was here, and with a quick thought I could sense Sabian was nearby, the extra senses courtesy of Ezra, I imagined. The hellhound was curled up behind my knees, and I was safe at home.

With that, I drifted back to a deep, healing sleep. Maybe I'd wake up to find the last day had been a really bad dream.

∞ ∞ ∞

I wiped steam off the mirror and leaned on the counter, my arms supporting most of my weight as I stared at my reflection.

"Fuck," I said quietly.

The demon prince was quiet but, just as I could see the red rimming my brown irises, I could sense his presence in the back of my mind. My only experiences with possession were from the other side, casting demons out and all. Still, I was fairly certain this was not what a possessed person normally experienced. The prince was keeping his word and trying to make this as easy as possible. Still, it wouldn't take much for him to take over.

I wiped at my eyes, brushing away a few tears. I'd woken up alone, except for the hellhound, for the first time since I'd met Mal and Sabian. I had no doubt it had something to do with the demon prince's presence.

If it helps, you're not alone. Clearly, he wasn't as distant from my thoughts as I had hoped.

Asshole.

The demon chuckled. *Is that any way to treat someone who saved your life?*

I sighed.

I am a prince. It is customary to address me as such.

Either you're oblivious, or you just don't know me that well yet. I'm an exorcist, and about as likely to address you with a title as I am to sprout wings.

Ezra sighed but didn't push the issue. Smart on his part.

The hellhound licked water from my leg that I hadn't yet dried off.

You need to name him.

What? Why? Why is he here, anyway?

Price, if you had named your damn dog, he could have prevented a lot of this.

What? I shivered as a chill ran through me. I could have prevented this? With a name?

Once you name him, the binding will be complete, and he will be able to fully manifest on this plane. Until then, he's trapped into his chosen form and unable to completely fulfill his duties to protect you. He's doing the best he can right now. He was instrumental in breaking the warding that had you trapped when you first met your angelic friend, and he was able to summon help in time to save you yesterday, but he could do so much more with a name.

Let me get this straight. I have to name my hellhound and bind him to me. And then he can eat all the bad things?

Ezra chuckled again. It was a good thing he found me amusing, or he'd probably get tired of me fast.

Yes.

That's some seriously fucked up movie shit. I am not *naming him Moon Child.*

I don't think he would appreciate that name anyway. Nor would he appreciate Mr. Fluffy Pants. He read my thoughts before I could voice them in this strange mental conversation we were having.

I sighed.

Why haven't you named him?

I don't know what to call a hellhound and I didn't realize it was that important. So how permanent is this binding?

The demon shrugged, and I felt the movement just under my skin. I shuddered.

It's breakable.

He didn't elaborate and I suspected I didn't want to know more. At least right now. That brought another question, did I want yet another demon bound to me? Darius was right, I was getting in deep and this was not the team I was used to playing for.

Warm, invisible arms wrapped around me, and a bare chest pressed against my back. I leaned into the contact for a moment before I froze.

I promise, in the coming conflicts you're on the right team. Ezra whispered in my ear, and a different kind of shiver jolted through me.

On one hand, I desperately wanted to run or at least shove him away. On the other...he was an awfully good kisser.

The prince went still. *I am going to blame the incubus,* he said. *I apologize.* He released me and his presence faded.

I groaned, before sagging forward. This entire situation was ridiculous.

"So, no Mr. Fluffy Pants?" I looked down at the Pomeranian.

He growled and mimed lifting his leg toward my foot.

"Hey, house broke hellhound, remember?"

He sat and wagged his tail.

"What about Mayhem?"

His fluffy little ears perked forward, and he wagged his tail cautiously.

"You like that?"

The creature yipped something that certainly sounded like an affirmative.

"All right, Mayhem it is."

I don't know what I expected, but the result of naming him was anticlimactic after what the prince had told me. He gave a full body shake, making him look even fluffier, before he went back to licking water off my leg.

I shook my head, grabbed a towel, and finished drying off. Once I was dry, I went into my bedroom and grabbed clothes, before digging around in a desk drawer and finding some pink tinted glasses. They were meant to be a fashion accessory, but they were light enough that I could wear them inside and hopefully it would hide the red in my eyes. No, I hadn't bought them. They'd been a gag gift years ago and I'd kept them mostly because I'd forgotten about their existence until now.

I threw them on and looked in my dresser mirror. It was going to have to be good enough unless I was going to start wearing actual sunglasses inside.

Steeling myself, I left my bedroom and headed for the living room, where I could sense Sabian. I presumed Mal was there if he hadn't left. This extra sense of the demons in the house was really weird. Even the hellhound was like a faint pull, though he trotted along my side.

"Chris," Sabian said hopefully when I came into the room.

Mal arched an eyebrow, I imagined at the pink tinged glasses.

"Hide the red?"

He studied me for a moment before inclining his head. "Well enough. If anyone noticed, they'd probably assume you went on a bender and had a bad hangover."

"Wouldn't be the first time," I muttered.

"Are you hungry?"

"Now that you mention it, I could probably eat an entire cow."

His smile was hesitant, but he got up from the chair and headed for the kitchen. "You slept later than I expected, but I made biscuits and gravy since that would be easy to reheat."

"Thank you." I went over to one of the stools, sat and leaned my elbows on the counter. I cradled my head and shut my eyes. "What the fuck have I gotten myself into?"

Mal slid a plate in front of me and put a hand on my shoulder.

The demon flinched, which led to me flinching. Mal pulled his hand away.

I grabbed his hand and pulled it back. "Wasn't me. Sorry, guess the prince either isn't used to being touched or doesn't like it."

"I'm sorry I attacked you," he said.

"I'm sorry I got you nearly killed. If it helps any, Mal, I didn't feel anything you did to me, and I knew what I was getting into." I twisted around on the stool until I faced him.

His face was drawn, and I pulled him against me.

The prince was basically quivering with distaste. I ignored him as best as I could.

Mal finally reached around me and held me close.

"Are you okay?" I asked.

"Yes."

We held each other for a few moments before I let him go.

"Are we okay?" I forced out.

Mal's lips twitched into a weak smile. "Yes. Though, I may sleep at home for a while since your guest doesn't like to be touched."

I clenched my jaw, but nodded.

I almost laughed at the prince's sigh of relief.

You'd better not be sticking around long if that's the cost. I'd gotten used to being held at night.

Ezra didn't reply.

Mal brushed his knuckles along my cheek before leaning over and kissing my forehead. "I have to head into the shop for a while, Chris. Don't go anywhere alone and I'll call you later, okay?"

"What about you, mate?"

His smile widened into something predatory. "I'm on to their tricks now. They won't catch me off guard again." Then his expression fell. "I'm sorry about that. I truly didn't expect to be attacked in the middle of the square. That kind of isolation spell is not easy. Clearly this occultist is far more skilled than I had anticipated."

"Hey, I was the one window shopping. Some occultists we are, huh?"

"Yeah, well, now we know." He kissed me gently on the lips then turned to leave.

"Hey, Mal. Guess we should practice some more roleplaying, since we may not be up to anything more interesting for a little while, huh?"

He turned back to me, his eyes lighting up with delight. "I'd like that."

I winked. "We'll have to teach the prince how to play. I'll call you tonight. Maybe a game tomorrow?"

He nodded and this time he did leave.

I turned my attention to Sabian. He wilted.

"I'm sorry," he whispered.

"You saved my life, Sabian. In theory I'm going to survive this, too. It'll be okay. Thank you."

He looked relieved, then his gaze darted down to the hellhound. "I thought you had named him. I shouldn't have assumed. I'm sorry for that, as well."

"It's not your fault, Sabian. I should have and my passenger informed me of my failure there. Mayhem. That's what I'm calling him now."

Sabian's eyebrows rose and he chuckled. "Fitting, I suppose. Okay, well that's handled. You should eat your breakfast before it gets cold. Then we need to figure out what is next."

I turned back to my plate, and groaned at the first bite. Damn that vampire could cook. "Where is Aaron?"

"He's hiding in his room."

"Okay. So, I'm assuming you're not going to be touching me, either?" I thought back to his absence last night.

Sabian didn't answer, but when I looked at him, he was staring at his hands, looking upset again.

"It's not your fault, mate. Not happy about it, but not blaming you. So, what are we going to do about keeping you from getting hungry enough to throw two random strangers into each other's arms?"

A hint of chagrinned amusement broke through his solemn expression. "Seems to have worked out for you."

"Yeah, but I'm not real anxious to share you, or Mal..." I broke off and frowned. Where had that come from? No, I didn't want to share them, but what the hell kind of say did I have in it? Especially since they seemed okay with sharing me.

"You're the only woman for me, Chris Price," Sabian said, voice quiet. "And I doubt Mal feels any different. You're our exorcist. Don't worry about me. I'll figure something out. If nothing else, your enjoyment of Mal's cooking helps some."

I patted my stomach. "Yeah, it's a good thing I have the metabolism of a racehorse because otherwise I'd have gained twenty pounds in the last few days."

"You'd be amazing no matter how much weight you did or didn't have. But let's not worry too much about it right now. I'm fine for a few days."

"Great. So, what's next?" I finished shoveling food in my face and put the dish in the sink.

"We need to know what the prince knows, and formulate a plan from there," Sabian replied.

I can draw him into our conversation so that you don't have to repeat everything I'm saying.

I sighed and repeated that to Sabian. He nodded in reluctant agreement.

Moments later the three of us were standing in that same blank space where I'd interacted with the demon prince before. The last couple of times I'd been distracted but this time I could truly appreciate how blank it was here. It was like standing in a white void, with only myself, Sabian, Ezra and...what the hell was that?

The dog-like creature was nearly as tall as I was, covered in short black hair that shone in the ambient light, muscular, with eyes that glowed red with flame. Horns curled forward around his cheeks and large pointed ears jutted up from his skull. A spiky fringe of hair ran down the creature's entire back, from head all the way down to his long, spike-tipped tail.

"Mayhem?" I said hesitantly.

The creature turned toward me and dropped his jaw in a doggy grin. His tail flicked, more cat-like than dog like, but otherwise this creature was all hellhound.

"Why...why on earth do you look like a Pomeranian?"

197

He sat and tilted his head, as if he couldn't figure out what my problem was.

"Never mind."

Ezra stood behind me, and he touched my back, fingers tracing a small circle between my shoulder blades.

Sabian's eyes narrowed, but he didn't otherwise object.

I wanted to tell him to stop. I also didn't want to tell him to stop.

The demon prince stilled his hand before dropping it to his side. Maybe he hadn't meant to touch me?

Regardless, we were all here now.

"Okay, what's going on?" I turned to face Ezra.

Sabian came up to my side and I slid my hand into his. Ezra got a pinched look on his face like he might physically be in pain, but he was just going to have to deal.

Mayhem came up next to me and sat, still almost as freaking tall as I was. He leaned over and pressed his body against my hip. After a moment I put my hand on his back. The hair that spiked down his body was surprisingly soft.

"As we've already discussed, there seems to be a power play going on in the demonic realm. Lott, who you're familiar with, is a more recently elevated prince. He's also quite ambitious. There is more to it than a simple power play, but I do not yet know all the details. He seems to have aligned with these humans to bind demons and help the criminals. Honestly, it's a strange thing because the criminals can't do much for him in return. I would have thought he'd choose a more powerful group of mortals."

"They're focusing on demons that fall under your control, right?"

Ezra nodded.

"They managed to summon you, yes?"

He frowned, but nodded.

"Seems like he might be getting what he wanted. You, and yours, tied up so you can't interfere," I suggested.

Ezra's eyes narrowed. "Perhaps. But to what end? My territory and power shouldn't be interesting to him."

"Is there any other sorts of power plays going on that you're involved with?"

Ezra pursed his lips before shrugging. At least this time I couldn't feel as if he were shrugging under my skin. "Nothing of real consequence. The last strong opinions I put forth were many years ago as the mortal plane counts them. I can't imagine it's important now."

I also got the impression he was not going to tell us what that was, so I didn't press. Not now, anyway.

"Okay, so Lott is pushing into your territory, or at least pushing you out of it. He's succeeded."

"He has merely inconvenienced me. To truly take over my territory he would have to trap me on Earth in a somewhat permanent fashion and show that I was incapable of defending myself and my territory. He nearly succeeded, unfortunately. Instead, I'm safe, though unfortunately on Earth."

"That's why you want to stay. So, he can't summon you again?"

"Yes, though my preference would have been to stay without actually being in possession of a mortal."

"Yeah, well, same here, mate."

Somehow, he caressed my back again, though he was facing me. He frowned, as if realizing he was doing it.

"So, we're caught up in a power play that seems simple on the surface, but doesn't make a lot of sense, so is probably connected to something much deeper. That about it?"

Ezra nodded.

"First step, we gotta stop that twatwaffle occultist and get the demons sent back to hell. Right?"

"Yes."

"Then what?"

"Then you and I part ways, and hopefully your involvement is done," Ezra said. "You've already claimed Sabian and you have one of my hellhounds and I will owe you that favor, so we will be seeing each other again. Though hopefully not longer than it takes for me to repay your assistance in this matter."

I sensed hesitation as he voiced the last.

"Sure. So, I get to keep Sabian and Mayhem?"

"As much as I'd enjoy fighting you, Price, I have more important things to worry about. Sabian wants to be claimed, and I am not losing anything by leaving him in your possession. The hellhound is a gift. He's from excellent bloodlines, by the way."

I had never considered that hellhounds might have breeding programs. Shaking my head, I sighed, though I dug my fingers into the creature's mane. He leaned against me a bit more firmly.

"Okay." I didn't know what else to say to any of that.

"Prince Ezra, what do we need to know, to fight this occultist and the other demons?" Sabian asked, voice far more respectful than I'd managed with Ezra. Perhaps that was because Ezra had outright told us I could keep Sabian without him fighting us. That had to buy some gratitude at least.

"We have to find her. Once we destroy her, it shouldn't be difficult to use my connection to the others to track down the amulets and destroy them. Either with that clever spell the vampire had in his collection, or if we can convince the angelic one to assist, he can destroy them simply by touching them. Then either Price or the Catholic priest can send them back to my realm. They will all want to go, so the rituals will not be difficult."

"Can I do an exorcism with you possessing me?" I shivered.

"If I'm not interfering, which I won't be."

200

"Almost seems too easy."

"Finding the occultist and defeating her will not be easy," Ezra said. "The rest shouldn't be difficult."

"Okay, so, how do we find this bitch and defeat her?" I hoped he had some ideas, because I didn't.

"It may take some magical detective work to find the woman. Defeating her likely will be as simple as killing her and as complicated. She will have many defenses."

"Great. So, what role are you going to play in this?" I was almost afraid to ask.

"I'm going to continue to keep you alive, Price. Hope I don't need to do more than that, as I'll have to act through you. The longer I possess you, and the more I act through you, the more significantly you will feel my absence when I'm gone."

"Do I even want to know what that means?"

Ezra didn't reply.

"So, you can't just step out of my body and be present on Earth?"

"Now that I've possessed you, I'd have to return to my realm before I could be summoned again and manifest as Sabian does. If you want to go that route, I can teach you to summon me."

"I feel like there's a catch."

"It requires sacrifice." Ezra smiled as if that idea didn't actually bother him.

"Right, that's a pretty big catch."

He shrugged.

"And if we send you back, they could summon you again and all the bad things you mentioned before could still happen, but if you're still here they can't do any of that?"

"It is theoretically possible for them to summon me again while I am in possession of you. However, I do not think they would succeed if they tried. Assuming you fought them, anyway. You are much stronger than their occultist."

Fight to keep being possessed. Right. That was tweaking my brain a little.

"Yeah, okay, let's hope she doesn't try that." I really didn't want to know what that sort of battle would do to me.

"I also hope they do not think of it. If they try the summoning they've been using, it won't work, regardless. However, if they discover you are alive, they might figure out what we've done, and that could convince them to try it. Still, you can't simply hide away if we're to stop them."

"Yeah, right, mate. Lay low, but don't?"

He nodded.

"Great."

Ezra tilted his head as if he were listening to something, then suddenly I was back in my living room, the sound of Darius' ring tone blaring from my phone.

I did not want to talk to him. The phone stopped.

"You guys okay?"

I twisted around on the couch. Aaron was standing in the doorway, staring at us.

"Yeah. We were just talking with Ezra. Got something of a plan going on."

"Are you okay, Chris?" Aaron came the rest of the way in the room.

I sighed and leaned back against the couch. "As okay as I can be. I'm not dead, at any rate. That's a bonus."

Aaron sank down into the chair and stared at me.

"Anyone have a chance to fill you in on your secrets?"

He raised his eyebrows. "No."

"Guess you got angel blood, mate."

If anything, his eyebrows climbed higher. "Really?"

The proper term is Nephilim, or half angel.

I relayed that to Aaron.

"But, neither of my parents..." he protested.

Likely his father is actually an angel. Also, likely, his mother didn't know. You don't have to tell him that, however.

"I don't know. Just, you've got angel blood. Pretty cool, actually. At least someone in this house isn't in thick with the demons." I tried to smile. It didn't work.

"Sure. This, really is going to take a lot to process." He shook his head and hunched his shoulders. "But I suppose we've got bigger things to worry about right now. What did you learn?"

I filled him in.

Before he could reply, my phone started ringing again.

"Damn it," I muttered and grabbed the cell. "What?"

"Price, could you and your posse please come down to the sheriff's office. We've got another one you really should take a look at," Darius said, voice neutral.

"Seriously?"

"Chris, it's important. I promise this isn't about you or your friends."

He's telling the truth if it helps.

"Yeah, sure, okay. Mal's not here, but I can bring everyone else."

"Yeah, that's probably fine. I'm not sure we need him."

"All right, mate. See you in a few."

I glanced at the others and seeing their agreement, stood and put the phone in my pocket.

"Why don't I drive?" Aaron offered as we headed toward the door.

I hadn't been awake long, but weariness dragged at my limbs and I agreed.

Side effect of almost dying twice. I'm doing the best I can, but it still takes some time to recover from that.

Probably still better than being dead.

At least you got out with your soul intact.

I shivered and hoped it stayed that way.

Dakota Brown

Chapter 16

Price

I stared at the holding cell in amazement. The demon had used his host's blood to paint the walls with symbols. Ezra was helpfully translating as I studied them.

The cops didn't know I was possessed, hopefully anyway, but they knew about Sabian. The incubus was flitting around the room, translating the symbols as he went, while one of the officers recorded everything. It amounted to a pictograph retelling of what had happened to the demon.

I actually felt sorry for it. This demon was one of the more innocuous types, almost more of a demonic nature spirit than a true demon. A trickster, but not particularly evil on the scale of demons. Still, his host had passed out from blood loss before it completed its tale of capture and imprisonment. It had begged to be released every few symbols or so, but the really interesting thing was that the tale gave us clues. Really big clues as to where to start looking for our occultist.

"You were right. This is important," I said once Sabian had finished performing for the cops. Ezra and I had already read everything.

"Are you up to releasing the demon?" Darius asked.

I almost felt like that was a test.

"Yeah, I can do it."

The demon prince didn't object, so I figured we were golden.

"What's with the glasses?" Officer McClellan asked as she led us to the cell where the possessed human currently resided under monitored restraint. They'd treated him then brought him back here, probably owing to the demonic possession.

"Bad hangover," I muttered and shivered as invisible hands caressed my back. Did he even realize he was doing that?

The hellhound trailed along behind us, ignored by everyone. That was a fantastic trick on his part.

"Surprised you were in any shape to drink last night. You looked pretty bad when Mal carried you out of that warehouse."

Damn, we'd finally gotten to the stereotypical warehouse and I'd mostly been unconscious for it. Bummer.

"Looked worse than it was. Needed a bender to come down from the adrenalin and actually get some sleep."

I could tell she didn't believe me, but I wasn't about to tell her the truth. Or anything else, for that matter.

The possessed human was a young man with shaggy black hair, sallow skin, and a desperate air about him that might have been his natural state even without a desperate demon.

"You couldn't take care of him before we got here?" I asked Darius.

"Wasn't sure if you would want to talk to him first," Darius answered. "This is the first one we've found in a while."

"Seems like most of their amulets hold pretty well. You only find the ones that are flawed," I said.

"That's what we were thinking." Darius studied me as I approached the possessed human.

He looked up, the familiar red rimming his irises. I fought to keep from rubbing at my own red rimmed eyes.

"Master! You're safe!"

I felt my eyes widen in surprise and I glanced at Darius and Deputy McClellan. Neither of them looked like they understood.

He's speaking in demonic. You understand because I'm translating for you. Don't reply. I will handle this.

They went back and forth for a bit. Ezra somehow communicating without using my body. Probably a perk of being a prince, and also not being bound into an amulet.

The end result was that Ezra's underling was more than happy to be sent back to hell, promised not to resist, and gave us basically the same information we'd had from his bloody artwork.

Proceed.

You're not my boss.

Ezra sighed.

Darius hadn't painted a protective circle this time, for which I was extremely grateful. We were going to do this without for a while. It wasn't nearly as dangerous with the demon prince riding along, as it would have been if I hadn't already been possessed. None of the demons we were dealing with were going to try and tangle with Ezra for my body.

Fuck that was weird.

I didn't even need the reveal spell to find the amulet.

I snatched the charm off the guy's wrist. Oddly, the human didn't react poorly to losing his demon. He simply sighed and passed out.

I debated just handing the thing off to Aaron. They'd told me what had happened when he touched them. Finally, I decided the cops had enough of our secrets and I'd do it the hard way.

"Want me to do this here or take it with me and do it at home?" I asked Darius.

"I have a room prepared," he replied.

Guess he didn't want me to inadvertently add to my collection. Three was plenty, but I wasn't going to bring that up in front of McClellan.

"Sabian, why don't you and Aaron and Mayhem wait while I take care of this." I didn't want to accidently banish the hellhound, either.

The hellhound cannot be banished in the same way, especially now that he is bound to you. Keep him at your side.

As if sensing that, Mayhem stayed with me. Aaron waited with Sabian and I followed Darius into the small office, hoping like hell that he wasn't pulling something to try and get Ezra banished. He'd have an unwelcome surprise if he tried.

Fortunately, everything was just as he'd promised. Minus a protective circle, though I could see where there had been one.

Eyeing him as I approached the table made me feel like shit, but I had reason not to completely trust Darius.

He held out his hands in surrender. "I promise, no tricks, Price."

"Humpf," I muttered.

"I thought you two were friends," Deputy McClellan said.

"We are," Darius replied. "But it's a complicated friendship. I've certainly done things in the past to earn a bit of mistrust on her part. It's fine."

"What could you possibly be trying to trick her with in this instance? She's the one that taught you the spell."

"Long story," I grumbled and placed the amulet on the table. I checked for the ingredients to the ritual and got ready.

Do you want me to show you an easier way? I believe I have discovered one.

Not right now, 'cause then I'd have to explain myself. Later, mate.

Ezra didn't reply and I settled into the ritual language.

Releasing the demon took almost no effort, and banishing him was nearly as easy as waving my hand in the creature's general direction and saying go home.

Darius stared at me in amazement.

I shrugged. "He really wanted to go home."

"I'm sure that's it," he replied slowly.

"Yeah, mate. Now, I really had a hell of a shit day yesterday. I'm going home."

"Thank you for coming down, Price. And please thank Sabian for translating all of that. I'm not sure how useful it was, but the more information we have, the better."

"You're welcome, Darius." I headed out of the office and took a deep, relieved breath when Sabian and Aaron flanked me.

Another deputy showed us out and I collapsed into the passenger seat of Aaron's new car.

By the time we got home, I barely had the energy to call Mal, but I did. We talked for a bit, before I bid Aaron and Sabian an early good night and fell into my bed, hoping to sleep soundly enough to not think about being alone. I'd spent most of my life alone in my bed, but damn it, I had gotten so used to Mal and Sabian holding me and now it just felt empty, even with a tiny puffball hellhound curled up at my side.

Even he got up, grumbling, after I tossed and turned for what seemed like forever.

I was about to get up when Ezra jerked me into the blank space.

"What's wrong?" He stared at me, arms crossed across his chest.

This time he wore some sort of silky looking dress shirt, in black, with the sleeves rolled up showing muscular arms. His slacks were also black and fit well enough that it probably should have been illegal.

"What do you mean?"

"You're trying to rest. I'm trying to rest. Why are you tossing about like a ship on stormy seas?"

"Didn't know you were a poet, too."

"I'm not," he practically snarled. "I'm a tired demon prince, who spent most of my energy keeping your ungrateful ass alive. And I've spent the rest of my energy attempting to be nice to you. I'd like to have a chance to recover and I can only do that while you're unconscious."

"One, I'm not ungrateful. Two, I'm exhausted." I glared back at him. "But because of you, no one will touch me, and I'm used to certain, uh, extracurricular activities, not to mention cuddles at night. Apparently, the lack is keeping me from sleeping."

"You need to be held to sleep?" He stared at me, incredulously. "That's a lot of touching."

"Hey, mate, you're the one that keeps running phantom hands up and down my back, or playing with my hair." I'd noticed that, too.

He opened his mouth to protest, then snapped it shut. "Incubi are bad influences."

"Yeah, is it actually his fault?"

"Of course, it is," Ezra protested a bit too insistently.

"Umhm." Shit, what was I doing? Trying to provoke him? "If you would let Sabian hold me, I'd probably pass right out."

"No. I will not be...held...by a subordinate, no matter the situation." Ezra shuddered.

"I could call Mal."

The demon prince glared at me.

"Sorry the hellhound isn't quite doing it for me. He's cute and all, but it's not the same."

Suddenly I was back in my body. "You're going to give me whiplash if you keep that up," I grumbled.

Shut up, and go to sleep. A heavy, warm weight settled over me, as if someone I couldn't see had wrapped themselves around me. Ezra's phantom arm slid across my stomach, his legs tangled with mine, and his chest pressed against my back. I swore his breath tickled my ear, sending shivers down my spine.

You're not sleeping.

"I mean, it takes a minute. Sorry. Follies of mortal bodies and all."

Price, your heartrate is even higher than it was before. You're supposed to relax.

"I, uh, sorry." Shit, now I was really awake. He felt awfully good pressed against me. That coupled with the memory of his lips on mine was sending me on a mental spiral into places I shouldn't be going.

The demon prince sighed. *If you tell anyone I did this...* He trailed off and before I could ask what he meant, Ezra slid the arm that was under me up until his hand gently gripped my throat. His other hand trailed down lower until it slid under my clothing, leaving traces of fire along my skin.

"Sabian will know," I blurted out, heart really racing now.

He needs to feed, too, and he will not say anything if he knows what is good for him. That last bit was likely directed at Sabian.

"But..." I gave one last weak protest, not quite getting the words out.

Your men will understand. Besides, this is all in your head.

"Really?"

211

Mmhmm. He kissed my neck, then bit me gently. I quivered, breath coming fast.

My protests fled as he rolled me from my side to my back until I was cradled against him, legs spread, giving his fingers access. He bit me again, harder, and I arched back into him, gasping. His fingers closed around my throat, enough to get my attention, but not enough to hurt.

I whimpered, as he stroked at my clit, then dipped a finger inside me, before going back to work on the sensitive nub. I shuddered against him, trembling as he worked me. Some part of me held onto the idea that this was all in my mind, but I could feel it so exquisitely, every press of his lips or nip of his teeth on my neck, the squeeze of his hand on my throat, his fingers as they dipped inside of me again, pumping, stroking, rubbing, until my body shattered, and I rocked against him as he fucked me with his fingers through my orgasm.

Once I could think again, I was almost surprised to find myself still cradled in his arms.

I took a breath, and then another, before I finally found my voice. "Do you, uh, need anything?"

Ezra chuckled, the sound vibrating through me. *Price, I'm inside you, your pleasure is my pleasure. Thank you for your concern, however.*

"Yeah, sure." Whatever else he'd done, the combination of endorphins and the heavy, warm weight of him curled around me was doing the trick. Even if it was all just in my head. My eyelids drooped, and I tried not to think about what he'd said, or my brain might really break.

Good night, Chris Price.

"'Night, Ezra."

That he had used my first name for the first time occurred to me right before I passed over the point of oblivion, but it didn't keep me from passing out into the deepest, most dreamless sleep I'd had in ages.

∞ ∞ ∞

I could barely meet Sabian's eyes the next morning and buried my face in the cupboard while I looked for something to eat. Mal had been in charge of food enough that I didn't actually know what I had in the cupboard and I wondered if he had actually been shopping because there was more fresh produce than I normally kept in my kitchen. Maybe Aaron? He was basically living here, too, for the moment. I kind of wanted to touch him just to see if I got the same electric shock the others did.

If you like touching electric fences, go ahead, Ezra grumbled.

I ignored him, grabbed some bread to make toast, turned around, and almost ran into Sabian.

"I feel like I haven't seen you in forever, and it's been like, a few hours," I admitted and threw my arms around him.

Ezra snarled and I shoved him down. I swear I heard him yelp in surprise, but for the moment I had a time alone with Sabian.

He clutched me tightly and I drank in his familiar warmth.

"You know," he said, "Prince Ezra is right. It's a convenient way for me to feed, and no one is going to be upset with you for any of that."

I relaxed into him.

"I'm positive, Chris," he answered my unasked question. "Okay, before he gets upset and freaks out on me later." Sabian released me. "Seriously, do what you need to do. Living with me, well, believe it or not, I try to keep most of it reined in, but my nature is going to leak out, and it is going to affect you." He grinned. "Usually, this is a good thing."

213

I sighed, already missing his warmth, but I didn't protest when Ezra surfaced from wherever I'd shoved him.

"Mal's on his way over, by the way," Sabian said. "We figured you'd probably need to go over to the restaurant at some point, and you're going to need him to get through the wards."

"Fuck," I grumbled. "This is freaking ridiculous."

I tend to agree.

Shut it.

Amazingly enough, the demon prince didn't have a response to that, and I went back to ignoring him while I made toast.

Mal showed up a few minutes later and I practically launched myself into his arms, ignoring the grumbling demon prince when Mal pressed his lips to mine. I wrapped myself around Mal and he sank onto the couch holding me against him.

I lost myself in the press of our lips, the dance of our tongues, and the feeling of being absolutely desired that Mal always managed to convey to me.

When I finally came up for air, I still didn't release him.

"Miss me?" He smiled, amusement dancing in his eyes, blackened with lust.

"Yes." I reluctantly climbed off of my vampire and Ezra sighed in relief.

I'm a better kisser, you know.

It's not a fucking competition, and no, you're not.

Yes, I am.

Fine, whatever. I hoped he wasn't about to jerk me away into that blank space just to prove his point, but fortunately, I remained firmly in my own thoughts.

Aaron cleared his throat and I jumped, startled. I'd forgotten about him. "Oh, hey, mate. Want breakfast? I'm making toast."

Mal gave me a horrified look and headed for the kitchen.

"Is that what the burning smell is?" Sabian laughed.

"Okay, so Mal's an amazing cook. Fine. I'll have you know I make a damn good pizza."

"We're sure you do, Chris, but somehow you're failing at toast." Mal unplugged the toaster, which was, admittedly smelling a bit burnt. Maybe I'd accidently used the bagel setting?

I put my hands on my hips and glared at Mal.

"Sure, breakfast would be great. I have to go deal with the insurance company and all that crap this afternoon. Are we still worried about them coming after me?"

Yes, Ezra supplied.

"Yep, take Sabian." I glanced at the incubus and he nodded agreement.

"Okay," Aaron accepted the assignment reasonably easily. He was accepting all of this pretty well, actually.

He likes you.

Wait, what?

You've caught his interest and he likes you. You're getting quite the collection. Angels, demons, vampires. What's next?

I didn't reply. I'd been trying not to go there in my thoughts about Aaron, but now I had to wrench my thoughts back to the present.

"Mal, are you busy today?"

"No. I told Olivia I wasn't available for a bit and she is fine with watching the store. I thought after we went by your restaurant, we should start looking for the occultist."

"Yeah, let's catch that twatwaffle, and get all of this over with."

You'll miss me.

Will I?

He didn't reply.

Dakota Brown

Chapter 17

Price

Mal grabbed my arm before I could crash into the wards around my restaurant.

"That might actually cause you harm. Let's not test it."

I hugged my arms to myself and tried not to flinch away while Mal traced his finger along my forehead in some sort of symbol and muttered under his breath. Since it looked like I was well and truly sucked back into the occult life, I was going to have to get Mal to give me lessons. I was good, but it certainly never hurt to learn from someone better.

"Okay, you should be good now." Mal turned and headed into the restaurant.

Hesitantly, I followed. Mayhem trotted along in front of me. The comforting smell of garlic, dough, and marinara hit me and I relaxed my shoulders a bit. I was safe here and this was familiar and comforting, despite the way my life had turned on its head.

It occurred to me, as I watched the hellhound trot along, that we had never invited Mayhem into anything except my house. *How does he get through the wards?*

Canines, felines, most other animals, and children do not have the same rules regarding wards as most everything else. It is a matter of their innocence and how it interacts with the magic. Well, felines simply can't be bothered to acknowledge or care about wards. There are wards that can keep hellhounds out, but they are fairly specific. Unless someone is expecting a hellhound, it likely wouldn't occur to them to use it.

So, in the case of wards, hellhounds are dogs.

Essentially.

Huh.

"Hey boss, what's up with the glasses?" Billy asked when I wandered back into my office.

I stuck with the drunken bender story. "Do not try to drink Mal under the table." I groaned and clutched my head. "It is not possible."

Mal chuckled. "You held your own pretty well."

At least he could play along with the small lie.

"Okay, well, you up for looking at some designs?"

"Sure, Billy. Whatcha got?"

I spent the next couple of hours catching up on paperwork and approving some designs for the new branding. Ezra was rather horrified, which made me that much happier about the turn my shop decoration had taken. Mal was pleased and we texted Aaron a few of the pictures and got Sabian and his approval, as well. Well, Sabian's, anyway. I wasn't sure how Aaron felt about any of this. I needed to get him alone so we could have a talk soon.

∞ ∞ ∞

"Okay, something is bothering you," I said later when we were driving back toward my place. We had taken Mal's hybrid. He was driving one handed, and I took his free hand and threaded my fingers through his.

Shut it, I snarled at the demon when I could sense him squirm in protest.

"What makes you think that?" Mal glanced at me before returning his attention to the road.

"You've been way quieter than normal."

He took a breath that he didn't really need, and I knew I was right.

For a few minutes I wasn't sure he was going to reply, but once we were back in my driveway, he twisted in his seat to face me.

"I nearly killed you," he said. "It's upsetting me."

Well, at least he was direct.

"Mal, I knew what I was doing. I had backup to keep me alive. If I hadn't, I'd have figured something else out."

"Would you, though?"

I blinked. He had a point. "Well, I mean, I wouldn't want you to accidently kill me, anyway. I'd probably try to avoid putting you in that sort of circumstance. I'd be dead and I'm sure it would fuck with your head a little bit."

He raised his eyebrows "A little bit?"

"A lot?"

"Yes," he admitted. "You accidently kill people when you first become a vampire. It's almost unavoidable. And I've killed a lot of other people through the years, too, both before I was a vampire and after. I'd rather not add you to the list."

"Well, I'd rather you didn't, either. I'm much more entertaining alive." I grinned at him. "Mal, it's okay."

He sighed and turned the car off. "I sometimes forget how fragile human life really is. Then I lose someone. Or almost lose them." He glanced at me, before getting out of the car.

My heart sank. I don't know if I could handle it if he left, but I didn't know what to say.

Finally, I settled for a bit of my classic snark.

"Yeah, well I'm currently damn near indestructible."

Mal arched an eyebrow and I wanted to run my fingers through his hair and kiss away all his worries, but I wasn't sure if he would welcome that or not.

"I will be okay, Chris. It's just weighing on me right now." He headed for the house and I followed.

"Okay." My tone must have reflected some of my worry because once we were inside the air conditioning, he pulled me into his arms.

"Don't worry, Chris, you're still my exorcist."

I melted a little.

Ezra, wisely, didn't object as I cuddled into Mal's embrace.

We stayed that way for a bit, just holding each other, before he released me.

"So, you want to teach a demon prince how to roleplay tonight?" I changed the subject. "And maybe a half angel?" I added when I heard Aaron's car pull into the driveway.

"Yes, that sounds fantastic." He perked up as I had intended. Then he frowned. "Half angel?"

"That's Aaron's big secret. He's a Nephilim."

"Ahh. I wondered if it was something like that. Very interesting."

We need to look for the occultist, Ezra reminded me. Though I hadn't forgotten. We still had hours.

"I'm going to see if Aaron wants to drive me around while we follow some of the clues Ezra's demon left us." I wanted some time to talk with him without the others around. "Maybe Sabian can make you feel better?" I suggested.

Mal blinked a few times, as if trying to process what I'd just said.

"Um, not like that, mate." I laughed. "I mean, Sabian would probably be into just about anything, but I meant you could talk with him, since you're both immortal badasses?"

Mal finally laughed. "Maybe."

Ezra ran phantom fingers up my back, making me shiver.

Mal tilted his head, dog-like.

I shook mine. "For someone who says he hates touching so much, he seems to *touch* me a lot."

I do not.

You just did, mate.

It is the incubus's fault.

Yeah, sure it is. Back to that argument again, were we?

Mal chuckled. "Enjoy, I suppose. I'm sure it's not everyone who has positive attention from a demon prince."

I sighed. "It's certainly better than a normal possession."

Mal brushed his fingers along my cheek. "Seriously, may as well enjoy the experience as much as you can."

"I'm getting the idea that you're thinking something along the lines of 'the longer he's around, the safer I am?'"

The vampire tightened his lips for a moment before he shrugged. "I won't lie, the thought has crossed my mind. Though, if he sticks around too long, he's going to have to learn to share."

Ezra shuddered.

I chuckled. At least that sounded more like Mal wasn't considering leaving once this was over. Some of the knots in my shoulders eased and Ezra caressed my back again.

I don't share what is mine.

Good thing I don't belong to you, mate.

He didn't reply, which was probably just as well. I was feeling uncomfortable enough with all the emotions I was having to deal with, that I'd probably start a fight with him, and I didn't need that at the moment. We could fight later.

Sabian and Aaron came in just then.

Sabian's eyes lit up like it was Christmas when he saw me. He hurried forward and, with a bit of flourish, dropped a rock into my hand.

Recognizing a gift when one was so obviously given, I studied it. He'd found a desert rose for me. From the bits of dirt still on the barite rose, I thought he might have actually found it, instead of buying it from a store.

"Thank you, Sabian. I love it," I replied with real gratitude in my voice. It was touching and very cool. It had been a long time since anyone had given me a gift. Especially one so heartfelt.

He preened with my approval.

I brought the rock into the living room and put it on the shelf where a few other treasures sat.

Sabian's grin broadened when I glanced at him. Now if only I could kiss him, but Sabian understood and he was probably just as uncomfortable with the idea as Ezra was.

"Okay, Aaron, if you're up for driving me around a bit, I was hoping to steal you away for a few hours. I want to use some of those clues we got to see if we can track the bad guys down."

"Sure, I've got the time."

"Great, thanks. Before we get going, though." I reached out to touch Aaron.

Ezra groaned in annoyance and I giggled internally. He'd compared it to an electric fence. That, I could handle. Hopefully, he hadn't been understating things.

The zap that arced through me when my skin touched his was a bit more than a standard electric fence but not bad.

I chuckled at Ezra's annoyed grumbling. "You feel that?"

Aaron stared at me, incredulously. "No. Other than maybe a bit of pressure."

"Great." I zapped myself again.

If you want me to stop shielding you from the full affects, do it again, Ezra growled.

I chuckled, but took his warning and didn't touch Aaron again.

"Are you okay?" Aaron asked.

"No, mate. But getting a rise out of Ezra is making my day."

Aaron actually laughed. "I'm glad to be of service."

I grabbed Mal for a relatively chaste kiss, blew one to Sabian because I wasn't willing to push my luck too far, and headed back out into the heat with Aaron.

∞ ∞ ∞

"So, what made you drag me alone out into the desert," Aaron asked.

I laughed. "Well, I can't do naughty things to you because I might not survive the electric shock, but I did want a chance to talk to you, relatively alone."

He blushed and cleared his throat. "Relatively?"

"Yeah, well, hellhound in the backseat, demon prince riding along for a case of possession, can't be completely alone."

"Point taken. How is that? Being possessed?"

"Well, this ain't typical, let me tell you. Ezra is behaving himself and intending on leaving. Usually by now I'd be completely consumed and beyond recovery."

"How have you avoided it for so long? Being in your profession."

"Well, I've got a lot of personal protections in place to prevent it. Ezra was able to slip in because I was basically dead."

You were very dead.

"You probably don't need to worry about it, though. Angel blood and all."

He shook his head. "I still don't even know what to think about that."

"So, you can tell when folks are lying. Melt demon possessed charms with a touch..."

"Hurts like a son of a bitch," Aaron interjected.

"And anything else?"

"Yeah, if I get really stressed out about something it gets kind of weird." He didn't elaborate and I didn't push.

223

"Great. So, you on board with helping us stop the occultist or should we leave you at home?"

"I'll help. I'm not sure what good I'll be. I'm just a physicist and a sports and chess coach."

His angelic nature will be very useful, and it will protect him from a lot of the danger.

"Ezra says the half angel thing will keep you pretty safe, well, probably not from getting shot, but from all the demon shenanigans, anyway."

Aaron nodded acceptance.

"And it'll probably be pretty useful in the confrontation. So, glad you're sticking around."

"You're very intriguing, Chris Price. I've never met anyone quite like you before."

"One of a kind, that's me."

He laughed, the rich sound going right through me and dragging me back to all those naughty thoughts.

"I'm not sure the world could survive two of you."

"Yeah, that's a terrifying thought. We'd either hate each other and destroy everything around us fighting, or be best friends."

"And destroy everything around you having a good time?" Aaron supplied.

I grinned, studying his profile. Smart. Handsome. Make that really smart. I wanted to trace those firm, lean muscles, explore those crazy eye markings, run my tongue along the wings draped along his back...Fuck me.

You do any of that and you're going to be unconscious, Ezra warned, voice dark.

It's your damn fault I'm not getting any.

You'll survive for a few more days.

I don't know about that.

Ezra, probably wisely, didn't reply.

As if sensing the turn my thoughts had taken, Aaron glanced at me. "Yes?" he prompted.

"Um, just, you know, living with an incubus is entertaining."

Sure, now you're blaming it on him.

You said I could!

The demon prince laughed.

Aaron shook his head. "I'm getting that impression. I like him. Mal, too."

"You sound surprised."

"Never met a demon or a vampire before," he answered. "Guess I never really thought about it. I like how they treat you. They seem like decent folks. Maybe once this is over, we can still hang out?"

"Yeah, mate. I'd really like that."

You know, Ezra said, *surrounding yourself with powerful men is not a terrible idea. Especially with as much as you seem to attract trouble.*

I ignored him. Pointedly. Though, yet again, I wondered why he cared beyond my usefulness in our current mission.

"So, we haven't turned off of this highway in a while, but I kind of feel like that dirt road needs exploring," Aaron suggested after a moment.

"If we hadn't already established that naughty things were off the table until I'm no longer hosting a demonic prince, I'd wonder what you had in mind." I laughed when he practically choked.

"It was more that something feels off, and I've learned to trust my feelings," Aaron stammered.

I'd have nudged him playfully, but when I went to do it on reflex, Ezra froze my limbs.

Jerk.

"Yeah, let's check it out," I said aloud.

Aaron gave me another long, searching look, before he turned back to the road.

"How are you defining your relationship with Mal and Sabian?" he asked, voice almost carefully neutral.

225

"We haven't really had time to figure it out yet. I didn't meet them too long ago and we all know we need to discuss it, but not getting killed, or, well, in my case, recovering from getting killed, has taken priority." I was trying pretty hard not to think about nearly dying too much, but I probably was going to have to have a good freak out session about it later. Even though I didn't want to think about it, I'd brought it up enough that it was clearly on my mind.

"Why?"

He shrugged. "Just curious."

He's far more than curious, Ezra chimed in. Unnecessarily.

Yeah, getting that idea, mate. Thanks.

Phantom fingers curled around my neck before trailing down my spine. I managed to hide my reaction outwardly, but Ezra stilled.

Sorry. He muttered and disappeared from my awareness.

"You have any family?" I asked as I studied the landscape. We were driving deeper into the desert. There were a few mesas nearby and this road twined between two of them, whatever was beyond them out of sight, and probably where we were headed.

Aaron's brow furrowed as he concentrated on the road and whatever feeling was nagging at him.

"Yeah, parents are still alive. They're down in Albuquerque. Got a sister in Colorado. Aunts, uncles, and cousins all over the place. Sister's got a couple of kids."

"No Mrs. Reed?"

He glanced at me before looking back at the road. "No. Why?"

I shrugged. "You're the one asking relationship questions." I deflected the question back at him, not really ready to truly go there.

"I've dated. Not extensively. The markings and other abilities make things awkward after a while."

"Know that feeling," I said. My markings were chosen, and my abilities crafted and honed, but even before I'd met Darius, I hadn't exactly been what most people considered normal.

Aaron chuckled. "I suppose you would."

"Do you think I'm someone you could take to visit your parents?" Okay, maybe I was going there a little bit.

Aaron frowned. "Yeah, sure. They're cool with a lot more than you might imagine." He shrugged. "I wouldn't even tell you to leave the exorcist part out. I do need to talk to them about the Nephilim thing. It'll explain a lot, but I didn't think it was something I should broach over the phone."

"Yeah, probably not, mate."

That he thought his parents would be cool with me blew my mind. That, I had not expected.

We fell silent after that, listening to the woosh of the air conditioner and the crunch of dirt under the tires. I thought about turning the radio on, but we were out of range of the good station, so I left it off.

After a long silence that wasn't completely uncomfortable, we rounded the mesa and Aaron hit the brakes.

We stared for a few minutes before he quickly turned the car around and we hurried out of there. Hopefully, we hadn't been noticed.

On the surface the place simply looked like a New Mexico style ranch. Adobe architecture, sprawling single story home, barns, other outbuildings, fencing, even a wall around part of the house forming a private courtyard. Very charming. I would have loved it normally.

It practically oozed with malevolence. The air over it shimmered, and I could convince myself I could see arcane symbols surrounding it in some sort of super powerful ward.

You can see them. Possibly because I can see them. Or they are simply that prominent.

"Okay, that's evil," Aaron declared when we were much further away, nearly back to the main road.

"Yeah."

Did they notice us?

I do not think so.

"That's way more what I expected demons to be like than the three you've got hanging out with you."

I'm quite evil, Ezra declared.

"Ezra says he is extremely evil." I kept my tone neutral.

Aaron chuckled. "Is he?"

"Probably." I shrugged. "He seems to be reasonably mellow in the evil department at the moment, but maybe he's just reining it in for our sakes."

Exactly.

I wasn't quite buying it, but I had no doubt he was far from good.

"Sabian could probably be quite evil if he wanted to be, but he seems inclined toward decency. The hellhound, well, he did choose the shape of a Pomeranian. I'm not sure what that says about him."

Hellhounds are protective and a bit chaotic. Their personalities often reflect the ones they are bonded with.

"Ahh, Ezra just said Mayhem will be chaos, but not particularly evil."

Both Aaron and Ezra laughed, though for slightly different reasons. I found myself grinning.

The difference between myself and what is going on at that ranch is that I have achieved my ambitions, and am relatively content to rule my corner of hell. The evil we sensed there is of the type that wishes to break onto Earth and cause actual destruction.

"Okay, Ezra says he's only evil if you piss him off. Whatever demonic presences are going on back there are evil because they want to break the world."

Essentially.

"I see."

"So, Ezra, you mentioned that there was something deeper going on than just an attempt to gain some territory on Earth. Anything else we should know about that?" I asked aloud so Aaron could hear.

I don't yet know the extent of this.

That was similar to the answer he had given me the last time I'd asked basically the same thing.

"What'd he say?"

"He doesn't know enough to say yet."

"Think he would tell us if he did?"

"Eh, probably not. He just wants to end this and head home. Guess as long as we don't have to deal with the rest of it, doesn't matter much to me."

"What do you think the odds of us not having to deal with any of the fallout are?"

"That's a good question." I leaned back in the seat, unsuccessfully trying to ignore the phantom fingers that trailed over my skin again. I did find it interesting that Aaron was still considering himself a part of the equation after this was dealt with. Especially since he'd felt what we were up against.

Chapter 18

Price

What is the point of this?

It's fun. It makes Mal happy. Shut up.

We should be planning our attack on the occultist.

Trust me, we will. Also, if you hadn't noticed, Mal has us storming a heavily warded dungeon. Think of it as practice.

Ezra grumbled.

We were playing characters closer to our normal selves this time. I was playing a heavily intoxicated sorcerer. Which, I found entertaining, because I didn't actually drink that often anymore. Even when I'd been younger, I'd saved the benders for really special occasions, usually involving breakups, or fantastic fuckups on my part. Being a drunk exorcist wasn't the best idea.

To appease the demon prince a little I brought up our mission. "What is the plan?"

"Tomorrow is a new moon," Mal said. "Conveniently, it will be dark. Inconveniently, you won't be able to see very well. I suspect the rest of us will be fine."

I can help with that.

"I think Ezra's got the 'Price is a human' problem taken care of, at least where my night vision is concerned."

"I see pretty well in the dark," Aaron admitted.

"Yeah, not a problem for me," Sabian confirmed.

"So, we sneak in. Severely injure or kill the occultist, send the demons back to hell, and break things to the point where the human authorities can handle it, then call the cops?"

"Damn, Mal, you're starting to sound like me." I chuckled.

He shrugged. "I'm not sure how extensively we can plan otherwise. You and I should probably have a bit of a talk about the wards before I leave tonight. I'll do some research and show up tomorrow prepared to deal with them. We can set Aaron loose on any demon possessed charms. They are mostly Prince Ezra's demons, so I suspect we won't have much of an issue with them once they're freed. They might even help us against any humans they've left behind."

Likely.

"Demon prince agrees," I supplied.

"And we do need a solid plan on dealing with the occultist. I have a few ideas. Once we finish assaulting this dungeon, I'll cook dinner and we can finalize a few things." Mal leaned back in the chair and studied me.

I nodded. "Sounds good, mate."

"Should we let Darius know what we're up to?" Mal asked.

"Naw, don't think he's up for this kind of chaos." Honestly, I didn't want to deal with him after. I suspected I was going to have to let Ezra out to play and he'd probably never forget that. I didn't want to let Ezra take over, but the extent of the demonic energy I'd felt was far more than I'd ever encountered before. I also didn't want to put him at risk. He simply wasn't as good at this stuff as I was.

Mal gave me a worried look before he nodded. "It will be easier if we don't have to worry about any objections the priest might have."

Aaron rolled his dice and sighed. "Yeah, your priest friend probably doesn't need to know I'm a half angel. At least not until we figure out what exactly that means."

"He seems unreasonably cool with demons," Sabian said, voice a bit dark.

"Yeah, at least leaving me with you lot. Not complaining, mind. Just agreeing with Sabian that it is a bit strange. I don't think Darius has gone to the dark side, but it is something we should maybe consider." I shivered. The idea of Darius aligning himself with evil was disturbing. "He also hasn't checked on me recently. Kinda strange."

I'm evil and you have aligned yourself with me, Ezra declared, a bit petulantly.

I have no doubt you're an evil badass, Ezra. You are, however, working for the good guys right now.

He sighed, and I took that as him conceding the point.

Mal brought our attention back to the game.

∞ ∞ ∞

That night I lay staring at my ceiling, running our plan through my mind. It was as solid as we could make it. This ninja shit was so not my cup of tea, however, and I was worried about tomorrow.

Ezra jerked me into the blank space. He was again wearing his silky dress shirt with the rolled-up sleeves and the black dress pants that fit him just right.

I jerked my gaze away from the red buttons on his shirt and the trail down his chest they led me on. My fingers itched for me to run them up and down his chest.

"Worrying about it won't make it easier."

"I know." I hugged myself, frowned, and glanced at myself. I was wearing some sort of badass evening gown. It clung to me in the right spots to accent my figure. The fabric slid across my skin in a way that was far more intimate than I would have expected.

"For real?" It also showed off a great deal of my ink. Yep, open backed, too, from the feel of it.

He shrugged and had the good grace to look embarrassed. "It matches my clothes."

I sighed. "I've never worn anything like this in my entire life."

"Pity. You can change it if you want."

Not having the energy to bother with trying to figure out how, and secretly enjoying the outfit, I simply turned my back and hunched my shoulders. I didn't want to deal with any of this. I'd quit. Gotten out. So many people important to me had died. And now I was putting people at risk again. Sure, they'd be a lot harder to kill, but still, they were putting themselves at risk because of me.

Ezra touched the small of my back, his warm fingers trailing fire up my bare skin as he stroked along my spine. I hadn't heard him move closer.

My breath came faster as he put one hand on my hip, the other caressing my bare neck.

"They're here by choice," he said, reading my mind. "Sabian would be involved regardless. The hellhound lives for this kind of conflict. Mal is a warrior despite his scholarly tendencies. Aaron is not at risk from the demonic energy, only human weapons and I'm certain Sabian will protect him as their role is to release as many demons as they can."

His breath tickled my neck and my stomach tightened. I managed to keep from leaning back against his chest, but it was one of the harder things I'd done recently.

"You are the most at risk in this fight."

"But I have you," I breathed out, voice raspy.

"You have me," he agreed.

We stood that way for a small eternity, neither of us making a move to come together, but seemingly unable to pull away from each other.

The more involved I got with him, the harder it would be to break away later. He was leaving. I'd probably never see him again. At least not like this.

"I should get some rest," I finally gasped out. My entire body was pulled tight, and I wanted nothing more than to lose myself in what Ezra seemed to be offering. It was just a really bad idea. I was good at bad ideas, but somehow, I managed to take a step away from his delicious heat.

"Yes, you should."

I couldn't read his voice as I managed another step away.

Moments later I was back in my bed, staring at the ceiling. Alone except for the Pomeranian curled up at my side.

I took a few shaky breaths, rolled over onto my side, and somehow managed to pass out. Though, briefly, while I was on the edge of sleeping and being awake, I was certain I felt Ezra curl himself around me.

∞ ∞ ∞

"Think it's a trap?" I followed Mal into the living room after letting him inside the house, trying not to stare at the way his jeans hugged his ass. I gave up and stared. The plain black T-shirt fit pretty well, too.

He set a bag down on the coffee table and sank down onto the couch. I told Ezra to shut it and curled into Mal's arms.

The vampire held me, resting his cheek against my head. Sabian looked on, expression peaceful. Aaron joined us a moment later, folding himself into the chair across from us. They were both dressed in jeans and dark T-shirts, too. Eye candy all around. I was not complaining.

235

"It's possible. Doesn't change anything. We have to assume they are prepared for us to discover them. They know I'm a vampire, they know Sabian is an incubus. I'm assuming they have some idea of what makes Aaron special since they are the ones that led us to him in the first place. What they might not know is that we still have Prince Ezra with us. I wouldn't count on that, either."

"Great. You're filling me with some extreme confidence."

Mal kissed me and chuckled. "We'll be fine."

"You don't think we need any other form of backup?" Aaron shifted uneasily in the chair.

"Such as?" Mal asked.

"The cops, I guess." He hunched his shoulders.

"We could simply tell them where to look. It would get a lot of them killed, however," Mal said.

"It's us or nothing," I added. "Let's get ready to head out."

Reluctantly I uncurled myself from Mal's embrace though I felt Ezra's phantom hands on me, as if he were holding me in place of the vampire.

Mal opened his bag and pulled a few things out.

"I made a few of our own charms for protection." He handed out some etched silver circles. The sigils on them were familiar and I thought with a bit of time I could decipher what he'd done.

"Yours was the most complicated, Chris. Protecting you from other demons while not affecting Prince Ezra, Mayhem, or Sabian was interesting. Especially Prince Ezra. None of these should harm Sabian or Mayhem, but I wouldn't touch Chris unless you have to, just in case I messed up. I left Prince Ezra off the rest of them because it does introduce some vulnerabilities that the prince can defend against, which will help Chris but not the rest of us."

I could feel the power in the charm he'd given me. "Did you even sleep, mate?"

"No. I don't need as much sleep as you do on a regular basis."

Everyone pocketed their protective charms.

"I made this for you, since you seem to have misplaced all of your own tools." Mal winked and handed me a black stole with protective sigils hand stitched in silver thread. It was very similar to the one I had made for myself years back, only much nicer and the stitching was far neater. The added protections were helpful when dealing with exorcisms.

I took it from Mal. Yeah, this one was much nicer. That was real silk and I bet the thread actually had a silver content. Mine had been put together with a hope and a prayer and a beginner's skills. That I'd kept using it once I'd improved probably wasn't my smartest move.

"Thank you," I said with a touch of reverence.

I felt Ezra squirm.

Gonna be a problem?

No. You should wear it. It will help protect you. It's simply uncomfortable for me, not detrimental.

I slipped the stole over my shoulders and grinned at Mal.

"The one thing we're short on supply of is holy water, but you may not need any with Prince Ezra riding along."

Ezra shuddered.

"Yeah, I got a little bit left in my squirt bottle if I get desperate. Would hate to burn myself, though." I was getting way too comfortable with the idea of being possessed.

Mal handed me a silver knife with sigils worked into the blade and a sheath I could slide onto my belt. That could also be really useful for protection and other ritual needs. As with the stole, it was far nicer than the one I'd made for myself years back.

"I'd avoid touching the blade until Prince Ezra has left us," Mal suggested.

"Yeah, had that figured out. He's squirming pretty hard right now." I shifted on the couch, made uneasy by his discomfort.

I slipped the blade into the sheath and slid it onto my belt.

I am glad we are on the same side. Malak does know how to construct quality tools.

High praise from the demon. I'd tell Mal later.

"How long before we leave?" Aaron asked after Mal handed him another silver blade.

"Half an hour. Anyone hungry before we leave?"

You should eat.

My stomach was churning, but Ezra was right.

"I should try to eat. How are you doing, Mal?"

"I'll be all right."

I held out my wrist and his eyes darkened before he looked away.

"If that's all it takes, Mal, you're hungry, too. We all need to be at the top of our game. I'll feed you, you feed me. It'll be fine."

"It hasn't been that long since I've had fresh blood. I really am fine." However, he did not object when I scooted over onto his lap. I threaded my fingers into his wavy hair and grinned when he met my eyes.

Mal ran his fingers along my jaw, before tracing them down my neck.

I shivered in pleasure at his touch. Now, more than I had been before, I was grateful that Ezra had spared me the full impact of waking Mal up from being staked. Because of that, I had no hesitation when Mal lowered his lips to my neck. He hesitated a moment before he sank his teeth into my skin.

Pleasure exploded through me, curling through my breasts and sliding its way down my belly until my stomach tightened, and heat pooled in my core. I quivered, groaning, just on the edge of release.

Hmm, I kind of like this. I can torture you a bit.

Jerk.

Ezra laughed, running phantom fingers over my body, teasing me, using his ability to control me to keep me from crashing over the edge into some much needed relief.

Beg me, he demanded.

Fuck you, Ezra.

I groaned when Mal released me from his power. Turned on, but denied relief by the freaking demon.

That's about enough to get you exorcised.

He laughed, the sound trailing through my body and lighting me up further.

"Are you okay?" Mal asked, brow furrowed.

"Fucking demon thinks he's funny," I grumbled.

Mal raised his eyebrows before pulling me into a hug. "Thank you."

"Yeah, any time, Mal. Hopefully next time without an asshole demon being a giant jerk." I said the last loudly, as if he couldn't read my thoughts.

Ezra chuckled.

"Maybe he is evil," I muttered.

"Why don't you let me cook dinner for you and Aaron, and then we can head out." Mal probably knew what my problem was. Scratch that, I was certain he knew, but he was kind enough not to rub it in.

"Sure." I climbed out of Mal's lap and collapsed back onto the couch.

Aaron was staring at me, his mouth open slightly in amazement. Oh, right, he was still here and had not yet experienced that particular aspect of having a vampire around. Well, guess he was really indoctrinated now.

239

"Sorry, guess I'm just used to Sabian being around. Didn't think about it."

Aaron snapped his jaw shut and shook his head. "It's fine." He didn't continue, though I had the feeling he wanted to say something more.

He's turned on and more than a little surprised by it.

Thanks, Ezra. You know, I'm fucking turned on, too. Asshole.

I'm well aware.

His amusement was about to get him sent back to hell.

You need me for a little while longer.

If I didn't, I'd be kicking you out for that.

He laughed and retreated before we could argue more.

Fucker.

Sabian watched me with a trace of amusement in his otherwise carefully neutral expression. I wondered how much of my conversation with Ezra he could overhear. I knew, to some degree, he could read my mind, as well.

Grumpy, I climbed off the couch and headed for my room. My underwear was soaked, and I had nothing to show for it except unrelieved desire.

I can help you with that.

If you had just left me well enough alone, I'd be fine. I was not about to ask the demon to get me off.

You'll enjoy it more later.

I don't want to enjoy it later, I wanted to enjoy it now. What if we all die and I go out with unrelieved orgasms because you denied me.

I promise, if you're about to die, I'll make sure you have a mind blowing one on your way.

"Seriously?" I blurted as I nearly tripped over my feet entering my room.

"You okay, Chris," Mal called.

"Just arguing with fucking Ezra," I snarled. "I'm going to fuck Mal later, whether you want me to or not, just for that." I said the last aloud, knowing Mal would hear me. Hopefully, he wouldn't mind me using him a bit. I wouldn't have minded.

Ezra didn't reply as I angrily changed into dry clothes and stomped back out into the living room.

Fortunately, by then, everyone was basically pretending like nothing had happened, so we settled into a quick meal for those of us who could eat it, before heading toward the door.

I gave Sabian a hug, just in case. Ezra didn't object, which was either an improvement or he was more worried than he let on. I gave Mal a much longer one involving a heated kiss and a great deal of tongue.

Ezra stayed quiet, though I suspected he was annoyed. He might actually be worried he'd pushed me a little too far with his last stunt.

He would have to get over it.

"I'd hug you, Aaron, but electric shock and all."

Aaron nodded. "I'll use my imagination." Then he blushed. "I mean...for the hug."

I grinned at him. "All good, mate."

With that, we climbed into my tank of a car and headed into the desert. Hopefully, we all survived.

I might not forgive myself if something happened to any of them.

Dakota Brown

Chapter 19

Price

We parked as close as we dared, then went the rest of the way on foot, until we stood on the edge of the warded area. Sweat dampened my T-shirt under my light leather jacket, and ran between my breasts. A slight breeze did little to dispel the lingering heat from the day. I really should have left the jacket in the car, but it had saved my ass so many times that I ignored the discomfort.

Mayhem had shifted to his hellhound form, getting quite a reaction out of Aaron and Mal, who hadn't seen him yet. I had trailed my hand along the mane of fur that ran along his back. It was every bit as soft as it had felt in that blank space Ezra took us to. Mayhem had rested his head in my hands for a minute and I'd scrubbed at the base of his horns. By the way he had leaned into my touch, he liked that a lot. Now he stood at my side, alert for danger.

The smell of sage was heavy on the air as Mal studied the ward. He drew a sigil in the air with his knife and made a pushing gesture. The sigil glowed briefly before it pressed against the ward and seemed to fizzle out after a few sparks.

"They're going to know we're here after I take this down," Mal warned. He drew the sigil again. Using the knife, he cut his palm, said something I didn't understand,

and pushed again, this time with a spray of blood that the sigil absorbed.

Shit, Mal knew real blood magic? That was a little dark. Blood marks were one thing, but this was a whole different level.

He's a vampire. It's natural for them.

Oh.

The ward shimmered and Mal held up both hands, intoning something else, before he went and stabbed the ward with the knife.

Direct, Ezra commented.

It worked though. The ward shattered with an audible pop.

The broken magic washed over us, feeling like someone dragged sandpaper over my skin.

"Yuck," I muttered.

"Very unpleasant," Mal agreed.

"Let's go," Sabian ordered.

We followed his direction and headed for the front door as fast as I could manage, since I was the slowest one.

Resistance met us at the door. Two men, clearly possessing demon amulets, charged out. They both looked a little ragged, the strain of hosting unfriendly demons clear in their sallow skin and sunken eyes. Even with the demons being contained in amulets they were clearly paying a price for the possession.

Since we were trying not to kill people unless we had to, Sabian and Aaron took point instead of having Mal lead the fighting. He'd step in if necessary.

Sabian darted forward, grabbed one of the men and jerked the amulet away from the guy's neck. Neither of us needed a reveal spell to find them anymore. Ezra's doing. They also only ever seemed to wear necklaces or bracelets so that also made it easier.

Aaron grabbed the charm, hissed in pain as the silver melted between his fingers, and Ezra shouted a command to the demon that was freed.

Most of the ones we were going to release would need an actual host to be useful, but I didn't want to have to do too many exorcisms, so Ezra was basically telling the released demons to do what they could to help our fight and wait for me to send them back to hell when we were done. This one chose to help by blasting through his former captor and knocking him out. That was extremely useful, and I approved.

The other guy realized what we'd just done to his partner and reached for a gun. Mal stepped in faster than I could see and had the guy in a solid arm lock before he could get the weapon out.

Though it was obviously painful, Aaron repeated the procedure with that demon charm and the freed creature took out the human. Mal dropped the guy to the ground, held up a hand warning us to wait while he inspected the doorframe for wardings that could harm us, and then gestured for us to follow him inside.

It actually was kind of like storming the dungeon had been last night in the game. Some brief fights that the guys took care of, Mal checking for traps as it were, and quick progress through the house.

I knew it wouldn't remain this easy, but for the moment things were going our way.

We worked our way into heart of the house. I couldn't tell from the outside, and maybe we should have gotten on the internet to see if we could find some aerial pictures, but this house had an interior courtyard. That's where things stopped getting easy.

Mal neutralized another ward, but when we stepped through the door, a burst of energy blasted into the vampire, dropping him.

"Mal!"

He'll be fine.

I didn't believe the demon, but before I could do more than take a step in the fallen vampire's direction, Mayhem slammed into me, knocking me to the ground as another burst of magical energy smashed into the doorframe behind me.

You would not have been.

The hellhound blocked some of my view, but once I'd recovered from slamming into the hard ass ground, I looked around him and sighed.

"That what I think it is?" I groaned.

Yes.

"Fuck."

Indeed.

The occultist hovered in the air, a nimbus of energy surrounding her. The energy crackled with red and black streaks cutting through the green of what had probably been her aura before she took on a demon.

I had no desire to know what mine looked like at the moment, come to think of it.

Her eyes blazed red, and her expression was wholly inhuman. While Ezra was along for the ride, she'd clearly completely accepted, or been consumed, by the demon she was hosting.

That is another prince, Ezra supplied.

"Awesome," I grumbled as I climbed to my knees. "Probably a rival of yours?"

Likely. He didn't elaborate but I got the feeling he knew exactly who it was, and it didn't surprise him one bit.

Right now, her gaze followed Aaron and Sabian as they struggled with a group of men off to one side. I glanced at Mal. He was still unconscious.

Her attention snapped back to me as soon as I got to my feet.

Mayhem leapt, intercepting another magical blast. He apparently absorbed the energy, before roaring at the occultist. A jet of flame arched out of his mouth and splattered against her aura.

I shielded my eyes as the energies warred. In the end, her shielding held, but I got the idea it was close.

"Well, that's cool as shit."

It'll be a while before he can do that again, but yes, it is a handy ability. You'll need to cast out the demon. I'll do my best to protect you.

Before I could ask him how he was going to do that, I felt Ezra stretch, as if he were just waking up for the day and sliding into a comfy robe. Except that comfy robe was me.

"Hey!" I yelped, as he settled more fully into my body.

Just get rid of the prince and make this quick.

Ezra gathered my powers.

The exorcism! He snarled when I hesitated.

Right. Fuck. I'd deal with him later. Figuring this was a time for pulling out all the normal measures, I pulled the squirt bottle of holy water out of my jacket and made sure my protective stole was visible.

Stalking forward, Mayhem flanking me, I began.

"*Exorcizamus te, omnis immundus spiritus...*"

"You are not strong enough to cast me out!" Her voice was also inhuman, low, demonic, echoing around us.

I'd heard it all before and I answered with a spray of the last of my holy water.

It splattered against her skin, smoke rising where it burned her flesh. She screamed.

I dropped the empty bottle and pulled out the blade Mal had made for me. "*omnis satanica potestas, omnis incursio infernalis adversarii...*"

My energy focused through the blade, amplifying it. Damn, I hoped I got to keep the vampire around after this. He was fucking good at making tools.

Something flew at me from the side, but Ezra manipulated my powers in a way I'd never experienced before, some of his own power burning through me, and deflected whatever it was. Tears sprang to my eyes as his power torched my aura.

Fuck, mate.

The quicker you get rid of that prince, the sooner I can stop hurting you.

The demon recognized my weakness. She laughed, the sound echoing around us. "You are weak, Ezra! Letting that one keep her mind? You fool."

I shouted out the next few lines of the exorcism, blade held in front of me, pouring all of my will at defeating that vile creature. That I wasn't concerned about preserving the occultist's life helped this entire process.

Though it hurt, I was able to mostly ignore Ezra deflecting the demon's attacks as it became something like a constant burn as opposed to the sharp pain I'd experienced at first.

One of the possessed humans came at me from the side, gun in his hand. Mayhem snarled and launched himself at the guy. The gun went off, but Mayhem must have handled it. I turned out the cries of agony as the hellhound tore the demon from the human and mauled the infernal creature.

"*Ab insidiis diaboli, libera nos, Domine. Ut Ecclesiam tuam secura tibi facias libertate servire, te rogamus, audi nos...*" I shouted.

She screamed as the final lines of the exorcism shoved at the demon prince possessing her.

Ezra added his power to mine, and the power I used to send demons back to hell amplified to a degree I'd never experienced. I screamed in pain as we shoved the prince out of her. I could actually feel the walls between our plane and hell buckle as we forced the demon away.

I collapsed to my knees as the demon was sucked away. All of the extra power whooshed out of me and I barely managed to catch myself before my face smacked into the hard ground. Hopefully, we had succeeded, because if I was attacked in the next few moments I was done. My arms didn't respond to my commands to move and I finally gave up and let myself rest.

I must have passed out, because I woke to a hot tongue licking my cheek. Cracking my eyes open revealed my hellhound looming over me.

"Hey, Mayhem," I rasped out.

He whined and nudged me with his paw.

Aaron came into view and knelt next to me. "Are you okay, Chris?"

"Maybe." I groaned and managed to roll onto my back. *Ezra?*

No answer.

I'd figure out what that meant later. For now, I held out my hand and Aaron grabbed it, hauling me to my feet.

No shock.

Our eyes widened at the same time as we looked at our joined hands.

"I didn't mean to send him back, too," I said. "I mean, I was going to eventually, but..."

I really wasn't ready to process that new bit of information.

"Yeah, you did a number on all the demons in the room," Aaron said softly. "Sabian is gone, too."

"I...Fuck." What had I done? Banishing Sabian had not been part of the plan. I needed him, damn it.

He pulled me into a hug, and I clung to him for a few minutes, trying to pretend everything was going to be okay, while tears leaked from my eyes.

Finally, I pulled back. "Mal?"

"I wasn't brave enough to try and wake him up, but I don't think he's dead."

"Well, that's a start. If he's not dead, blood will fix anything that happens to a vampire."

Though my legs wobbled, and I had to put a hand on Mayhem's back for stability, I made it over to Mal's side. He was still sprawled on his stomach, his wavy hair obscuring his face. He wasn't breathing, but that was normal.

"Hey, Mal?"

I knelt next to the vampire and hesitantly touched his shoulder.

"Mal?"

He twitched, but I didn't jump back fast enough, and before I could comprehend that I was no longer on my feet, Mal had me pinned between him and the ground, eyes black, teeth bared, a low growl vibrating through me.

Or maybe that was Mayhem. The hellhound didn't interfere, but he was clearly ready to.

"Mal," I gasped out.

He blinked a few times, eyes clearing.

"Chris. I'm sorry." His grip on my arms softened and he leaned back, looking me over. "Are you okay?"

"Yeah, fine. You?" I wasn't, but I didn't want him to think he had hurt me just now.

"Head is killing me, but I'll be all right before long. Did I miss the rest of the fight?"

I forced a smile. "Yeah, slacker."

He helped me up then looked around before frowning. "Where's Sabian?"

"Uh." I waved my hand helplessly and burst into tears.

Mal tightened his jaw, before pulling me against his chest and let me cry while Aaron filled him in on the particulars.

"He's not dead," Mal said gently. "There's that at least."

"Yeah," I agreed through choked sob.

"We can get him back, you know."

I nodded. That we could simply summon him back had occurred to me. I wasn't sure if I was ready to go down that road or not, but there was hope. We would figure something out.

"Chris, we need to retrieve that book, make sure there's nothing else dangerous for the police to have, and get out of here. Can I hand you off to Aaron while I take care of this?"

"Yeah, mate. You're right. Sorry." I wiped at my eyes and rubbed my sleeve along my face, just now noticing the jacket was basically shredded. It had saved me again. I almost burst into tears again at the loss, but I managed to remind myself it was just clothing. It could be replaced, Sabian couldn't.

I stood with Aaron while Mal checked on the occultist–she was dead–and swept the room for anything we needed to take with us. He grabbed a couple of things before making a quick check of the rest of the house and pronouncing it as clear as he could manage without a much more detailed exploration.

Then we trudged wearily back out into the desert. He used his vampire speed to rush ahead and get the car, and by the time we met up again, I was dragging my feet so badly I was tempted to ask Aaron to carry me. I wasn't sure if he felt any better than I did, but he wasn't acting like he was in bad shape.

Still, Mal got me into the passenger seat. Mayhem shifted back to his tiny form and curled up on my lap, and Aaron got in the back. He put his hand on my shoulder and I rested my cheek against it while Mal drove, grateful for the comfort.

I drifted in and out of sleep. The magical blast of energy I'd used to push the demon prince back to hell had really wiped me out. I didn't want to sleep, afraid I would dream, and I kept jerking myself awake.

Mal pulled into the driveway, and was at my door before I could climb out. He opened it, undid my seatbelt, and lifted me out.

I tried to protest that I could walk but he smothered my objections with a gentle kiss.

Aaron opened the door, and we all went inside. The house felt empty without Sabian.

"Do you want anything to eat? Or do you just want to go to bed?" Mal asked.

"I...I don't want to dream," I admitted, feeling ridiculous, but I didn't want to be alone in my head right now.

Mal nodded. "Let's get you something to drink then."

We went into the living room and Mal set me gently down on the couch.

Turns out, Mal knew how to make hot chocolate from scratch and that shit was better than whiskey to knock me out into a dreamless sleep.

Chapter 20

Price

"So they're gone?" Darius asked the next day.

Mal and Aaron had contacted him after I'd finally fallen asleep.

He and Deputy McClellan sat on my couch, while I was curled up in the armchair, Mayhem warming my lap. Aaron had gone to work, but Mal was still here.

"Yeah, mate. They're all gone." I even managed to keep my voice relatively normal. I didn't want Darius to know what all we had done to banish the demon prince and defeat the occultist, so I didn't make an issue of his callous attitude.

If he had taken a look at my fractured aura, he would have known how much of a fight it had been, however he didn't seem to have noticed. That was also probably just as well. I'd recover, but it was going to take a little time. Ezra had burned through my energy pretty badly. It had been necessary, but even thinking about shifting into the headspace that allowed me to see all the pretty, and occasionally not so pretty, colors surrounding people made my head hurt.

It would also be a while before I could even think about trying to contact Ezra or Sabian. Mal probably could have done it, but I still wasn't really sure how we should proceed. I missed Sabian, a lot. I knew he'd be okay. He was most certainly in Ezra's good graces and I imagined Ezra had gained considerable standing when we had defeated our rival.

I didn't even know for sure if Sabian would want to be summoned back. I suspected he wanted to return, but I didn't know. It surprised me how much I missed Ezra, too. I did not want to be possessed again, but I certainly wouldn't mind seeing him again, as fucked up as that was. Exorcist drooling over a demonic prince. Smart, Price...real smart. Lusting after an incubus was bad enough.

I did feel really alone in my head though, and that was tweaking me out.

"You're not going to summon Sabian back, are you?" He frowned.

"Why would I do that?"

Mal was standing in the kitchen area, leaning against the counter. I saw his hands curl as if he wanted to punch Darius. I kinda did so I didn't blame him one bit. Neither Deputy McClellan or Darius could see Mal's reaction from where they stood.

Mayhem growled softly, but I put a hand on his fluffy back and he quieted.

"Any idea if there are more demon charms out there?" Deputy McClellan asked.

"I don't know," I answered. "Maybe. If I come across any, or find out there are more, I'll take care of it." Just, not for a week or two. I wasn't even sure if I could exorcise a willing demon right now, let alone one that might fight me.

"Well, Ms. Price, we certainly appreciate your help in all of this," Deputy McClellan said.

I stood when she did, Mayhem jumping to the ground from my lap, and shook her hand.

"You're welcome."

Darius studied me for another moment before he also got to his feet. "Stay in touch, Price," he said.

"Yeah, mate. If I need something, I'll be sure to let you know."

He winced but nodded, accepting the jab that he only came to me these days when he wanted help. I wasn't sure if we'd ever even try to bridge the gap that the years and bad experiences had built between us, but he would probably be there if I did need him. And I'd be there if he needed me. That's what best friends did, even ones with our fucked up relationship.

Darius exchanged a slightly strained goodbye with Mal and Deputy McClellan gave them both an appraising look before giving him a nod and they left the house.

Mal put his arm around me and I leaned into him as we watched them pull out of the driveaway and hopefully out of my life. At least for a while.

"Are you okay?" Mal squeezed his arm.

We hadn't had much of a chance to talk since last night.

"No. But I will be."

"Do you want to talk about it?"

I turned until I could bury my face against his chest. He held me, not speaking, just waiting on me.

"I don't know. I didn't expect to lose Sabian. I mean, I almost banished him once, but I guess I just didn't think."

"We did the best we could, Chris. Hell, I was unconscious for most of it." He sounded a bit chagrined.

"We wouldn't have gotten in without you, and I wouldn't have survived that hit, so thanks for taking it for me."

Mal rubbed small circles on my back. "Any time."

"I am surprised at how much I miss Ezra." I didn't want to admit it, but if I could tell anyone, it would be Mal.

"He seemed like a decent sort, for a demon prince."

I chuckled. "Yeah. He was kind of growing on me."

Mal returned my laugh. "Yeah. I hear that's what happens when you're possessed."

I snorted. "Guess so. Hoping to avoid that again, but he did save my life and all. Guess, if I do run into him again, I hope it's under slightly different circumstances. What are we going to do about Sabian?"

"Get him back, of course," Mal replied. "I've got a few ideas. Your aura has gone to shit though, and I'm guessing you're out of energy, so let's give it a couple of weeks."

"Seriously?" I tilted my chin so I could look him in the eyes.

"Yes, Chris. He's good for you. I like him, too. We just have to figure out the best way to go about getting him back."

I grinned, but then I remembered we needed to talk about the two of us as well and my expression fell.

"What about us?" Best to just get the emotional stuff over with.

Mal smiled. "I'd like to officially call you my girlfriend, if you want." He traced his fingers along my cheek, and I melted a little.

"Yeah, mate, that sounds great. You over the whole Chris is a fragile human thing?"

"No, but you've got a properly bonded hellhound now, you'll have your incubus back in a few weeks, and a half angel living in your guest room. Between them and me, you're as protected as you can be. Not to mention, you are pretty badass on your own, if you can avoid getting stabbed or shot."

I grinned. "Yeah, don't you forget I'm a badass, either."

"Trust me. I won't."

"So if I'm your girlfriend, am I still allowed to have Sabian?"

Mal blinked as if he hadn't even considered that as an issue. "Of course, Chris. Honestly, you should see if you can snag Aaron, too. He likes you."

I raised my eyebrows. "You know, you might be open minded about sharing me with other guys, but the thought of sharing you is making me see red."

Mal's grin widened. "You're the only exorcist for me, Chris. Trust me, you won't have to share my affections and I'm fine with sharing yours with Sabian and Aaron, if he decides to join us. They all bring something to our group, and to be honest, I would be very surprised if this mess with the demons is over with."

"So, surround myself with powerful men?"

"Just run them by me and Sabian first." Mal winked before pulling me back into a tight hug. "You are extremely badass, but if my gut feeling is correct, we are going to need all the help we can get. We're on the radar now, and I very much doubt we're going to be left alone. The stronger we are as a group, the better chance we'll have to be able to stand against forces no mortal, or vampire, should truly have to face."

I shivered at the seriousness in his voice. He was worried, and if he was, I probably should be, too. "Okay, mate. We'll stick together and build ourselves a nice roleplaying group in the process."

Mal sputtered. "That's not..."

I cut him off with laughter. "Side benefit, right?"

He sighed, then chuckled. "I suppose."

"All right, Mal. It's a plan. So, we've got a few hours before I should go check in at the restaurant. Care to entertain me for a while?"

Mal's lips curled up into a seductive smile.

I thought about making a joke, but before I could, he swept me off my feet and was striding toward my bedroom.

Whatever was coming, I wouldn't face it alone. I knew Mal, Sabian when I got him back, and Mayhem would never leave my side. And there was a chance I'd be able to add Aaron to that list of people I could truly trust with my life, my heart, and even my soul. And who knew, maybe, just maybe, there was a certain demon prince that I could add, as well. Time would tell.

Epilogue

Price

Sweat drenched my T-shirt, making it cling uncomfortably. I was almost ready to pull my jeans off, even though I'd get a massive sunburn, and dig in just my shirt. I also regretted turning down Mal's offer to help.

Still, this was something I probably needed to do myself. Maybe I should have waited until sundown and a full moon?

Stop bitching, Price, you're the idiot who buried all your shit in a crate on the mountainside.

I went back to digging.

No one would disturb me up here. It was private property and remote enough that it wasn't common to even get random hikers.

Still, I paused when my shoulder blades itched like someone was watching me.

I shielded my eyes and looked around, though all I could see in the hazy desert heat was an equine form. Usually, the horseback riders rode earlier to avoid the heat and it didn't look like this horse had a rider.

Maybe it was lost?

I put my shovel down, climbed out of the hole I'd dug, and turned back toward the apparition. Wavy in the heat, much like I imagined a mirage would be, the horse lowered its head and pawed at the ground.

I took a step forward and it threw its head up, turned, and bolted. I assumed the flaming mane and tail affect was due to the heat and possible dehydration, but it was clear, if there was actually something there and not my mind playing tricks on me, that there was no way I was catching that horse.

Shrugging, I took a long drink of water from a jug I had nearby and went back to digging.

The metallic thunk of my shovel hitting one of the two chests I'd buried all of my occult tools and books in distracted me completely from what I'd seen.

Renewed enthusiasm fueled my limbs as I uncovered the last of the large crates. I'd pull them out with my car. They were heavy, though I could lift them into the back seat and trunk on my own.

I'd get everything back down to my place, get together with Mal, and see about getting Sabian back. Surprisingly, even Aaron was onboard with this plan. Then we'd have to start working toward preparing for whatever else was coming at us, because Mal was right. Something was coming. I could feel it down to my very core. And it wasn't going to be friendly.

The End

Watch for book 2, The Price of Exorcism

Author's Note

Thank you so much for reading my reverse harem tale! More is coming soon! Reviews are so very important, especially to new authors and are greatly appreciated! Even a line or two will do!

About the Author

Dakota has two passions in life: writing and cinnamon tea. Tea so strong she ought to be able to see her future when she drinks it, and the writing? Well, she hopes it makes you see stars when you read it. She creates reverse harem romance novels filled with things that go bump in the night. That handsome werewolf walking down the street? The suave vampire you're just dying to get a taste of? You'll find them enraptured by charming, smart ladies ready to make those bad boys work for their affection. When not writing, Dakota can be found on the back of a horse out on the trail or tending the animals on her farm.

Other Works

Mountain Magic Trilogy (complete)

Becoming
Demon's Touch
Reckoning
The Men of Mountain Magic Novellas

Pizza Shop Exorcist (complete)

The Price of Possession
The Price of Exorcism
The Price of Magic
The Price of Souls
The Price of Rebellion
Demons Don't Do Christmas
Monster's Price

Horsemen Against the Apocalypse Duet

Seeking War
Apocalypse Interrupted (forthcoming)

Dreambound Trilogy (Complete)

Nightmare's Dance
Nightmare's Fall
Nightmare's Flight

Pizza Shop Monster Hunter
Monster's Price (stands alone)

Companions of the Convergence
Only Human in Strangeville (stands alone)

Hearts Hounds and Haunts (stands alone)